MW00989579

The
Bluebell
Girls

BOOKS BY BARBARA JOSSELSOHN

The Lilac House

To
Cam,

The
Bluebell
Girls

BARBARA JOSSELSOHN

I hope you enjoy the book!

Barbara Josselsohn

Bookouture

Published by Bookouture in 2020

An imprint of Storyfire Ltd.
Carmelite House
50 Victoria Embankment
London EC4Y 0DZ

www.bookouture.com

ISBN: 978-1-83888-967-8
eBook ISBN: 978-1-83888-966-1

To my mom, the original Sweet.

CHAPTER ONE

It took a mere ten seconds to drive across the old Jason Drawbridge that separated Lake Summers from the rest of the universe. But the difference between the two was so vast, there might as well have been an ocean, and not an inlet, dividing them. Life in the wider world moved at a feverish pace, the people quick to ask, "How are you?" but too harried to wait for an answer; in Lake Summers, life was calmer, and people always had time to listen.

At least that's how it felt to Jenna, as her wheels left the rumbling steel transverse and she spotted the town's iconic welcome sign, a miniature outline of the lake etched into copper. Opening the car's front windows, she breathed in the subtle wintergreen of the nearby yellow birch trees, and suddenly all the thoughts weighing her down felt less heavy. More manageable. Her ex-husband's engagement, her sister's words, her mounting expenses, and the toll the past year was taking on her eleven-year-old daughter, Sophie—on this side of the bridge, she thought she might actually survive it all. It had something to do with the way the shimmering late-afternoon sun slowly descended behind the Victorian-style buildings along Main Street. Something about the warm breeze that ever so slightly kicked up from the lake and seemed to whisper, *You've been missed.*

She glanced over her shoulder at the back seat, where Mo was curled up in a furry black ball and snoring peacefully, then faced front and breathed in again. *You've been missed...* It was a greeting she heard every time she returned to Lake Summers, and today, finally, she could reply as she'd always wanted. It had been nearly a year since Matt had walked out on her, admitting he'd fallen in love with one of his clients, and while she had felt like she was in freefall for most of those months, she now had a foothold and a route forward. She was moving to Lake Summers, back into the stone-fronted house where she'd spent the summer months when she was growing up, and where her mother now lived year-round. She was moving with Sophie, no matter how hard her ex-husband and her sister might protest. She was going to reinvent her life.

Traffic slowed on Main Street, and Jenna gently braked, watching the blend of vacationers and year-round residents converge upon the town center as they always did when summer got underway, eager to absorb every drop of afternoon sunshine. Up ahead was the Smoothie Dudes shop, where kids holding baseball gloves or skateboards waited in line near the walk-up window, and Pearl's Café, where families gathered around the outdoor chalkboard, reading today's varieties of fresh-baked muffins. A short distance beyond, she spied the turnoff for the footpath that led to the lake. She could almost see T.J. on that late-August night so long ago, his feathered hair blowing onto his face as he rounded the path's wide bend to meet her. The anticipation of seeing him had propelled her to sneak out that night despite the big storm heading into town. How often she'd relived that glorious moment when he touched her jaw and dipped his chin…

Her cell phone rang, blasting her out of her daydreams. She was glad for the interruption—she never liked thinking about how that night ended. But her relief vanished when she looked at her dashboard and saw it was her sister. She tapped "Ignore" and accelerated to make it through the next intersection before the light turned red, then eased her foot up from the gas pedal, noticing the speedometer approaching forty miles per hour. Lately the thought of speaking to Chloe could cause quite an adrenaline rush. But it wouldn't do any good to get a speeding ticket.

In the back seat, Mo let out a low growl. "Okay, bud, hold on a sec," she said as she scanned the road ahead. Miraculously, a car in the middle of the next block was leaving, and she pulled into the space.

"Here you go, Mo," she said as she opened the back door and gathered him into her arms, then set him down and watched him walk stiffly for a few steps before lifting his leg. Her sweet little poodle was fifteen now and had returned home last Friday after two nights in the hospital receiving intravenous fluids to combat pancreatitis. He was still weak, and so thin that he looked almost two-dimensional. No doubt he'd have been better off without the four-hour drive here, but she couldn't bear to leave him in anyone else's care. He looked so sad these days when she left the house, and so heartened when she returned, even if she'd just run out for groceries. She'd find him sitting on the floor in the front hallway, his ears pressed back and his body trembling, as though he feared she'd never come home. The time in the car notwithstanding, she was sure he'd enjoy three days here while she made initial plans to relocate. Besides, this town would be his new home, too. It made sense to introduce him to the streets and smells.

Because she was not changing her mind, not for anyone. Rye, where she and Matt had settled after Sophie was born, was a very nice town, and their split-level house was roomy and comfortable. But without Matt, it no longer felt like home. Jenna missed having a complete family at the dinner table, missed having someone to go downstairs and make coffee for in the morning. She didn't think she'd ever get used to the long, solo walk upstairs each night, listening only to her own footsteps. When they first moved in, she and Matt made a routine of shutting off the lights and walking upstairs together, arm in arm.

She hooked Mo's leash onto his collar and strolled back toward the center of town, to give him a chance to stretch and herself a chance to clear her mind. The breeze felt good on her bare legs and her collarbones, just above the neckline of her gray jersey sundress. She set the end of Mo's leash beneath her sandal, found an elastic band in her pocket, and pulled her hair into a ponytail, so she could feel the breeze on the back of her neck as well. Picking the leash up again, she spotted Pearl's Café just across the intersection. Suddenly an iced coffee seemed like an awfully good idea. Reaching the shop, she tied Mo's leash to a bench just outside the front door, where two other small dogs were sunning themselves on a patch of grass. Mo sniffed at them absentmindedly before settling down alongside them. "Be a good boy," she said and opened the screen door.

Inside, the air was cool and smelled lightly sweet, a little like vanilla and a little like toasted almond. She weaved among the tables and ordered an iced skim latte from the ponytailed young man behind the rustic light-wood counter. She was taking a bottle of water out of the refrigerated case for Mo when she heard a melodic voice behind her.

"Is that a bluebell girl?" the voice said, and when she turned, she saw Mrs. Pearl pushing open a gray swinging door near the register. She smiled and raised her shoulders with excitement. Mrs. Pearl looked cheerful and energetic, just as she did when Jenna was a teenager and would play with Mrs. Pearl's two little girls, making houses out of the sugar packets on the tables, as Mrs. Pearl stacked loaves of bread and rolls atop the wooden shelves that lined the back wall. She still wore the same outfit she'd always worn—a crisp brown chef's apron with small brass buttons where the neck strap hooked on, over an open-necked white blouse and slim white pants. Her hair was pulled back into a messy bun, although now it was more white than blonde.

"It's me," Jenna said, the phrase "bluebell girl" resonating like a familiar song. It was the name Mrs. Pearl had given the Clayton girls—her, her mother, and her sister—because of the garden of Virginia bluebells that burst out in color every spring

on the side of her mother's house. Jenna remembered spending
countless hours dancing barefoot among the blossoms there when
she was young, making up poems or daydreaming about boys or
reading a book or simply twirling with her arms outstretched,
breathing in their light perfume. Her mother had tended that
garden so lovingly for as long as Jenna could remember. There
was something poignant in her devotion, since the blossoms had
such a short life. They reached their full bloom in late May and
were gone by midsummer.

Mrs. Pearl embraced her. "You missed your mom and Sophie,"
she said. "They were here about an hour ago. What a pair!
Your mother was telling some wild story about disappearing to
California when she was seventeen, and Sophie was eating up
every word."

"Oh, no, did she really tell her that?" Jenna said. "I hope she
didn't give Sophie any ideas."

"I think she might have," Mrs. Pearl said. "She made it sound
so good, I wanted to be seventeen all over again, so I could run
off to Los Angeles too! I kept refilling their lemonade just to get
another earful."

"She's a great storyteller, that's for sure," Jenna said. "Although
I think you should take that one with a grain of salt. I never heard
any story about running away. She probably was trying to keep
Sophie entertained."

"I don't know, it sounded awfully real to me. I thought I knew
everything about your mother, but this was a new one. Leave it
to Sweet!"

Jenna smiled when she heard Mrs. Pearl refer to her mother as
Sweet. Jenna had no idea how or when her mother had acquired
that nickname. It was not even close to her real name, Frances.

Mrs. Pearl waved to a couple of women in running clothes
who were leaving the store with their iced drinks, then turned
back to Jenna. "But enough with that, let's talk about you," she

said. "I understand congratulations are in order! You're joining the *Lake Summers Press* in September!"

Jenna startled. "How on earth did you hear that?" she said. Nobody other than her mother was supposed to know her plans, not until Sophie was fully on board. Jenna had decided to introduce Sophie gradually to the idea of moving here. Her first step had been to have Sophie spend two weeks alone with her grandmother, in the hope that she'd start to fall in love with the town and the way of life. But if the phone calls she'd had with Sophie these last two weeks were any indication, it might take some work to win her daughter over. The last thing she needed was for Sophie to hear that she'd already accepted a job.

"The editor holds her meetings here, and you hear a lot when you're topping off the coffee," Mrs. Pearl explained. "They all love that you used to work for a national magazine. And that you published a book, too—"

"Oh, that book—it was nothing—"

"It most definitely was not nothing! I bought a copy, and I loved it! I even sent copies to my daughters for Christmas that year. Anyway, it sounds like they're already lining up assignments for you. Oh sweetie, I'm sorry if I wasn't supposed to know this yet."

"No, it's fine, it's nothing," Jenna said, shaking her head. "I just have some things still to work out. Sophie's going to need some time to get used to the idea, and then I have to deal with Matt." She felt her phone buzz and saw her sister's name when she glanced down. "Chloe's going to need convincing, too," she said, putting the phone back in her pocket.

"Well, I hope nobody gives you too hard a time, because Sophie will love it here," Mrs. Pearl said. "She's going into sixth grade, right? The parents all say the sixth-grade teachers are excellent. The math teacher is so cute, she's getting married this fall and is always showing me pictures of her wedding dress. That is, when she's not complaining about the taste of skim milk in her coffee.

She used to take half-and-half but now she's so worried about her waistline—"

"Mrs. Pearl?" the ponytailed boy called out from behind the counter. "The buzzer went off!"

"Thanks, Jake," Mrs. Pearl said with an acknowledging wave. "I'm sorry, sweetie, I have to go pull out those muffins," she said. "But I can't wait to hear more about all your plans. Oh, I'm so excited! It sounds like a perfect new beginning for you and Sophie."

She went back to the kitchen, and Jenna paid for her coffee and the bottle of water, then took a paper cup from the counter. Back outside, she poured the water and knelt, tipping the cup so Mo could drink. It wasn't as easy as it would have been if he had his bowl from home, which was decorated with cartoon images of baseballs and mitts. Mo had been named after Matt's favorite pitcher, the Yankees' Mariano Rivera, who was having one of his best seasons when they adopted the little guy from the shelter. That was back when Mo was a puppy, and Jenna was still naive enough to think it charmingly boyish that Matt chose to name the dog after one of his heroes. Not that she minded—to the contrary, it was cute that her small, shy dog had a tough-guy name. Still, Matt's preferences had prevailed in so many decisions—to live in Rye rather than closer to either her mother or sister, to buy a house near the highway instead of the coast. Again, it wasn't that the decisions were bad; but it troubled her that over the years, she had learned to trust his voice way more than her own.

She patted Mo's back until he lay down again and steeled herself to return Chloe's call. She dreaded hearing what Chloe was going to say, but she didn't want to wait and have the conversation hang over her head. She was making the right decision about moving, just as Mrs. Pearl had said. Her mother agreed, too; she was the one who'd suggested that Sophie come up alone for two weeks, to get a feel for the everyday rhythm of the town and even meet some kids her own age at the lakeside day camp. Still, Jenna wished she had her older sister's approval—or, at the least, acceptance. Chloe was loud and assertive, and she liked to give her opinions. Jenna didn't need the extra stress of knowing Chloe thought she was making a mistake.

She answered on the first ring. "Okay, let me be clear," she said, sounding as though they were already in the middle of an argument, and Jenna was refusing to concede an obvious point. "Mom belongs in assisted living—I know it, and you do, too. She told me when I called this morning that you were on your way to pick Sophie up, so it's perfect. Just tell her what we want to do, and make it sound good. You can even show her the Ocean Vistas website."

"I'm not doing that—"

"Tell her she'll love it, the apartments are very nice, they have lots of activities, and… and then you…" Chloe went quiet, and Jenna visualized a light bulb switching on atop her head. She braced herself for a fresh assault.

"Wait a minute, wait a minute," Chloe said. "You're not actually thinking what I think you're thinking, are you? You can't literally be thinking of moving in with her! Mom hinted at something, but I thought she was just getting confused, as usual—"

"As usual? Since when does she get confused?"

"Are you kidding me? She didn't even recognize my voice when I called this morning."

"Maybe it was the cell service. It can be spotty here."

"Look, the last thing she needs is an angry adolescent storming through the house. Or an old dog who'll bark all night because he doesn't know where he is."

"We're not staying that long," Jenna said. "Only until I can find us our own place."

"Not to mention that your ex-husband will blow a gasket when he hears. You haven't told him yet, right?"

"Chloe, you're making it sound so much worse than it is. I can take care of Sophie. And I can handle Matt, and I can take care of Mom, too—"

"Please, you can barely take care of yourself. The house was a mess when I stopped by last week, the sink was full of dirty dishes… not to mention it was over ninety degrees, and the air conditioning was broken again—"

"It's expensive to get things serviced, and I was taking the dog back and forth to the vet, which is not exactly cheap either. And I'm alone and in the middle of—Chloe, why are you trying to make me feel horrible?"

"Because I'm going to be the one to pick up the pieces. And I'm so tired of picking up the pieces!"

Jenna sighed and sank onto the bench near Mo. It was true—everything Chloe was saying about her life right now. Her silence evidently gave Chloe pause in a way all her protestations hadn't. She heard Chloe sigh too, and pictured her in her kitchen, tapping her lips with her fingertips, the way she always did when she was strategizing what to say next.

"Jenns," she finally said, using the nickname she'd given Jenna when they were little. "If you want to move, then move near me. It's only forty-five minutes away from Rye. Sophie will still be able to see her friends, and Matt can't fight you so much about forty-five minutes. You'll find a house and Mom will be in Ocean Vistas and we'll all be close. And that way I can keep an eye on you all."

Jenna leaned forward and put her forehead in the palm of her hand. It was hard to argue with that logic. Chloe lived in a very nice part of Long Island, just a few miles away from the ocean. Jenna missed living near the water—the lake had been so much a part of her summers when she was growing up. And Chloe's heart was in the right place, too, even though she could be so abrasive. But moving to Long Island would be admitting that she was a failure, that she couldn't run her own life, that she couldn't trust herself with any decisions. And she wasn't going to admit that. At least not yet.

"What is it, almost six?" Jenna said. "I told Sophie I'd be at Mom's in time for dinner. Look, Chloe, I can't talk now. I'll call you when I'm there, okay?" She hung up without waiting for a response and reached over to pet Mo, who was watching her, his chin on his paws. Her phone buzzed, and she ignored it. Chloe was so much like Dad had been—strong and determined.

Her phone buzzed again as she stood up and untied Mo's leash. Evidently, Chloe was not going to be ignored, which left Jenna with the choice of answering, hearing that buzz endlessly all evening, or silencing the thing, which would put her out of reach to everyone. Rolling her eyes, she brought the phone up to her ear. "Chloe, please stop calling. I told you I'd call you back—"

"Mom! *Mom!*"

Jenna froze. "Sophie!" she shouted. She heard a siren in the background. "Sophie, where are you? What's going on?"

"Mom!" Sophie repeated. "Oh my God! We just got to the hospital. Mom, it's Sweet!"

CHAPTER TWO

Sophie was so distraught that, at first, Jenna couldn't get anything out of her except "Mom!" and "Oh my God!" mingled between gasps and whimpers. But eventually the full story came out. Sophie had heard some loud bangs in the house when she was in her room changing, and when she went to investigate, she found her grandmother lying at the bottom of the basement steps. It sounded like she'd fallen, and although she was conscious, she still looked badly hurt, and Sophie felt it was serious enough to call for help. Jenna pushed her phone into her pocket and scooped up Mo. Her mother was strong, but she was getting older. The sound of Sophie's panicked voice, and the thought of her eleven-year-old having to deal with this all by herself, made Jenna dash down Main Street faster than she'd ever run through town before.

She made a beeline for the car, murmuring "I'm sorry," and "Excuse me," as she zigzagged among the shoppers and families planted in her path. It would be bad enough if her mother had tripped or stumbled. But it sounded like she fell down the whole flight of steps. Why would she be going down to the basement, anyway? There was nothing down there except old furniture—a sofa, a couple of tables, and Dad's old office desk and file cabinet. And Sophie said that she was awake but wasn't saying anything. Could she have had some kind of seizure or stroke? A heart attack? It didn't make sense—her mother had looked the picture of health when she dropped Sophie off at the house two weeks ago. Gorgeous, in fact, in her peach dress with the wide skirt and the fabric belt, and with her peach button earrings and the matching lipstick. She'd just come back from her stroll by the lake; her wide-brimmed hat was still out on the kitchen table. Jenna had been so hopeful that Sophie would enjoy all her grandmother had planned for her—weekdays at the lake learning to sail and making new friends, and afternoons and evenings meeting up with those friends at Smoothie Dudes or the Ice Creamery, or Penny Treats for old-fashioned candies or solid chocolate they sold by the block. And lots of long walks talking with her grandmother. She'd hoped that Sophie would learn what a go-getter her grandmother was, something she had no way of knowing before, since up until now she'd come here for holidays or short visits. Jenna had imagined that Sophie would fall so much in love with Lake Summers that she'd… well, if not jump at the chance to move here for good, then at least be open to a conversation about it.

But now, all those hopes were gone.

Finally, she reached the car. She set Mo on the back seat and slipped behind the wheel. Her mother was a young seventy-five, that's what everyone said. She didn't look anywhere near that age. And if she did get confused, as Chloe said, it was only because she got so carried away sometimes. Jenna still remembered all the times her mom had been late picking her up from swimming lessons at the lake because she'd lost track of time while planning a July Fourth block party for the neighborhood kids after the town fireworks, or organizing the summer theater program at the green, or starting some other big project. She'd never minded waiting or starting on the walk home by herself. She loved how her mother dove so deeply into whatever she was doing. Mom had always been ruled by her heart and not her head.

She started the car and drove toward the lower end of Main Street, telling herself not to imagine the worst. Maybe it was something simple, like dehydration, that had made her mom feel lightheaded and lose her balance. After all, she'd probably spent much of the day in the garden, watering the bluebells and checking on the hostas and coral bells, which would bloom in rich golds and pinks later in the summer, after the bluebells were gone. Or maybe she was coming down with something. If she wasn't feeling well, she'd never have gone to the doctor. She was always saying she didn't have time to sit in a doctor's waiting room, watching some inane talk show on a ceiling-mounted TV and feeling her life tick away.

As long as she didn't break a hip or hit her head, she'd be fine, Jenna thought. Maybe bruised up a bit, but fine.

The light ahead changed to red, and Jenna slowed behind a string of cars. She tapped her toes against the footbed of her left sandal, as she assured herself that true emergencies were rare in Lake Summers, so the odds were against this being something terrible. The one big exception was the night of that late-August storm, when Mr. Jason next door had a heart attack. She'd sat alone on her bed in the dark that night, watching the ambulance through her window, its rotating red light blurry because of the rain. What she saw more clearly were the faces of his four sons at the graveside service on that windy afternoon a few days later: T.J., so stoic; Steven, his eyes narrowed like he was itching for a fistfight; and the twins, Cal and Clay, with their quivering lips. Jenna wanted to move close to T.J. and hold his hand or rub his shoulder. But she couldn't.

The light turned green, but up ahead, the next two lights were yellow. Of all the times to get caught in traffic. Jenna heard Sophie's panicked voice in her head. She thought about the sound Sophie described, the bangs she heard from her bedroom. Once, years ago, a driver had lost control of his car and careened off the road and onto the sandy bank of the lake not too far away from where Jenna was jogging. She didn't see the accident, and thankfully no one was hurt, but she could still hear the thump, could still feel the echo reverberating deep in her stomach, could still sense that sudden knowledge that something terrible had happened. She worried that Sophie was now remembering the awful sound of her grandmother falling.

Finally, the lights were green again, and she made the turn off Main Street and started down Route 12. Ten minutes later, Adirondacks-Lake Summers Hospital appeared. It was a wide, low brick building set back from the road, nestled among tall birches and broad oaks. She rounded the corner, sped down the driveway, and pulled into the closest spot she could find to the emergency room entrance, then cracked open the windows for Mo. At least it looked to be a coolish evening, and there were trees blocking the slantwise sun.

"Be good, Mo," she said as she got out of the car. "I'll be back as soon as I can."

The glass doors to the emergency room parted as she approached, and she walked through the entranceway and scanned the waiting room, the faces of strangers indistinguishable as she searched for her daughter. Then she saw Sophie on a slim, gray-cushioned chair in the corner, her knees drawn up under her chin, circled by her arms, her thick red hair cascading over shoulders and toward her face.

"Soph!" Jenna called, and Sophie looked up, then ran across the room and into Jenna's arms.

"Mom, what took you? I've been waiting so long!" she said, pressing her face into Jenna's chest as she burst into tears.

Jenna hugged her daughter. "I know. I'm sorry. I came as fast as I could."

"They told me to wait here because they didn't want me to see what they were doing. Oh God, Mom, do you think it's really bad, do you think—"

"Honey, calm down. Let me try to find out what's going on."

Sophie nodded and Jenna went to a long desk at the far end of the room, where a woman in pink scrubs was tapping at her computer.

"Excuse me, my name is Jenna Marsh," she said. "My mother was brought in a little while ago, Frances Clayton—"

"Oh yes, Mrs. Marsh, they're taking care of her now," the woman said. "I'll see if I can get a doctor to come speak to you."

Jenna clasped her hands in front of her chest as the woman exited through a set of swinging doors. She looked over at Sophie, who was staring back at her, eyes wide and terrified. This was a lot for her daughter to take in. She wanted to distract Sophie for a bit, especially while she talked to the doctor. Pulling out her keys from her bag, she motioned Sophie over.

"Mo's in the car," she said and pointed toward the window. "I'm parked right outside. Why don't you let him stretch his legs? Take him over to that grassy area. I'll come get you as soon as I hear something."

Sophie took the keys and left the building. A few moments later, the woman in scrubs returned through the double doors. "Mrs. Marsh?" she said. "I can bring you back there now."

She led Jenna through the doors and into a brightly lit emergency room, then motioned for her to wait. Jenna nodded and watched the nurses and doctors and other professionals calmly going about their jobs, moving equipment and wheeling beds, studying beeping monitors, and conferring—even smiling occasionally—with one another. She moved from foot to foot and knocked her fists together in front of her chest, and counted forward and backward from one to ten, to try to make the minutes pass faster. She couldn't remember the last time she'd been to an emergency room.

Finally, a young doctor approached her.

"Mrs. Marsh?" he said. "I'm Dr. Banes, I've been taking care of your mother tonight. It looks like we were pretty lucky. She's going to be fine."

"Oh, thank God," Jenna said. She closed her eyes for a moment, feeling a wave of relief work its way through her body.

"We performed a CT scan and took some X-rays," he said. "She does have some significant bruising on her right leg, and a bruised rib that was giving her some pain. We gave her some painkillers, and she's resting now. I don't expect we'll find anything more. Looks like it was a garden-variety fall, and you'll be taking her home tomorrow or the next day at the latest."

"So she's okay? She was able to talk and everything?"

"Yes, she was talking. Mostly insisting she was fine. Oh, and she also mentioned that I was nice-looking and she hoped I had someone special in my life."

Jenna laughed and shook her head. "That's my mother," she said. She took her phone out of her pocket to send a quick text to Sophie: *Everything's fine. I'll be out soon.*

Just then another doctor, older and taller than the first, came up alongside them. "I'm Dr. Roberts, the chief of internal medicine," he said. "I take it you're Mrs. Clayton's daughter? I was checking in on Dr. Banes when he was treating your mom. If it's okay with him, I'll take you down to see her."

The younger doctor nodded, and Jenna thanked him, then followed the older one deeper into the emergency room. He strode past curtained-off beds and around desks and large, rolling devices, and then stopped near the last curtain.

"The painkillers will have kicked in, so she's probably very groggy," he said. "My advice would be to say a quick hello and then let her rest. You can give her a hard time about going down those basement stairs alone after you get her home." He smiled, his white mustache spreading beneath his nose.

Jenna rolled her eyes. "I don't even know why she went down there. She never goes to the basement."

"Well, I'm sure she had her reasons," he said. "At any rate, I would guess you could use a good night's sleep, too. Everything will look better in the morning. We'll take good care of her, okay?"

Jenna nodded. The younger doctor seemed knowledgeable and pleasant, but she appreciated the older doctor's warm, fatherly tone. She'd never had a physician talk this way to her before, let alone someone so high up—but then again, she'd never talked to any doctor about her mother before. "Thank you," she said, breathing a bit more easily. He patted her shoulder and then proceeded back down the hall.

She peeked around the curtain, where her mother lay on the narrow bed. Her face had none of the colors that always made her so interesting to look at—the creamy tan of her complexion, the pale peach of her favorite lipstick, the apples of her cheeks with their delicate pink glow.

"Mom?" she said, as she approached the bed, hoping her mother was alert enough to hear her. She reached over the metal bars and lightly stroked the top of her mother's head. Her mom opened her eyes. They looked watery and unfocused.

"Hi, Mom," Jenna said, trying to steady her voice. "How are you feeling?"

Her mom attempted to smile and the lines along her forehead deepened, as though even smiling was painful. Jenna reminded herself of what the older doctor had said, that things would look better in the morning. "The doctors say you're going to be fine," she whispered. "Hang in there, and get some rest. I'll be back tomorrow."

Her mother closed her eyes, and Jenna walked out. On the other side of the curtain, she paused and placed her hand over her mouth, trying to absorb her emotions so they wouldn't spill out. She didn't want to make a scene. She knew there was no reason to cry. This all could have been so much worse.

Wiping her cheeks, she went back through the double doors and into the waiting area. This was not how things were supposed to go. Even as Matt threatened to leave and then left for good, even as he started to make plans to marry again, even as the air

conditioning in the house broke and the dog got sick and Chloe
started haranguing her about all her bad decisions, she'd always
believed that her mother was here for her. She realized now that
she'd been counting on it. Maybe she'd been planning to move
back here ever since Matt left; maybe she'd been hoping to do it
for even longer but hadn't realized it until recently. She'd never
anticipated that her mother would be lying in a hospital bed rather
than standing outside the front door of the old Lake Summers
house, waiting to welcome her home. Yes, it was ridiculous and
childish. Selfish. She was a grown woman. And her mother would
be fine. But this was a bad year, and she needed her mom.

She passed the desk, and the woman in scrubs looked up and
rested her chin in her hand. "Try not to worry, Mrs. Marsh," she
said. "She's in good hands, and Troy's got your dog. So you have
nothing to worry about except taking care of your daughter and
trying to get a little sleep."

"Thank you, I appreciate—" Jenna stopped short as she
registered what the woman said. "What? Who has my dog?"

"Your mother's friend, the one who brought Sophie here.
We didn't know how long you'd be, so I called and asked him to
come back and get him."

"But my dog… he's been sick, and he needs special food—"

"He knows, your daughter told him. Don't worry, Troy's a
veterinarian, he works at the animal clinic on Main Street. He
said he'll keep him as long as you need."

"But… but who…" Jenna started, and then sighed. She had
enough to worry about, and if Mo was staying with a vet, it
wasn't worth carrying on. Apparently Sophie knew the person.
Wherever Mo was, she and Sophie could pick him up on their
way to the house.

"Thank you," she said and walked across the room to Sophie,
who was sitting on her knees, facing the window. She went to tap
Sophie's shoulder. But she stopped when she got close enough

to see that Sophie was on her phone—and to hear who she was talking to.

"But Daddy," Sophie was saying. "I'm really upset. Can't you come here? Just for one day?"

Jenna backed up, pretending to look at her own phone so that if Sophie turned around, she wouldn't know Jenna had overheard. It felt like a gut punch, harsh and unexpected, hearing Sophie begging Matt to come and see her. Was Chloe right—was she unable to take care of herself and her daughter? Did Sophie feel that way, too?

No, she thought. She couldn't let her mind go in this direction. If her mother was hurt, then she needed to be stronger, and if her mother was struggling, then she needed to be steady. After all, she'd always known she was her mother's daughter.

Except that now, she had to figure out exactly what that meant.

CHAPTER THREE

Troy pulled into his driveway, shut off the engine, and looked at the little black dog in the passenger seat. "Any suggestions on how I can avoid your mom?" he asked.

The dog perked up his ears and gave a loud, wet sneeze.

Troy chuckled. "Big help you are."

He got out of the car and walked around to open the passenger-side door. The dog scrambled onto all fours, sliding on the leather seat before securing his footing. Then he studied Troy intently, and within his wide-open eyes, Troy could see a battle raging between friendliness and suspicion. Confidence and trepidation. The dog's tail, lowered yet wagging, laid bare this internal conflict. Sometimes Troy couldn't believe how open dogs were with their emotions. They were lucky that way. There was a freedom in having no choice but to let the world know exactly what you were feeling, moment to moment. But people were different. People knew that being open left you vulnerable. And that was a consequence nobody could accept.

He ruffled the hair on the dog's head. "Mo—that's your name, right?" he asked. "Bet you've had enough of being in a car. Come on, let's get you acclimated to the place. Then we'll fix you something to eat."

Evidently consenting to the plan, Mo placed his front paws on Troy's forearm and allowed himself to be picked up. The dog felt light for his size—too light, Troy thought. Sophie had mentioned he was recently sick, and Troy now wondered if it was more serious than she knew. He looked the dog over as he carried him to the small patch of lawn in front of his house. He was clearly mostly poodle, but the shape of his snout suggested another breed or two mixed in. Some kind of terrier, maybe a Wheaten? Or something smaller—Shih-Tzu? Havanese? Cavalier King Charles? All possibilities. These days everyone wanted a poodle or poodle mix. And no wonder—poodles were good dogs, smart and easy to get along with. Hooking the leash Sophie had given him onto Mo's collar, he placed him on the grass. He could tell the dog was an old-timer. The hair around his face was gray, and his haunches had a salt-and-pepper appearance. And he favored one side as he walked, the telltale limp of arthritis. But he was an appealing little guy, curious and alert. He looked up at Troy and wagged his tail with more enthusiasm than before. He was eager to make friends. No doubt he came from a loving home. Although what else would anyone expect from Jenna?

Mo sniffed around and squatted, and then allowed himself to be led up the front steps and into the house. He circled the small blue rug in the entrance hallway, before sitting down and fixing his eyes once again on his host. "Hungry?" Troy asked. Mo wagged his tail and let out a high-pitched bark. "Well, rumor has it you're still recovering. That presents a bit of a challenge, my man. Let me see what I've got."

He went into the kitchen and over to the pantry at the far corner. Opening the double doors, he looked inside and grimaced. He didn't keep much food in the house, choosing most evenings to bring home a pizza or Chinese from downtown, or to slap some chicken or a couple of hamburgers on the barbecue grill on the deck. But even so, it never failed to surprise him how empty the shelves were. Back when he was a kid, this very pantry would be overflowing with cereal and beans and rice and condiments, with carton upon carton of pasta and oversized jars of sauce. And there'd be snacks—family-size bags of potato chips and tortilla chips and pretzels, and canisters of popping corn, alongside loaves of white bread and enough jars of peanut butter and grape jelly to fill a grocery store aisle. Not to mention the baking ingredients that always lined the top two shelves—bags of every type of flour and sugar imaginable, packages of semisweet and milk chocolate chips, cylinders of rainbow sprinkles, jars of honey and molasses and caramel sauce, tubs of shortening, and canisters of ground cinnamon, nutmeg, ginger, and other spices. His mom always liked having something dense and sweet baking in the oven, especially in the winter, when the summer folks were gone and the town was quiet, when he and his brothers could no longer spend most of their time outdoors. While the rest of them preferred summer, his mom loved the winter months.

Now the pantry held just one box of spaghetti, a small jar of marinara sauce, and a few cans of soup. And a plentiful supply of dog food, since he often brought home dogs who'd been boarded at the clinic, hating the thought of leaving them by themselves overnight. Troy spotted a couple of cans of prescription food that he'd been storing for Roxie, a lively cocker spaniel who stayed over from time to time when her owner, Cara, one of the nurses at the hospital, worked an overnight shift. The low-fat recipe would be suitable for a guy with pancreatitis, too. He opened the can and spooned the contents into a bowl.

"Here, boy," he called, as he placed it on the floor. Mo sniffed the grayish-brown chunks encircled in brown jelly, then sat back on his haunches and shot his host an accusing look. "Not to your liking?" Troy asked. Mo gave a hopeful tail wag. "Can't say I blame you. Maybe I can doctor it up a bit."

He went to the refrigerator, which was mostly empty like the pantry, and spotted the small package of lean ground beef he'd intended to use for himself this week. He showed the package to Mo, who licked his chops.

"Okay, you can have it," he said. "But no greasy burgers for you. You're gonna need your portion boiled. Don't worry, it'll still make the canned stuff tastier."

Mo slid his front paws forward until he was on his belly, his chin between his paws, and Troy brought a pot from the cabinet over to the sink. Filling it with water, he glanced out the window at Sweet's house, which he could see through the spaces between the tall birches that separated their yards. The lights were off inside, which was unsettling since Sweet was always home in the evenings. He ran his hand through his hair. Hopefully Sweet was okay. He liked her. He liked having her next door. She was exactly the way he remembered her when he was growing up. Older, sure, but with that same spirit. Like last Saturday, when he'd gone to change a light bulb he'd noticed had gone out on a fixture above her back door and she'd come out to offer him a glass of iced tea and ask what he was doing that night.

"Nothing planned," he'd said, and he took a few gulps, then put the glass on the table.

"Nothing?" She'd sat down on an upholstered patio armchair and looked at him from beneath her wide-brimmed hat. "Aren't there any nice girls you've met since you've been back?"

He'd dropped his chin and shook his head as he climbed up the ladder. "Don't you have something to do with Sophie?" he'd said.

"She's at the lake with her friends," she'd replied quickly, then pursed her lips and gave Troy a playfully disgruntled look. "Now don't try to distract me, Troy Jason. I have no doubt you meet plenty of nice women at the animal clinic. Plenty of single women who own pets and would like to know you better. Isn't there one you'd like to ask out to dinner?"

He'd unscrewed the old bulb. "Sweet, this is not a conversation I choose to engage in."

"Oh, please! This is a conversation everyone chooses to engage in, whether they know it or not!" She'd tucked a strand of white hair behind her ear. "I get it, you're the serious one. I remember how you were, always watching out for those three wild brothers of yours. You're too sensible for love. At least, that's what you think."

"Love?" He'd leaned his elbow on the top rung of the ladder. "I thought we were talking about dinner."

"It starts with dinner and leads to love. A candlelit dinner, over at that Italian place across the lake. A nice-looking man like you has no business being a bachelor for the rest of your life. Don't you ever think about love?"

He'd screwed in the replacement and then climbed back down and squeezed the rails shut, trying to show her that like the ladder, the conversation was closed. But he knew it wouldn't be closed until *she* decided it was. When he was a kid, there was something called the Lake Summers Theatrical that happened every July, when theater pros from Broadway would come up to Lake Summers for two weeks to help the local kids stage a musical. Sweet had single-handedly arranged the whole event each year, convincing shopkeepers and business owners and residents to contribute money to put the actors up in a hotel, pay for sets and costumes, and hire local contractors to construct the temporary stage on the green. He'd heard the program fizzled out a few years ago when Sweet no longer had the energy to manage it. The town couldn't find anyone who could work the magic she always had.

He'd hoisted the ladder onto his shoulder. "Anything else need fixing while I'm here?"

"All I'm saying is that people aren't meant to be alone," Sweet had told him. "A person's job on this earth is to find someone to love. Over and over, if that's what has to be. Otherwise, what are you? Just a pile of unfinished work." She'd tilted her head and studied him then. "But you weren't always this difficult, were you?" she'd said. "You had a girlfriend growing up. That lovely blonde with the doe eyes."

"She wasn't my girlfriend—"

"Of course she was. You took her to the Alumni Dance at the resort the night of the big storm. We came outside to see you. How handsome you looked in your suit, with that starched white shirt and that blue tie."

Troy looked down. "No, Sweet. I didn't—"

"But why do I remember that night being so sad?" She'd looked past him toward the woods behind her yard, and the lines across her forehead deepened. "That's strange. It was a happy night, wasn't it? Jenna came home so late, I thought she was upstairs already. I would have worried so if I'd known she'd been out in that dreadful weather. Why do I remember her crying? Why was that, Steven? I mean... wait, you're Troy, right?"

Troy had looked at her then. "Stay there, Sweet," he'd said. "I'm going to put the ladder away and then I'll help you inside." He went around to the garage and planted the ladder against the back wall. He hadn't worn a suit to the Alumni Dance. It was a casual event, the guys in khaki shorts and boat shoes. It was at his dad's funeral later that week that he'd worn the suit Sweet was talking about. But she was right about that night of the storm, how sad it turned out. How Jenna had snuck out of the house without her parents knowing. He thought about going back and clarifying her memories. But he didn't want to upset her, and he didn't want to talk about Jenna or that night or even that summer. When he came back around, she'd already risen from her chair and picked up his empty iced tea glass from the table. He'd opened the back door for her, and she carried it inside and proceeded to tell him that Jenna was coming up on Wednesday for a few days, and she hoped he'd join them for dinner one night.

"She's thinking of moving back for good," Sweet had said. "Just like you did."

He'd said he was busy next week, and promptly went home and made plans to take a few days off from work and use Steven's cabin near the Canadian border. He didn't want to see Jenna. Not even to say hello, and if Sweet thought that made him a pile of unfinished work, so be it. He'd closed the clinic early to change his clothes and get started on the trek up north before dark, and that was when Sophie had come tearing across her front yard over to his house to tell him of Sweet's fall.

He went back to the stove to put the water on to boil, then squatted down and gave Mo a good scratch behind the ear. Mo stretched his limbs and rolled onto his back, front paws lolling above his chest, eyes narrowing dreamily.

"A dog's life, not too shabby," Troy said and rubbed Mo's muted pink belly until the water boiled.

He put the ground beef into the pot, then pulled a slotted silicone-handled spatula from the utensil holder on the coun-tertop and swished the meat around. The most recent renter of the house had moved last year, and Joanna, Steven's wife, an interior designer with an upscale clientele in Connecticut, had taken it upon herself to freshen up the house in anticipation of putting it up for sale. She'd done a nice job. The small ranch-style home, which felt homespun and cozy when they were kids, now had a decidedly modern, beachy vibe. The old, dark-wood furniture and jewel-toned upholstery throughout the house had been replaced with either leather, light wood, or glass. Track lighting had supplanted all the table lamps, and cool, white window blinds now hung where floral or plaid curtains used to be. It wasn't that Troy didn't like the new look; it just made him feel like a visitor. He knew that Joanna was aiming to make the place more marketable, but a part of him also thought he was meant to feel out of place. Lake Summers had become a hot commodity in the last few years, and real estate prices were high. The house had been left to all four boys, and his three brothers were ready to sell.

When the beef was cooked, Troy took the pot to the sink and poured the contents into a colander. Then he rinsed it with cold water to drain off any remaining fat. It was essential Mo avoid as much fat as possible: the little guy was old and way too thin—another bout of illness could very well prove too much. He picked up the dog's bowl and mixed in some of the beef, then set it back down again. Mo sniffed the food and began chowing down.

Leaving the dog to relish his meal, Troy grabbed a beer from the fridge and walked out onto his deck. He rotated a lounge chair so that it faced the lavender sunset that filtered through the trees and stretched out on it. He preferred the wrought iron furniture they used to have back here, but at least the aluminum set Joanna had selected was lightweight. The bottle top unscrewed easily, and he took a swig of beer. It was the only beer he drank, Adirondack Gold, made by a family-owned brewery a few hours west of town. The taste was nice—light and crisp, a little bitter but not overwhelmingly so. It had been his dad's favorite, too—the fridge had always had a good supply. There was nothing his dad liked more than to come out here on summer evenings, lean back in his favorite deck chair, take a long pull from an ice-cold bottle, and share some simple lesson about happiness or family with his boys. These days Troy picked up some six-packs from Main Street Provisions every few weeks.

He put the bottle down on the side table and reached into his pocket for his cell phone so he could call Claire and tell her he'd be at work the rest of the week after all. Claire, his part-time associate at the clinic, was eight months pregnant with twins, and while she had insisted she felt perfectly fine and could hold down the fort while he took a couple of days off, he was glad he could give her the option of easing up.

"Sorry to bother you after hours," he said when she answered. He could hear the low murmur of people talking and glasses clinking in the background, and he figured she was out having dinner with her husband. She had told him she was determined to go out as much as she could into these last few weeks, since she'd be staying close to home once the twins came. "But I'll be in the office tomorrow. I canceled my trip."

"Oh? Everything okay?"

"There's a neighbor who needed some help. And a dog that needs watching. I'm not sure how long he'll be here."

"You're watching their dog? Why don't you just drop him off with me? We'll be home pretty soon, or I can drive over and get him. I hate to see you cancel. You sounded like you wanted to get away."

"It's fine. It's my neighbor's dog, I promised I'd watch him. It's no big deal. But as long as I'm coming in this week, you might as well stay home."

"What? No, I told you, I feel fine. Why don't you take the time off anyway?"

"There's nothing else I want to do. And the schedule looks light. Doesn't make sense for us both to be there."

"Hmmm," she said. "Okay, if you're sure. But call me if you change your mind. I still have a couple of weeks before these two little monsters will be fully cooked. And if I do stay home, I'll keep working on the fundraising drive. If we can get twenty more pledges, we'll be in the top five practices in the region."

"Hey, that's something," he said. Claire and Zoe, the tech at the clinic, were working on a major pledge initiative for the Mountainside Rescue, an Adirondacks-based animal rescue charity. "You should be proud of that."

"It's all thanks to you," she told him. "When they hear that you're involved, everyone in town is happy to give."

"I doubt that's the case."

"No, it is. Anyway, Troy, thanks about tomorrow. Call me if you need me. See you next week."

He nodded and put down the phone. Then he looked next door again. The house was still dark, and that had to be a bad sign. He'd been hoping that Sweet would come home tonight, maybe with a few bandages at the most. But she did look pretty bad, lying there by the stairs. It was all he could do to keep Sophie from becoming hysterical. He didn't have a lot of experience with kids, but he figured they were a lot like animals and took their cues from the humans they trusted: if you stayed calm, they stayed calm. As he followed the ambulance to the hospital with Sophie next to him, he repeated over and over that Sweet could be going to no finer place, that the doctors at Lake Summers Hospital were as good as it got.

He wondered now if he should have called Jenna after that day on the patio when Sweet got mixed up about the storm and called him Steven. He supposed he could have simply said he was concerned. Maybe she would have come up sooner. Maybe he could have prevented this whole thing.

Then he exhaled loudly, admonishing himself. It was crazy to think he could have saved Sweet with that one call. Why was he always so convinced he could make things better? He'd learned long ago that he wasn't good at that. He wasn't equipped for that. And the more he tried, the more of a disaster he always created.

He took another swig of beer. That's why he left Sophie at the hospital, after making sure that Cara, who'd been working at the emergency room desk, knew to keep an eye out for her until her mother arrived. He didn't want any more entanglements. He came home intending to pack quickly and still head out to Steven's cabin. But then Cara called about Mo, and before he knew it, he was offering to take the dog home and keep him as long as they needed.

He reached down to scratch Mo, who had followed him onto the deck and was now dozing on his side, clearly contented with the warm evening and his full belly. "How do I help your family without getting too involved?" Troy asked.

Thanks to the moonlight, he could see Mo lift his head and look at him with wide-open eyes. Then the dog yawned and dropped back down on his side. "Beyond your pay grade, huh?" Troy said. "I guess I'll have to find the answer myself."

CHAPTER FOUR

"I figured it out!" Sophie said. "Oh my God, Mom! I know what it is!"

"You know… wait, what?" Jenna lifted her eyes. Sophie was looking at her, her half-eaten burger in one hand and the last of her fries dangling from the other. "I'm sorry, honey, I wasn't paying attention…"

"Mom, concentrate! This is important!"

They were sitting at a small table on the outdoor deck of the Grill, the water from the inlet lapping softly below them as it sparkled beneath the orange sunset. It was past seven-thirty by the time they'd left the hospital, and she and Sophie were famished. They both wanted nothing other than a Deckside Burger Platter, the Grill's most popular dish, which came with a pretzel bun, double layer of Jack cheese, ketchup-laden twin patties, and sweet potato fries. They could barely wait to place their order. Everyone in town agreed the Grill made the best burger platters on the planet.

Jenna drank some water to wake herself up. She was relieved by what the older doctor—Dr. Roberts, was it?—had said about her mother, that things would look better in the morning. Still, her plans were all up in the air now, and the reorganization ahead felt overwhelming. She and Sophie were supposed to be on their way back to Rye in two days, so they could pack up and get ready to move to Lake Summers for good. But Jenna wasn't sure how long it might be before her mother could be here on her own. She might need some help around the house, making meals or even getting dressed, for a few days or possibly a couple of weeks. It could take a while for a bruised rib to heal. What if her mother needed them through the summer?

"Okay, I'm awake now," Jenna said. She clenched her fists to demonstrate her resolve, even though she was sure she could easily doze right off here at the table. The long drive to town, the unexpected rush to the hospital, and the big meal she'd just consumed were catching up with her. Dr. Roberts had recommended a good night's sleep, and that sounded like heaven. Still, she couldn't cut her daughter off. The last year had been so hard on Sophie, with her parents splitting up and her dad moving out. And it would get even harder when Matt finally stepped up and told Sophie the truth—that he wasn't living in a hotel in Connecticut, as he'd said, but had moved in with his fiancée, Felicity, and her two little girls. Sophie had been quiet in the car on the way to the Grill, and Jenna suspected Matt had said on the phone that he was too busy to come to Lake Summers. Now that she had perked up, the last thing Jenna wanted to do was rain on her parade.

"What is it?" Jenna said. "What do you know?"

"I don't know for sure, I mostly just *think*, but I'm pretty sure I'm right," Sophie said, finishing off the last of her fries and wiping her mouth with the back of her hand. "I *think* I figured out why she went downstairs."

"You know why Grandma went to the basement?" Jenna said. The question had been simmering inside her all evening. Even Chloe had found it inexplicable. "There's nothing she could possibly need down there," she'd said when Jenna called her just before they left the hospital. "See? This is what I'm telling you. She's not in her right mind."

It hadn't even occurred to Jenna that Sophie might have the answer.

"I don't call her Grandma anymore, I call her Sweet like everyone else," Sophie said. "And I was just remembering what she said when we were at Mrs. Pearl's. Something she never told anyone else in her life, that's what she said. And it's going to sound crazy to you, because she was really young, and you don't get stuff like that anymore. So you have to promise not to be all judgy—"

"I don't get young stuff? But your grandmother does?"

"Because she was young when it happened. And you're not young like that—"

"And I never was?" Jenna feigned offense.

"Mom, come on. Just promise, okay?"

"Fine," Jenna said, pretending she was still insulted. Then she laughed. "I promise. No judginess."

Sophie tilted her head and narrowed her eyes. A moment passed. Then the hint of a smile started to appear, as her cheek-bones rose and her eyes lit up. "Okay, Mom," she said, with a deliciously conspiratorial tone that Jenna wished she could bottle. "So, you know how she's always talking about love and falling in love and stuff?"

Jenna nodded. Her mother adored love stories—about regular people, about people from storybooks, about anyone. She never tired of telling the story of how she and Jenna's father had met and fallen in love, on a subway platform after a rock concert they'd both attended at Madison Square Garden. She was going uptown with her friends, he was going downtown with his, but their eyes met, and they smiled and said hello, and they stayed there on the platform talking as the trains rushed past on either side of them.

"Like the way she and your grandfather met?" Jenna said. "They fell in love in an instant, she always said."

"Yeah, but this was way earlier," Sophie said. "She was talking about her first love, her first *real* one, way before Grandpa. It was this movie star she met the summer she ran away, and she fell in love because he said these two words—she didn't remember what they were, but she said they were almost magical. And she was mad at herself because she couldn't remember more about him, and she forgot what the two words were. So I think there's something about him in the basement.

"I think she went down there to look for it."

*

Twenty minutes later, Jenna pulled into the driveway of her mother's house. The beams from the headlights glided along the adjacent bluebell garden, making the dense clusters of trumpet-shaped, deep-purple flowers look translucent, almost ghostlike. She reached the top, and the headlight beams formed two white-hot circles on the house's darkened stone facade. Shifting to park, she took advantage of the light that bounced back from the house to look at her daughter in the passenger seat. Sophie was dozing, her head against the window, her thin bottom lip quivering slightly. She looked peaceful. Of course, it was late to be bringing Sophie back, especially after such a long and draining day. Matt would have said she'd been irresponsible. But they'd stayed out so she and Sophie could talk.

Jenna turned off the engine and focused on the sound of her daughter breathing. Having had the drive to think things over, she wondered now if this story Sophie told about her mother's first love—her first *real* love, as Sophie called it—could be true. For as long as Jenna could remember, her mother had been completely in love with her dad. Even now, she could picture them from when she was a little girl: how closely they held each other as they danced under the stars during the Jazz in July evenings on the green; how her father would rest his head on her mother's lap, and her mother would stroke his forehead, when they all spread out on the beach blanket to watch the fireworks explode over the lake each July Fourth. She remembered the surprise party she and Chloe had planned for their parents for their fortieth wedding anniversary, how her father—the calmest person Jenna had ever known—had choked up as he raised his champagne flute, his eyes glistening behind his wire-rimmed glasses, and told the guests that his life began on the day they crossed paths on that subway platform. She remembered her mother's devotion to her father the summer before he died, how she held his hand and encouraged him to walk with her by the lake, how she was the only one who could get him to muster enough strength to leave the house.

Could her mother have had another love, a previous love? Someone so important to her, she'd kept something from their time together hidden away in the basement, as Sophie suspected? Were people allowed to have two all-encompassing loves in their lives? And after sharing forty-two years of marriage with Jenna's dad, was it right for her now to reminisce with Sophie about someone else?

It sounded so far-fetched. Her mother had often said she'd had a sheltered upbringing, that Jenna's grandfather was controlling and overprotective. If that was true, how could her mother have run off to California? Wouldn't her father have stopped her before she left, or tracked her down, or called the police or something? Wouldn't she have needed money and a place to stay? Jenna remembered now what Chloe had said on the phone, how she thought their mom was no longer "in her right mind." Had she gotten confused, thinking a story she'd once heard was actually *her* story? Or had she made it sound like the story happened to her in order keep Sophie entertained? That's what she had suspected when Mrs. Pearl brought up the story at the shop earlier today—that her mom had simply been trying to hold onto Sophie's attention. It was sweet that Sophie believed the story, and a huge relief that she and Matt hadn't soured Sophie completely on love. But Sophie would feel awful if she got caught up in this story, only to find out that it never happened.

Jenna looked again at her daughter, with those reddish-brown freckles and that gorgeous mess of thick, red hair that cascaded

down her back, a chaotic mix of waves and spirals. She loved that
Sophie never asked to get a hair treatment at the salon, the way
many of her friends did. She loved how Sophie felt comfortable
with her hair, with herself. She was like her grandmother that way.

She stroked Sophie's cheek to wake her up, then got out of the
car. Using her phone's flashlight to light her way—she couldn't
remember ever arriving here at night and not seeing the full range
of outside lights ablaze—she pulled her overnight bag from the
trunk and wheeled it up the front walk. Sophie teetered alongside
her, yawning loudly as Jenna unlocked the front door. Inside,
Jenna turned on as many lights as she could find—the small table
lamp on the hallway console, the kitchen high hats, the table
lamps and wall sconces in the living room. Her mother never
liked overhead lights, and only tolerated them in the kitchen.
She said table lamps and sconces were dreamy and romantic. She
liked her home to be dreamy and romantic.

Hoisting her bag over her shoulder, Jenna led Sophie up the
stairs. The staircase was her favorite part of the house—an elegant
mahogany focal point for the entrance hallway. The steps were
wide and made a sweeping curve, hugging the back wall as they
ascended to the second floor. The banister was smooth and shiny,
and it curved around the post on the bottom-most step. When
she was young, she'd often pretend the staircase was located
deep within a palace. She'd pretend that she was a princess being
summoned downstairs to help save a prince from some dreadful
fate, flying down the stairs as she grasped the curved banister with
one hand and pretended to lift the skirt of her long, bejeweled
dress with the other.

She turned on the lamp in the bedroom that Sophie was using,
the one that she and Chloe used to share when they were young.
It was furnished the same as it had been back then, with sheer
white curtains on the windows and two twin beds with coverlets
patterned in pale yellow peonies. Though the house was spacious,

it had only three bedrooms. Her mother had insisted that she and Chloe share a bedroom because she wanted an empty bedroom for guests, even though they rarely had overnight visitors. Jenna suspected her mom just liked the idea of her daughters sharing a room. Still, by the time Chloe started high school, she'd had enough and moved into the guest room. Jenna remembered being a little sad those first nights alone. The room felt empty with her sister gone.

"You okay, honey?" she asked Sophie. "Awake enough to get into pajamas and brush your teeth?"

Sophie nodded and trudged toward the hall bathroom, and Jenna went down the hall to her mother's room. The queen-size bed was made up perfectly, with crisp, white sheets, a white comforter with a coral-rose print, and a row of lacy pillows lined up against the headboard. It was the same bed her mother had shared with her dad every summer before Dad passed away. How strange it must have felt to her mother at first, not to have her husband beside her. Jenna knew what that was like, to feel an emptiness in bed. Although it was different when someone chose to leave. Her father hadn't wanted to leave them. He'd clung to life for months, hanging on in the hospital and then in the hospice, even after her mother told him he could go. It was funny, Jenna thought—she'd spent years in marketing communications, writing about beds, mattresses, box springs, foundations. Memory foam, air, springs. But she never wrote about the most important thing. How someone came to be in your bed, and how that person came to leave it.

She put on a tee shirt and pajama pants, brushed her teeth, then faced the bed again. Should she sleep in it? Or take the guest room downstairs? Or the second twin bed in the room Sophie was using? Years back, she and Matt had stayed here while her parents were in New York, and they'd slept on the full-size bed in the guest room downstairs because Matt said that being in her parents' bed made him uncomfortable. But now things were different. Surely her mother would encourage her to sleep here, hoping she'd feel cozy and safe. But would she feel guilty instead, knowing that her mother was in a hospital bed?

Before she could fully wrestle with that question, Sophie decided for her. She came into the bedroom in blue plaid shorts and an oversized white tee shirt, her red hair piled in a bun on the top of her head. "Mom, can I sleep here with you?" she asked.

"Of course," Jenna said. "Climb on in."

She went downstairs to turn off the lights, then came back and got into bed, stretching out an arm to invite Sophie to snuggle. Sophie curled up alongside her, and Jenna stroked the wisps of hair that didn't reach her ponytail. What a strange day it had been. It had started off as she headed out of Rye, anticipating taking the first steps toward a new life. She'd been so happy to cross the old Jason Drawbridge, so glad to see Mrs. Pearl, so relieved that poor Mo had had an uneventful trip up here. Poor little Mo, who'd been so sick just last week…

She shot up in bed. "Oh no!" she exclaimed into the darkness. Mo! She'd forgotten all about him. She had no idea where he was. She had no idea who was watching him, if he was safe, if he had eaten, if he was lying somewhere, wide-eyed and trembling, because he didn't know where she was.

She nudged Sophie's shoulder. "Soph? Where did you say Mo was? Who has Mo?"

Sophie didn't even open her eyes. "He's fine, Mom," she mumbled. "He's with Troy."

"With who?" she asked. Yes, now she remembered, the nurse at the hospital had mentioned that name. It rang a bell, because she'd been thinking of a Troy just that afternoon—Troy Jason, the oldest brother of the family that used to live next door, the boy she'd met on the footpath to the lake. Although everyone called him T.J.

"You don't have to worry," Sophie said. "He's a vet."

"But honey, he's been sick. Soph?"

Sophie didn't answer. She was already asleep.

Jenna sighed and settled back down in the bed. It didn't matter if she got more information from Sophie or not. It was nearly midnight now. There was no way she could go making calls or knocking on doors at this hour to get her dog.

All she could do was try to sleep. So that tomorrow she could find Mo and take care of Sophie. And see her mom. And talk to the doctors.

And figure out how she was going to manage this next chapter of her life.

CHAPTER FIVE

The sun was pouring into the bedroom when Jenna woke the next morning. Her mother kept the sheer white curtains on both windows pushed to the side, preferring an unobstructed view of the sky and insisting the thick woods behind the house provided more than enough privacy. Lying in bed, Jenna couldn't help but remember how she used to greet a morning like this when she was Sophie's age—throwing off the covers, pulling on a bathing suit and shorts, swallowing a few mouthfuls of cereal to humor her mom, and then dashing outside to find Steven, from next door, and debate what to do first: ride bikes into town? Explore the woodsy trails behind the Lake Summers Resort? Climb the rock formations adjacent to the lake? No matter what, the day always ended with a race to the Ice Creamery for the IC Special, a large vanilla milkshake with chocolate and caramel layered on the bottom and mini-marshmallows and brownie bits sprinkled on top. Back then, there were no organized activities, like the day camp Sophie was enrolled in. There were only wide-open days that zipped by in a flash and left you so tired, you could barely make it upstairs and into bed.

She glanced at her mother's nightstand clock—seven o'clock—and then looked across the bed at Sophie, who was fast asleep on her back, her legs splayed out and her mouth open. Sophie was like her dad, a big sleeper. Jenna had spent the whole marriage curled up on the edge of her bed, or tucking herself into the spaces Matt created for her—the spot beneath his outstretched arm where

her shoulder neatly fit when he slept on his back, the curve of
his neck just above his spine where she could snuggle her head,
draping her arm around his chest, when he slept on his side. In
the early years, she felt comforted by these nooks and crannies.
But over time, his limbs took up more and more of the bed, and
she felt small and slighted, having to conform to the portions of
the mattress he left her. Having to minimize her impact on their
shared space. She'd considered suggesting they buy a king-size
bed, but gradually realized that what she was struggling with,
what they were struggling with, was much, much bigger than
the surface area of their mattress.

She tiptoed downstairs, wanting to let Sophie sleep a little
longer. It seemed a good sign that no one from the hospital needed
to reach her overnight. In the kitchen, she made a pot of coffee,
then poured some into a mug and took it outside to the patio.
She was anxious about Mo, but even if she woke Sophie up to
ask again where he was, it was probably too early to go calling
a stranger about her dog. She should wait at least another hour.

She strolled off the patio and over to the bluebell garden. It
was her favorite part of the house, right beneath the window of
her old bedroom. There used to be a huge oak tree there as well,
but now there was a small bare spot where the trunk had been,
and at this time of year, the bluebells were so lush that the bare
spot was completely hidden. The garden had been Jenna's favorite
place to run barefoot and play pretend games when she was
young. If the mahogany staircase inside was the place where she
would come running down to save her prince, then the bluebell
garden was where he'd thank her with a kiss when she completed
whatever mission he'd needed her for, whether it was rescuing
the kingdom's kidnapped children and returning them to their
parents, or finding the prince's dog, who'd gotten lost in the forest.

She took another sip of coffee and went back to the patio.
Sitting down on a tan-cushioned lounge chair, she stretched out

her legs and looked over at the Jasons' house, which she could see just past the trees on the far side of the yard. She'd never noticed it when she was a kid, but it was actually much smaller than her house—although it made sense, since hers was originally the main residence of a long-forgotten horse farm, and theirs, the carriage house. Still, the Jasons' house was where she and Steven would go when it rained or they needed a break from the sun. Mrs. Jason always had cream cheese sandwiches or baked treats waiting—brownies or chocolate-chip cookies or homemade caramel candies. Plus, there was something fun about a house with so many brothers and a big golden retriever and a dad who owned some kind of a local store—was it a print shop?—and could come home during the day. Her house was so quiet by comparison. Her dad stayed back in their regular home near New York City during the week so he could commute to the office, coming up to Lake Summers on weekends, and her mother was often out working on whatever musical she was organizing that summer. And Chloe was usually with her friends and wanted nothing to do with Jenna or Steven.

She took a sip of coffee. It was strange, how all those summers seemed to meld into one. She barely remembered returning every June. Was everyone's childhood like that? She supposed she'd realized from time to time that they were all growing up. The twins must have graduated from tricycles to two-wheelers at some point, and the older boys—first T.J. and then Steven—they must have started changing, too, their voices getting deeper, their chests broader. At some point, T.J. and then Steven learned to drive. Then T.J. got that part-time job at the Lake Summers Resort, parking cars, and a second job working the cash register at Mr. Miller's dry-cleaning store. One summer, college brochures started showing up on the Jasons' kitchen table. But still, through it all, they'd remained the same old family next door.

Until that August, the year of the big storm.

Sophie came outside, still in her pajamas. "Aren't we going to get Sweet?" she said. "Why didn't you wake me up?"

"I wanted to let you sleep," Jenna said. "We'll go there right after we eat and get Mo. Unless you want to go to the lake," she added. "You can go to camp and be with your friends. There's no reason you have to come with me to the hospital."

"Why don't you want me to come to the hospital?"

"I didn't say that. I'm just saying you don't have to."

"But I want to tell Sweet I can help her find what she was looking for in the basement."

Jenna sat up and planted her feet on the ground. She was even more certain today than she had been last night that the Hollywood love story could never have happened. It didn't make sense. Her father had been her mother's one true love, her only love. Even now, she could see her mother telling the story of how they met to Mrs. Jason and a few other moms from the neighborhood who'd come over for coffee on the patio one morning. "We finally left the platform and found a twenty-four-hour coffee shop on the corner of Madison Avenue," she said. "I just sat there drinking in his dreamy brown hair and those long eyelashes. And when he told me that his dad had died and he'd sacrificed his plans to go to law school so he could help his mom take care of his younger sisters—that's when I knew I wanted to marry this man."

So either her mother had made up the Hollywood story to amuse Sophie or her memory was playing tricks on her. Either way, it felt wrong to continue to let Sophie believe in this fantasy. On the other hand, she was reluctant to burst Sophie's bubble now. Talking about her grandmother's so-called love had put Sophie in such a good mood.

"Honey, I love that you want to see her," she said. "But she'll probably be home this afternoon. Don't you think you'll have more fun at camp?"

"But I want to talk to her about that guy."

"Yes, but she may not remember it the same way now. Or she may not want to talk about it. Maybe it was more like something she was… just imagining…"

"I knew you were going to do this!" Sophie said. "I knew you weren't taking me seriously, even though you said you were. Listen, I know she wants me to find out about this guy because I was there yesterday, you weren't. So maybe *you* don't want to be there. Fine, drop me off. *You're* the one that doesn't have to stay. I'm getting dressed."

"Soph—" Jenna called, jumping up from the chair and spilling the remains of her coffee all over her shirt. But Sophie was already heading upstairs. Jenna went back into the kitchen and grabbed a dishtowel, thankful that the coffee wasn't still hot. She sighed and hurled the dirty dishtowel onto the countertop. The truth was, the way for Sophie to help her grandmother most would be to get close with her new friends at the lakeside camp, so she'd agree to move to Lake Summers for good. But Sophie didn't know that. She believed the story her grandmother had begun yesterday at Pearl's was true; she was charmed and intrigued by it. And Jenna had encouraged Sophie at the restaurant last night because it was so good to see her excited and revved up to learn more. If she now seemed skeptical or unsupportive of Sophie's plan, she'd drive her daughter away.

She went to the refrigerator to take out the eggs, milk, and bread, so she could make a quick breakfast of French toast. Once she and Sophie were finished eating, she cleared the table while Sophie went upstairs to brush her teeth. She wanted to get Mo before they went to the hospital, and she hoped Sophie remembered how to contact the person who had him. Otherwise, she'd have to call the hospital and try to track down the nurse who'd been at the emergency room desk last night. She hated that she'd have to leave Mo all alone today in the house, but she didn't have any other choice. If things were okay at the hospital, then she could come home before it got too late and take him for a nice walk by the lake.

She loaded the dishwasher and headed outside to haul the cartons of Mo's prescription food from her car before going upstairs to get dressed. But when she opened the front door, she noticed a rolled-up sheet of paper looped through the door handle. She pulled it off and unrolled it. There was a short, handwritten note:

Jenna,

I figured you got home late last night, so I didn't want to wake you and Sophie up. Don't worry, Mo's fine. I'll take him to work with me, so he won't be by himself all day. We can meet up later. I'm sorry about your mother. I hope she's feeling better.

Troy

She read it again, confused by the tone. Who was this guy? It sounded like he knew her. But she didn't know any Troy who lived here in Lake Summers. The only Troy she'd ever known—not just here, but anywhere—was T.J., the boy who lived next door. But the Jasons moved out of town when she was in her senior year of high school.

She stepped inside, holding the note. "Hey, Soph?" she called upstairs.

"I'll be right down," Sophie called back.

"Who did you say is watching Mo?"

She came out of the bathroom and leaned over the railing. "I told you. Troy."

"Yeah, but Troy who?"

"I don't know. The guy who lives next door. Although Sweet said you called him something else. T.R. or T.Y.…"

"T.J.?"

"Yeah, that's right. T.J."

"*T.J.?* That can't be right. He moved a long time ago."

"I guess he moved back. I have to get a hair tie…"

She left the banister, and Jenna went to close the front door. Then she paused and looked again at the small converted carriage house beyond the line of trees. T.J. had Mo? T.J. moved back?

Re-rolling the paper, she pressed it against her chest, wondering why she was suddenly finding it hard to breathe. Was it just the surprise of it all?

Or was it the uncertainty of how she would feel, what she would say, when she saw him later?

*

At the hospital, they took the elevator to the fourth floor. They'd gotten no information when they arrived at the main desk; the attendant had simply handed them passes to attach to their clothes and pointed toward the elevator bank. Jenna squeezed Sophie's hand as they traveled upward. She hoped her mom was feeling better this morning, and that the doctors were ready to release her. She hoped they could all get back to normal, as though the last eighteen hours or so had been nothing more than a hiccup. The elevator doors opened, and she put her arm around Sophie's shoulders and led her down the hallway.

They arrived at Room 424, and Jenna slowed as she approached the threshold, taking a breath before plunging forward. It was a small but sunny private room. The bed, which took up most of the space, was empty.

Then she heard her mother's voice. "Finally, my bluebell girls!" she said. "Coming to rescue me at last! I am decidedly not the hospital type. Isn't that true, Henry?"

Her mother was sitting on a straight-backed chair by the window, opposite a young man wearing blue scrubs and sporting a tiny gold hoop through one earlobe. There was a rolling tray table in between them with some playing cards arranged in piles.

"That is for sure!" the man said, tossing the cards in his hand onto the table. "Most patients don't win nearly so often."

"Oh, you're just letting me win because you feel sorry for me," she said. "And by the way, don't call me a patient! I'm simply a guest and I'm leaving as soon as they let me go. Henry, this is my daughter and my granddaughter. Girls, this is Henry, my savior. I would not have gotten through this morning without him!"

"Hi, Sweet!" Sophie said as she ran over and kissed her grandmother's cheek. "You look like you didn't even fall at all!"

"Nice to meet you both," Henry said as he gathered up the cards and put them into his pocket. "Don't forget to say goodbye before you leave, Sweet."

Jenna watched him leave, then turned back to her mother. The difference between now and how she looked last night in the emergency room was breathtaking. It was hard to believe something as simple as a few hours of sleep could work such magic, but there was no other explanation—other than, maybe, her mother's sheer force of will. Even wearing a blue-checked hospital gown, she looked beautiful. Elegant. She must have recruited a nurse or hospital volunteer to go down to the gift shop to get a hairbrush, some hairpins and a tube of her favorite color of lip gloss, because her hair had been gathered into her regular small bun at the back of her neck, and her lips had a subtle peach shine to them. Jenna felt almost silly for worrying so much yesterday when she arrived at the hospital. Her mother would never have let even a fall down the stairs set her back for more than a day. The only visible remnant of her fall was a thin bandage around her ankle.

"I think you have an admirer," Jenna said, kissing her mother's cheek.

"Oh, Henry? He's one of the helpers here. Studying accounting at night at the community college. Very sweet."

Jenna sat down on the edge of the bed. "You look good, Mom," she said. "A lot better than you did last night."

Her mother grinned, showing off her tiny teeth. Jenna had always thought that was one of her most charming features. They looked like little seed pearls and made her seem young, no matter how white her hair got or how deep the lines on her forehead and around her mouth grew. "I'm glad to hear that. And I'll look even better once I can get out of this silly gown and into some real clothes. When do we leave?"

"As soon as I talk to the doctor. So no more pain?"

She touched her side. "This hurts a little. And moving around is a little rough, but not too bad. Mostly I'm embarrassed. Falling down like a child. Those old stairs are terribly slippery. Next time I keep a tight grip on the banister."

"Next time? Why were you going to the basement anyway?" Jenna said.

"Why did I go to the basement? Why wouldn't I go to the basement?"

"Because there's nothing there—"

"Well, sometimes you have to go to the basement. Sometimes a person goes to the basement."

"What? But I'm asking why. Why would you—"

"Mom, stop!" Sophie said. "Sweet, Mom doesn't believe there's anything in the basement about the movie star and the two words."

"Sophie, I didn't say that—" Jenna said.

"But don't worry," Sophie continued. "Because even if she doesn't believe us, I know that's why you went to the basement—"

"Sophie, that's enough—"

Just then there was a knock on the open door, and a young doctor with a mop of brown curls strode into the room. "How are you all doing this morning?" she said. "Sweet, how are you feeling? How was breakfast?"

"Not nearly as delicious as my own coffee on my own patio," she answered. "I am extremely ready to go home."

"Oh, I don't blame you a bit," the doctor said. "I'm working on getting you out of here as soon as we can." She turned to Jenna. "I'm Dr. Tanner. Are you Mrs. Clayton's daughter?"

Jenna nodded and introduced Sophie.

"I've taken over your mother's care from Dr. Banes," she said. "Your mom said it would be fine if you and I went over some information. Why don't we step into the hallway for a minute? Let's let your mom keep enjoying her granddaughter."

Jenna followed the doctor out of the room, surprised she wanted to talk to her without her mother there. "Is everything okay?" she asked when the doctor stopped and turned to face her. "She can go home today, can't she?"

"Everything looks good," the doctor answered. "But it was a significant fall. Because of her age, we'd like to monitor her one more night."

"Okay," Jenna said. "If that's what you think is best."

"And I also wanted to let you know that she seemed a little confused this morning. She didn't know where she was or what had happened yesterday until we reminded her. Have you ever noticed anything like this? Forgetting where she is or what recently happened?"

Jenna shook her head. "Although my sister mentioned something. And actually…" She thought back on the discussion they'd had a moment ago. "Actually she sounded strange just now. Like she forgot why she went to the basement but didn't want me to know she didn't remember. Although she's never had a great memory. She's the kind of person who's always thinking of a zillion things."

"Yes, but being absentminded is not the same as forgetting what happened a little while ago."

"So you think there's a problem?"

"I'm not sure," the doctor said. "After all, she has been through a trauma. But it's something to keep an eye on. I understand she lives alone?"

Jenna nodded.

"That may be something you want to reconsider, what with the fall and this new concern we want to watch. I can have the social worker call you and she'll be able to discuss some options. Very nice to meet you, Mrs. Marsh. The nurses can find me if you have any questions."

She smiled and Jenna thanked her and went back toward her mother's room. Outside she paused and leaned her back against the wall. She was going to have to tell Chloe what this doctor had said, and that would reinforce Chloe's argument for the place on Long Island. She'd probably want to start making calls and filling out applications right away. But Mom loved Lake Summers, and she loved her house. She loved the white linens on the beds and the stone patio that looked out onto the woods, and the bluebell garden that burst out with color so reliably every spring. She loved the lake and the stores and the concerts on the green, and stopping for iced tea and a muffin at Mrs. Pearl's. How could they force their mother to leave? But after what the doctor said, how could they let her stay?

"Jenna?"

She startled, so deep in her thoughts that she hadn't noticed Dr. Roberts approaching. But she recognized him as soon as she looked up. His white hair and mustache were unmistakable. As were the curves that formed around the sides of his eyes when he smiled.

"How's she doing this morning?" he asked.

"She's good," she said. "Much better."

"But you look concerned," he said. "Something wrong?"

"No, it's just…" She paused a moment, holding her breath while she thought. "It's just this is all more complicated than I realized. The other doctor feels my mom shouldn't live alone anymore. She wants the social worker to call me with options. I guess I wasn't prepared for that."

He nodded. "I'm sure it came as a shock. You were here for a regular visit. Life can sometimes knock your socks off."

"It wasn't a regular visit," she said. "I was coming to make plans to move to Lake Summers in September. But if my mother is no longer safe living alone, maybe I should move in now. It'll be hard to do it so fast, but I can do it if that's what she needs. Do you think that would be a good idea?"

He crossed his arms over his chest, his white coat hiking up on his shoulders. "I wouldn't make long-term decisions right this moment," he said. "The top priority is to help your mother recover completely from the fall. So yes, if you and your daughter can stay in town for now, I'd make every effort to do that. In my experience, there's a lot to be said for being home and close to family—especially for someone turning seventy-six in August."

He raised his eyebrows, confirming that yes, he knew she had a birthday coming up. "Not that it's possible all the time. But given that she's more banged up than anything, I'd say she'll be more comfortable and have a better recovery at home.

"In fact, just look," he said. "I'd call that the best medicine in the world."

He gestured toward her mother's room, and Jenna peeked in. Sophie was sitting on the armrest of her mother's chair, her knees gathered up by her chin. Her mother was speaking, her hand resting on one of Sophie's knees, and Sophie was smiling and nodding.

The doctor smiled. "Take care, Jenna. Don't hesitate to call me if I can help in any way."

He reached into the pocket of his white coat and drew out a card, then handed it to her and strolled toward the nurses' station. She heard him say a few words, something about an Italian dinner he was cooking, and the nurses laughed and shooed him away. She wanted to believe him, that bringing her mother home was best. He was so calm and encouraging, both last night and today, and she trusted him. He even knew how old her mother was, and that her birthday was coming up. She supposed he'd learned that from her records, but it was nice that he'd mentioned it.

She walked back into the room and caught some of what her mother was saying. "Yes, that's right, there were two words," she said. "Oh, I wish I could remember them. He explained so beautifully why they were important. And that was the moment I knew that my life was changed—"

"Sorry to interrupt, but Sophie, that looks awfully dangerous," Jenna said. "You'll fall backward and land on your head, and next thing you know, we'll be coming here to visit you."

"Ugh, Mom," Sophie said as she pulled her legs up over the armrest and stood. "You're interrupting us. Tell her, Sweet. You were looking for something you hid away in the basement. You were looking for stuff about your first real love. I told you, Mom," she added. "She was trying to find it so she could show me."

"It was deep inside something," her mother said. "A closet or a drawer. Some enclosure of some type, that I remember. It had a little chip on it, like a crack or a mark. That's where the rest of the story is."

"Don't worry, Sweet," Sophie said. "I'll find it, no matter how long it takes. We can stay here all summer, I don't have to be anywhere until school starts. I'll find the stuff and then I'll find the guy. And then you can be with him forever."

CHAPTER SIX

Troy turned onto Main Street and made his way alongside the green, acknowledging with a resigned nod all the smiles and chuckles levied in his direction. He didn't like attention and never usually garnered it on his way to Pearl's and then over to the office. But he knew there was no escape today, because the expressions of amusement weren't about him.

No, they were about his four-legged companion, who was trotting alongside him, his tail high and his nose proudly turned upward.

He stopped at an intersection to wait for the light to change, and Mo stayed by his side, studying the people around him, his eyes reflecting bits of gold from the sun. Out of caution, he'd done a quick check with his stethoscope before they left the house, and despite the little guy's age and recent health scare, his heart sounded good. Troy figured that Mo would nap for most of the morning, while he saw patients, and then they could take a walk by the lake around noon. He'd given Mo a small breakfast and had brought in his backpack some leftover boiled beef, which he could sprinkle over the prescription dog food he stocked in the office, in case Mo got hungry during the day.

Arriving outside of Pearl's, he scanned the daily muffin varieties. They had the mixed-berry with crumb topping today, one of his two favorites—his other was cinnamon swirl with a brown sugar glaze—and he decided to pick up a couple, along with his normal coffee order. He was tying Mo's leash to the outdoor bench when a little girl with high blonde pigtails came out of the shop and walked over to him, her father watching from a few steps away, a cardboard tray with two coffees in his hand.

"Can I pet your dog?" the little girl asked.

"Sure," Troy answered. Having spent the whole night together, he knew Mo was friendly. He squatted down so he was eye to eye with the girl. "Do it like this," he said and held out his hand toward Mo's nose, palm up. "That's how he likes to meet new people."

The little girl followed his directions, and Mo placed his nose in the girl's palm. She jumped up and shook her hand. "He sniffed me!" she squealed.

The dad put the tray on the bench and picked her up. "No, he kissed you!"

"No, Daddy, he sniffed me!"

"That's how dogs kiss!"

Troy nodded as he stood back up, even though the dad was wrong and the girl was right. Mo had most certainly sniffed her, probably captivated by smells of breakfast still on her fingers.

The little girl wiped her hand on the front of her yellow dress. "Yuck! Why is it wet?" she asked.

"The wetness helps his nose smell better," Troy said. "And helps him stay cool."

"Helps him smell better? Helps him *smell* better?" The little girl started to giggle. "The water helps him smell better? Like… *flowers?*" She threw her head back and laughed out loud.

"No, that's not what I meant," Troy said. "It makes him better at smelling. It's not really water. It's actually mucus…"

"Mucus? *Haaa!*" She threw her whole body back this time, and it was all her dad could do to keep her from tumbling out of his arms and falling on her head.

He pushed her upright. "I think someone had too many chocolate chips on her waffle this morning," he said. "Come on, let's go bring Mommy her coffee. Thanks," he called to Troy over his shoulder as he picked up the coffee tray with his free hand and proceeded down Main Street.

Troy squatted beside Mo and stroked his back to encourage him to lie down. He was glad no one he knew had seen that encounter with the little girl. Because what he'd said to her was ridiculous. He had tried his best, squatting down and demonstrating what to do with her hand, but that said more about his knowledge of dogs than of kids. He didn't know how to talk to young children. Of course she'd mistake what he meant about the dog and smelling. And of course she'd find the word mucus funny. Who used a word like mucus around little kids, unless you *wanted* them to laugh? Talking to kids was an acquired skill. His brother Steven had three kids, and his other brothers, the twins, had two each, with Cal expecting a third in a few months. They all knew how to speak to kids. They talked to their kids the way this dad had, kind of talking about them rather than directly to them. *Someone had too many chocolate chips. Somebody's up way past her bedtime. Somebody isn't going to get dessert if somebody doesn't finish her vegetables.*

What was that all about? Did it make the kids better listeners, or just help the parents avoid having to make direct accusations? Troy wondered if anyone had actually studied the effects of talking like that. He knew how to talk to dogs because he was around them all the time. He hardly ever talked to children. A long time ago, he'd expected to have kids and a wife, as well as a big house where his brothers and their families would come for backyard barbecues and Thanksgiving dinners. He was the oldest, so he'd assumed that would be his role. Not that he regretted not having kids. You can't miss what you don't have. Ignorance didn't hurt. But it could make you feel foolish. Like when you said the word mucus to a four-year-old.

Although he wasn't bad with older kids. After all, he'd taken care of his three younger brothers all those years ago, and they didn't turn out so bad. And he'd had a pretty good relationship with Sophie these last two weeks. She was a sweet kid. Kind of guarded when he first showed up, but she'd relaxed after some time had passed and she saw him more often, when he was outside watering his lawn or fixing odds and ends around Sweet's house. "My poor Sophie," Sweet had said to him one morning as she stood by herself in the street, watching her granddaughter head down the block on her way to camp. He'd gone next door to wheel her trash bins to the curb and then walked over to make sure she was okay. She'd meandered back toward the house with him, explaining that Jenna's husband had left a few months ago, throwing both Jenna and Sophie into a tailspin.

"Sophie doesn't understand what's happened to her parents, and she's so lost," Sweet said. "I hope she'll find her smile while she's here."

Troy watched Mo circle the small patch of grass outside of Pearl's and then settle into a ball. "I'll be right back, little guy," he said, and then went into the shop and over to the coffee line. He was glad that Mo had slept well last night and looked so content this morning, as he had no idea how long Jenna would need his help. The house next door was dark when he went to bed last night, and while he'd seen a car in the driveway this morning—an SUV with the name of a Rye car dealer on the bumper, so it had to be Jenna's—he didn't want to risk waking anyone up. So he'd left a note and brought Mo to work.

He thought about Jenna on and off all night. She'd always been so close to Sweet, closer than Chloe, who would often complain about how impractical and unconventional their mother was. Jenna and Steven's shenanigans had sometimes gotten Jenna into trouble with her dad, but as far as he knew, Sweet was never harsh with her. Instead, she had tried to channel Jenna's energy into creative projects, like helping with the Lake Summers Theatrical's production of *The Wizard of Oz* one summer. Even though that backfired when Jenna and Steven tried to balance on the lighting bar across the top of the stage as if it were a tightrope, and both ended up plunging straight to the ground. Jenna broke her wrist and Steven wound up with a severely bruised kneecap. But that didn't settle them down. It just made the grown-ups more careful to assign them projects that kept them away from high places.

And yet now, Jenna was a single mother whose ex-husband, according to Sweet, knew just how to make her doubt herself, how to target the small shards of pride and self-esteem she had left. A part of him wanted to scoop her up and build her back into the person she once was. But he told himself not to think like that. Who was he to rescue anyone? He'd come back here to get away, not to trade one set of entanglements for another.

"Coffee?" the young guy behind the counter asked.

He nodded. "Two medium regulars, milk and sugar," he said. "And I'll take a couple of the mixed-berry muffins, too."

"Sorry," the guy said. "They haven't come out of the oven yet."

"No, no, we have them," a voice shouted from the kitchen. Then the swinging doors opened and Mrs. Pearl appeared. "I made a few early for him, Jake. They're over on the last shelf. Anything for Lake Summers' favorite son."

Troy gave her a sideways look. "I've told you before, it's going to take a lot more than muffins to get me to forgive you for dragging me back here," he teased.

"My, my, we're awfully grumpy before we have our coffee," she teased back. "Jake, make his a large. Because… hey, wait a minute, aren't you supposed to be at your brother's cabin?" she asked. "Don't tell me Claire went into labor! She's not due for a few weeks yet. Did you have to stay and cover for her?"

"No, nothing with Claire," he said. "Something else came up. I'll get back to the cabin later this summer." He paid for his order and took the bakery bag and a cardboard tray with the coffees. "Thanks for the muffins. Appreciate it."

"My pleasure," Mrs. Pearl said as she went back into the kitchen. "Anything for the guy who rescued the animal clinic!"

He nodded and went back outside and put the bag and tray on the bench so he could untie Mo's leash. "Okay, my man, do me a favor and walk nicely," he said. "No pulling, or we'll both end up wearing these coffees."

He slipped his wrist into the loop of Mo's leash and proceeded along Main Street, away from the hubbub of the town center. His practice was a little off the beaten path, in a converted Victorian house on the corner of Main and Walnut. What had been the living room was now the reception area, while the downstairs bedrooms were examining rooms. The dining room was his office, and the upstairs was all storage. It was a far cry from the animal hospital where he worked when he lived in Philadelphia, a three-story facility with four vets and two state-of-the-art operating rooms. But he had been ready for a change when Mrs. Pearl called to ask him to come home. The old vet from his childhood, Dr. Munoz, had died suddenly, and his pregnant associate, Claire, was planning to cut her hours dramatically once the babies were born.

"I heard your tenant is moving out," she said. "So you have your old childhood house to live in. This town needs its own vet, Troy. It'll change everything if the clinic closes and people have to drive a half-hour to Lyons Hill for the nearest animal hospital."

He'd agreed pretty quickly. He didn't want to turn her down, and he had nothing keeping him in Philly, anyway. He'd missed Lake Summers. No other place had ever felt like home.

He reached the clinic and pushed open the door. Mo trotted inside as if he knew exactly where he was going. "Hey, Zoe," he said. "Brought a friend for the day."

A young woman with red-framed glasses and a crown of jet-black hair in a high bun atop her head came around from behind the wooden desk. "Oh, how adorable!" she exclaimed.

"Who is this? And what are you doing here, anyway? I thought you were going away."

"Nope, you're stuck with me, I'm sorry to say. And this is Mo, my house guest for now. I didn't want to leave him alone all day."

"Well, of course not," she said, coming down onto her leggings-covered knees. Mo rolled onto his back, and she scratched his belly. "Hello, Mr. Mo. Would you like to hang with me and be a greeter?"

"You don't have to watch him," Troy said. "I can keep him in my office—"

"No, I won't let you take him!" she said. "He is too cute."

"Okay, if you're sure." He handed Zoe the leash. "Don't give him anything to eat—he's on a special diet. Otherwise, he shouldn't be any problem. He's a real sweet dog. Thanks, Zoe."

"No worries. I put the schedule on the desk. Mrs. Sally canceled, so your first appointment isn't until ten thirty. Although when I got here, there was a voicemail from Art Grayson saying he was going to stop by this morning. I was about to call him and tell him you weren't coming in. But since you're here, do you want to just see him?"

Troy sighed. "Sure, that's fine," he said. He supposed it was inevitable that Art would track him down. Art owned several buildings in town and, according to Mrs. Pearl, had purchased the Lake Summers Resort, a 100-year-old inn that sat on a huge swath of land, a few years ago for cash. You didn't get that successful by allowing people to avoid you.

He took his coffee and pulled a muffin and napkin from the bag, then went into his office and set his breakfast on the desk. It was an old-fashioned wooden type, large and boxy, with wooden drawers that were coming apart. The reclining wood desk chair seemed fragile, too—so much so that Claire no longer sat on it, convinced that it couldn't withstand both her and the twins she was carrying. But Troy resisted. It meant something that

Dr. Munoz had sat in this very place for years—no, decades. He remembered it from when he was a kid and would take his family's golden retriever, Cody, here for shots and checkups. And the truth was, he didn't need anything modern or new. He had enough modern stuff in his house, thanks to Steven's wife, Joanna.

He looked at the appointment list Zoe had left for him. The Wellmans were coming in to get their new puppy vaccinated, and then Mrs. Kim was bringing in Josie, her Jack Russell terrier, who had taken a bad jump off the sofa and seemed to have torn her ACL. If he were still in Philadelphia, he'd have been able to repair it, but the Lake Summers office wasn't equipped for surgery, so he'd probably have to send them to Lyons Hill. He was sorry he couldn't operate—not so much because he liked surgery, but because when someone needed him, he wanted to do the complete job. Still, he was glad he was here. He had had enough of the Philly house after Stacia moved out, taking the dachshunds, Tick and Tock, with her. He'd been ready for a change.

A couple of quick knocks sounded at the door. "Hey there, Doc," a voice said. "Mind if I come in?"

The door opened wider, and a well-toned man with a gray newsboy cap and the whitest smile of anyone Troy had even known, let alone someone in his seventies, appeared. "My apologies for stopping by on such short notice, but I can't seem to get you to return my calls. Were you this much of a pip when you were a kid?"

"Hey, Art, sorry about that," Troy said, standing up to shake the man's hand and then motioning for Art to sit in the worn leather chair opposite the desk. He didn't like people to think him rude. But he'd had a funny feeling ever since Art spotted him on the sidewalk a few weeks back, recognizing him from when Troy was in high school and would tutor his eighth-grade son in math. Art said he had a new town project that he wanted to tell Troy about over drinks, and that's when Troy had decided to keep his distance.

He liked Art, as everyone in town did. Despite his wealth, he was down-to-earth, and although he'd traveled all over the world, he had grown up in Lake Summers and never wanted to live anywhere else. But he was also known to be remarkably persuasive. And Troy wasn't interested in getting involved in any new projects.

"How's the resort doing?" Troy asked. "Enjoying the hotel business?"

Art took off his cap and twirled it around on a finger. "What I like is keeping Lake Summers as Lake Summers," he said. "Out of the hands of the big corporations. Last thing we need is a hotel chain altering the whole complexion of the town."

He put his cap on Troy's desk and rubbed his hands together. "My problem is my staff," he said. "The bright kids, the ones with the best ideas—they stay a year or two and then go down to New York or east to Boston to work. The town needs young blood to grow and prosper. The resort does, too. Not everyone is a Troy Jason, you know? Not everyone has this town in their blood, and will come straight home when the call goes out."

Troy shook his head. "It was the right time, that's all. I was ready to make a change…"

"The kids I have working for me, they're always looking for 'meaning,'" he said, putting the word in air quotes. "They're like my son used to be, the one you tutored when you were in high school. He didn't care a whit about money—he was out in Seattle campaigning for a guy running for Congress on a platform of workplace safety. The guy had no political experience, no organization, no funding, and my son was pleased as punch to knock on doors and eat chips for dinner. He wanted to help make the world a better place, you know?"

"He was a good kid," Troy said. "Hey, Art, I've got a dog with a sore leg coming in soon. Is there something you needed?"

"You bet there is," he said. "You see, I'm putting together something big this year, something the kids working for me can get behind. A major local history exhibit at the resort. Museum-quality lighting, poster-size prints on the walls, the works. There'll be a huge grand opening—music, raffles, food. Make the whole town proud they live here, give the people who work for me something big to get behind."

"Sounds great," Troy said. "Put us down for something for the raffle. A couple of jars of dog treats or even a free wellness checkup. Zoe can set that up—"

"Is that why you think I'm here? No, what I have in mind for you is much bigger. I want you to be the honorary chair of the big event."

"What?" Troy froze. He had not seen this coming. "No, no, Art. I don't know anything about history. I'm not the guy—"

"Are you kidding? You're exactly the guy. You're smart, you're a leader, your name means something in this town. The picture of you and your brothers at the dedication of the drawbridge still hangs in Village Hall. You're like that guy my son worked for. Nobody will ever forget the sacrifices your family made."

"That's about my dad, not me."

"Don't be so modest, you're a chip off the old block. You have plenty to be proud of. And besides, you saved this clinic. You're Lake Summers' favorite son, like Mrs. Pearl says."

"Art, no. I don't have time—"

"That's the beauty of it. It's honorary, that means it won't take any time at all. Let me put your name and your picture on a couple of posters, come by to check out the installation once in a while if you feel like it, and show up for the grand opening on August 8th. You'd come anyway for that, it's a town celebration. You care about this town, you wouldn't have come back if you didn't."

Troy rubbed his forehead. He didn't want to do this. He didn't want the attention. But Art was right. He cared about the town. It was his refuge after Stacia left. It was home. And he agreed with Art; he liked the town the way it was. He didn't want big corporations buying up businesses. Art had a point, people needed to understand what they had here. And if he could help accomplish that just by lending his name, was that so hard?

It was something his dad would do. His dad would have been thrilled to be asked. It was something his dad would want *him* to do.

He put his palms on the desk. "Okay," he said. "If you think it can help to put my picture on a poster, then I'm good. And sure, I'll show up on August 8th."

"Good man!" Art said, grabbing his cap and standing up. "Your dad would be proud."

They shook hands and Art left, and Zoe called to him that the Wellmans had arrived. Troy took a quick sip of coffee and a bite of muffin, then brushed the crumbs off his hands as he rounded the desk. He supposed it wasn't a big deal, helping out Art and the town in this way. He only hoped there wouldn't be too many posters. He hated the thought of seeing his face all over town. But he supposed he'd be fine as long as he didn't have to make a speech or shake too many hands.

Because he wasn't his dad. He liked flying under the radar. He'd been living the quiet life he wanted for months now, with little disruption other than Sweet's observations about his social life and Steven's increasing pressure to put the house on the market. Why did everything have to change? Suddenly he was worrying about Sweet and taking care of Mo and getting blindsided by Art. And on top of that, now Jenna was back in town. He was going to have to see her. He was going to have to return Mo and ask how her mother was doing, and how she was doing. He was going to have to offer to help more if she needed it.

He wondered for a moment just how much longer he'd be able to stay in town. How soon it would be before he left Lake Summers once again.

CHAPTER SEVEN

"So the older doctor says she'll do better with us at home, but Chloe wants her to move straight into this assisted living place she found. Oh, and then there's Sophie, who thinks that somewhere out there, there's a movie star from sixty years ago who'll want nothing more than to swoop in and carry her away."

"I'd go with the movie star," Mrs. Pearl said. Then she reached across the table and took Jenna's hand. "But seriously, sweetie. What do *you* want to do?"

They were sitting at one of the café's outdoor bistro tables, a large striped market umbrella shielding them from the sun and two tall glasses of half-finished iced coffee sweating in front of them. Jenna sighed as she drew her hand from Mrs. Pearl's and clasped both hands together, pressing them against her chin. Less than twenty-four hours ago she'd been in this very spot, celebrating her decision-making and imagining a new future. She'd known there would be a struggle with Matt and possibly some resistance from Sophie, and she'd already begun to endure Chloe's objections. But she'd been sure that in the end, everything would work out. Now she wondered if her plan had always been a pipe dream. As precarious as the sugar packet houses she'd once built with Mrs. Pearl's daughters, which always collapsed sooner or later.

"I don't know," she said. "I don't know who to listen to." She'd dropped Sophie off at day camp after they left the hospital, wanting her to have some fresh air and a bit of normalcy, and called Chloe from the car to give her all the news. Chloe's gentle tone from last night disappeared when she heard Jenna explain Dr. Roberts' reasoning. She could still feel the sting of Chloe's outburst: *What are you, delusional? She fell down a flight of stairs, and now they think she may have dementia. You can't handle all that! Don't do anything, I'll be there tomorrow!*

"How does your mother feel?" Mrs. Pearl said.

"She just wants to come home," Jenna told her. "Oh, you should have seen her at the hospital, with her hair all fixed as best she could and lipstick on. And then she was telling Sophie that running away story, and they were snuggling on the hard hospital chair. That's why Dr. Roberts said she'd recover better at home. She was so sad when I told her they wanted her to stay one more night."

She clenched her fist and lightly struck the table. "You know something? I *do* know what I want. I want her home. I want to move here with her. I can take care of her. I can make a good life here for the three of us."

"There you go," Mrs. Pearl said.

"It all makes sense," Jenna said. "I have a job lined up, and Sophie's made friends. She feels at home here, and I think she'll come around to the idea of moving here. She loves being with my mother, the two of them get along so well. The only thing that's changed since yesterday is that my mother needs me—she needs me now and she needs me in the house. And that's okay. I don't have to be in Rye to make plans to move. I can start the ball rolling here."

"It does sound like a perfect life," Mrs. Pearl said. "Oh, Jenna, it'll be so wonderful to have you here year-round. And you'll make new friends, too. You'll join some clubs, maybe some volunteer groups. Maybe get on some boards. Who knows?" she said, wrinkling her nose. "Maybe you'll even meet someone."

"I don't know about that," Jenna said. She rested her chin on her hand. "I just want to feel at home again. I haven't felt like that in a long time. Matt and I were growing apart for so long, and I kept thinking I could make it better. But I wasn't the person he wanted, and there was nothing I could do to change that. It'll be good to finally be comfortable. And be myself and not have to feel guilty about it."

Mrs. Pearl smiled. "I agree completely," she said. "So why do you still look concerned? Is it Chloe? You think she's going to try to change your mind?"

"I know she will," Jenna said. "She thought my decision to move here was wrong to begin with, and now she thinks it's crossed into the absurd. Especially since one of the doctors noticed that Mom wasn't remembering things she should have been." She shook her head. "She's not going to change my mind, I'm set now. But I'm not looking forward to going around and around with her. The way we always do."

Mrs. Pearl pressed her lips together. "Jenna, your sister's not a bad person," she said. "She's just used to being the big sister. So, fine. But she didn't see Sophie with your mother, she didn't hear what that doctor said. Tell her what you saw and what you heard. Tell her everything you told me."

"But she sees things her own way. I know she feels that we should have moved my mother out years ago. I know she feels that Mom would have been better off if we had gone along with her plan from the beginning."

Mrs. Pearl waved her off. "Oh, please, this town is exactly where your mother belongs. She loves her life. She stops by here every morning for an iced tea on her way to the lake or to go shopping, looking so lovely with her big sunglasses and that sun hat of hers with the peach-colored ribbon. And she chats with the runners and the moms with strollers and the shopkeepers on their way to work. She loves it here, and we all love her! She's not that old, she can get back to the way she was. Look, your mother's always gotten lost in her thoughts, that's part of her charm."

She lifted her arms, palms up. "But where is all this concern coming from? When you were a kid, you were a force to be reckoned with!"

Jenna smiled at Mrs. Pearl's staunch support of her. Then she leaned forward, her eyes narrowed, as though she were trying to solve a math problem in her head. "Is that really how you saw me?"

"Absolutely. My girls couldn't wait for you to come back each summer, once you got old enough to babysit. You were always inventing pretend games or taking them on scavenger hunts or making pirate costumes from the old aprons and dishcloths in the kitchen here. Just like your mother—that's what people always said. Remember how everyone thought she was in over her head when she wanted to bring actors from New York to help the kids here stage a full-out Broadway show? Then the Lake Summers Theatrical became an institution!"

"I was never like *that.*"

"You don't remember setting up all those relay races on July Fourth? You couldn't have been more than Sophie's age when you and Steven Jason dreamed that up. And it's not like you were a whirling dervish. You were smart, and you thought things out. When you put your mind to something, even a brick wall couldn't stop you. I mean that. Not even a brick wall."

Jenna shook her head in disbelief. Yes, she was stubborn when she was a kid and wanted nothing more than to outrun or out-bike or outthink Steven. She supposed the two of them did start the tradition of July Fourth races, but that couldn't have been as important as Mrs. Pearl made it out to be. She never saw herself as all that impressive. She mostly remembered feeling driven—a lot when she was young and even more so when she got to high school. Always needing to prove something or capture something. And never quite sure what she was after.

She looked up as Mrs. Pearl's words brought another old memory to mind. "Actually, I did once crash into a brick wall," she said. "Literally. The Public Works Building, around the corner."

"You did?"

Jenna nodded. "I ran my bicycle straight into it."

"How did I never hear about this?"

"I didn't tell anyone. I was so embarrassed. It was because I was trying to keep up with Steven, as usual. He did this crazy thing one day—we must have been about twelve or so, and he rode his bike really fast down the slope on the side and stopped maybe inches away from the building. He did it twice and then said it was too dangerous for me, and he said we should go get ice cream. So he left but I didn't because, of course, I had to try. So I got on my bike and didn't brake soon enough and went headlong into the wall."

"Oh my God," Mrs. Pearl said. "You could have killed yourself."

"I know. Somehow I tumbled sideways when the bike crashed, and I ended up only with a scraped elbow and a big cut on my knee." She paused, remembering how it was to lie there on the grass, stunned and staring at the sky, hoping no one saw her. Hoping Chloe would never find out, or else she'd make fun of her forever.

"See?" Mrs. Pearl said. "Like I said. A force to be reckoned with!"

Jenna looked across the street in the direction of the Public Works Building. It was while she was lying on her back on the grass that T.J. had showed up, somehow suspecting when Steven took off that morning that he was up to mischief. He was only three years older than she and Steven were, but so much more responsible. He checked that she was still alive, then ran to the house across the street and came back with tissues and bandages. He patched her up and walked her home.

She turned back to Mrs. Pearl. "Did you know T.J.'s in town? Steven's older brother?"

"Of course I do," she said. "Although he calls himself Troy now. He's working at the animal clinic down the street. He's a vet."

"That's right, they told me that at the hospital," Jenna said. "When did he come back?"

"Just this past winter. Old Doc Munoz passed away, and his associate didn't want to take over the clinic because she's having twins this summer. Everyone was upset because nobody wanted the clinic to close. But then I remembered that Carole Cline—remember her, the music teacher?—she had a cousin in Philadelphia who knew Troy, so I got his number and told him we needed him."

"You asked him to come back?"

She nodded. "And luckily enough, their renter had just moved out. He was able to move right into his old house next door to you."

"But I thought they sold that house after Mr. Jason died."

"A lot of people did. But no—they've been renting it all these years. I heard they planned to sell it this spring. Now I guess they're going to keep it for a while."

"So T.J.—I mean, Troy—he came back just like that?"

"I don't think he had much keeping him in Philly. At least, that's the impression I got from Carole. Honestly, Jenna, he sounded pretty glad when I called. Sometimes coming home is exactly what a person needs." She smiled. "Interesting, right? All you kids fanned out across the country years ago. And now you and Troy are back. Who would have thought it?"

Jenna finished her iced coffee. Yes, she and Troy. The girl who ran into the brick wall. And the boy who came to bandage her up.

*

She helped Mrs. Pearl clear the table, then headed up Main Street in the direction of Lake Summers Market. She had two hours

before she needed to get Sophie and thought she'd pick up some
food for dinner. Her mom had a beautifully stocked kitchen full
of pretty, mismatched plates and cups, most of which she had
bought at antiques stores and quirky thrift shops while traveling
on vacation. Cooking at her mother's house was fun, unlike at
her own house, where dinners had become so tense in the months
before Matt left, and so quiet and sad after he did, that she came
to dread calling Sophie to the table.

Looking toward the lake, she could see the traffic circle adjacent
to the Lake Summers Animal Clinic, where Troy was working.
She wondered why he'd been so willing to uproot his life when
Mrs. Pearl called him. Yes, Mrs. Pearl was right—coming home
could be a perfect remedy. She was proof of that. But her life in
Rye had become intolerable. Had Troy felt the same way? She
was so curious to see him that she considered walking there to
say hello and take Mo off his hands. Then she thought better of
it. It would be rude to surprise him. If he had wanted her to stop
by, he would have invited her in his note.

She reached the market but continued on her walk without
stopping in. She didn't know where she was headed—she only
knew she wanted to keep going. But then she reached the footpath
that led to the lake. And she realized that was where she'd been
heading the whole time.

Turning onto the path, she smelled the familiar scent of
wild grasses and honeysuckle. The thick green canopy overhead
softened the daylight, and although the air had been warm on
Main Street, it felt decidedly moister and cooler here, and the
breeze raised goosebumps on her bare shoulders. Approaching
the bend just ahead of the lake, she spied the diamond-shaped
boulder resting a few yards away from the trail, surrounded by
tall white birches. Exactly where it had always been. She ran her
hand over the gritty stone, then sat down on the edge. The noises
from Main Street faded behind her like the sound of an exhale.

Meet me at the footpath, he'd whispered to her that evening when no one was paying attention, when his father was trying to load film into the camera and his brothers were playing basketball. When his mother was exclaiming how lovely Bethany, a friend he'd offered to drive to the Lake Summers High Alumni Dance at his mom's insistence, looked in her frilly yellow sundress, and Jenna's parents were coming outside to see what the excitement was all about. He was nearly twenty and about to start community college, after taking a year off to help manage his father's print shop, and she was seventeen and a few weeks away from starting her senior year in high school. *Ten o'clock*, he'd told her with a nod.

She'd nodded back and watched as he and Bethany drove off, then had dinner with her family and spent the evening in her bedroom, waiting until it was time to go. Waiting for the moment when her life—her real, adult life—would begin. He was the prince she had envisioned, the one she had to save when she ran down the stairs of her house pretending she was a princess. She knew her father would be mad, but she suspected deep inside that her mother would understand. Her mother believed in following your heart. That's what she'd always advised.

At a quarter to ten, she opened her window, tucked her ballet flats into the square neckline of her favorite dress—the sleeveless pink one with the buttons down the back—and reached with her foot to the closest branch of the twisted oak tree outside her bedroom. She grasped the branch with her hands and brought her other foot to the branch. Then she climbed down, branch by branch, squatting when she reached the lowest one and jumping to the grass below. She put on her shoes, checked that her suitcase was safe behind the trash cans on the side of the house, and ran silently across the lawn.

The air was heavy and humid as she reached the center of town. A major summer storm was approaching, with the first bands of rain expected before dawn, so Main Street was unnaturally quiet. Some shop windows were covered with wooden planks or cardboard, as shopkeepers had taken protective steps in anticipation of rough winds before they closed for the night. She turned onto the footpath, and as the glow of the streetlights on Main Street dissipated behind her, she turned on the small flashlight she'd brought along. When she approached the bend, the dirt trail grew soft and pliable beneath her shoes. She found the boulder and the circle of birch trees and looked at her watch. Two minutes after ten.

"Jenna!" She heard him call her right before she saw the beam from his flashlight, right before she made out his long, dark hair the color of graphite, and the slightly lopsided smile she had hardly noticed when she was young but that she now found so beautiful. Her cheeks were hot, and her legs felt achy in a delicious kind of way. She leaned against a tree and he touched her bare shoulders, then ran his fingers down her arms as he dipped his chin. She felt as if she'd never been kissed until he'd kissed her for the first time five days ago, his kisses velvety and tender and now familiar, too. She tilted her head at just the right angle, so his mouth fit neatly against the curve of hers, as she reached around his neck and felt the soft ends of his hair against her fingers.

And then the rain came. It came suddenly and powerfully, seeping through her ballet flats, streaming down her arms, pounding her nose and eyelids. She knew they had to leave; the storm had arrived early, the first streak of lightning separating the sky, the first round of thunder rumbling through. But all those thoughts were muffled by the words that repeated in her head: *I love you. I love you. I love you.*

She didn't know then that the first blast of lightning had struck a transformer, setting off a massive fire at the Lake Summers Resort, where the dance was going on. She didn't know that the kids at the dance would soon be evacuated. She didn't know they'd all be accounted for, except for Troy. She didn't know that in just a few short moments, the whole town would be looking for him. And that his father was among the volunteer firefighters who'd be called in to search the burning building.

She looked at her phone and realized she didn't have much time left until she had to meet Sophie. Reversing course, she went back to Main Street and over to the market to quickly get groceries. She loaded them into her car and drove on to Shore Road. The lake shimmered in the sunshine as she parked and went to sit on the stone wall by the sandy bank. She kicked off her sandals, and the breeze cooled her toes and brushed the space below her collarbones left exposed by her V-neck top. It had been strange—chilling, even—to be back on that footpath, her first time since that night with Troy. She couldn't help but wonder how different their lives would have been if the storm hadn't arrived early. Maybe they'd have made it out of Lake Summers. Or maybe they'd have thought better of it all and turned back for home before their parents even found the notes they'd left. Maybe they'd still have gone their separate ways after that summer night. But it left an emptiness inside her that everything stopped, that they never talked about it afterward, that their story ended before it began. Her mother would have called that emptiness the place where unfinished work still remained.

The sound of giggles drifted toward her, and when she looked up, she saw Sophie and a group of friends coming up from the lake. She was glad that Sophie looked so relaxed with these girls, so much a part of the group. It was remarkable that she'd gotten so close to them, considering that she'd only met them two weeks ago. That was something she'd always admired about her daughter—how easy she was to get along with. It felt like a promising sign for the future that Sophie seemed so connected. If she liked her new friends, she'd feel good about staying and be more likely to agree that living with her grandmother was a good idea.

Jenna watched Sophie say goodbye to the girls, then got up from the stone wall to greet her. "Hey, you. How was camp?" she said, putting her arm around Sophie's shoulders.

"Great," Sophie answered, sounding even more enthusiastic than Jenna expected. They reached the car, and as Jenna started the engine, Sophie unzipped her backpack and stuck her hand inside. "I was telling my friends all about the movie star, and they all want to help me find the guy. Even the counselors," she said.

She pulled a slip of paper out. "Okay, so we know she went to the basement even though she's not sure what she was looking for. She kind of didn't remember what stuff she put there, which is kind of weird, but I didn't want to say that to her. But she did say at the hospital she was looking for something with a chip, right? So we made a list of the places she could have been looking that could be chipped. Like a desk or an old dresser with some wood chipped off, or some paint chipped off, or some kind of box, big like a moving box or little like a jewelry box, with a corner chipped off. Or a closet, if there's a chip in the paint…"

"This is what everyone wanted to do at camp?" Jenna said. "Didn't anyone want to swim or anything?"

"We swam," Sophie said. "But we wanted to do this too. Because my friends all want to meet this movie star when we find him. If he's still alive. I mean, I guess he could be dead, but I really, really hope he's not. And then some people were wondering if maybe he was famous, if maybe he got big and famous after they fell in love. Like maybe he's in movies that we know. Wouldn't that be awesome?"

She turned back to her list. "So when was the last time you were in the basement, Mom? We have to go down there when we get home. Did you say there's furniture there? Do you know if there's a closet? I swear, I didn't even know there was a basement until Sweet fell. And I didn't pay any attention to what was down there yesterday because I was worried about Sweet…"

Jenna rubbed the inside corner of her eye. It was good to see her daughter so energized. If things were different, she'd have thrilled at Sophie's enthusiasm. But the way the doctor said her mom didn't even know where she was this morning—that made her even more convinced that the movie star story couldn't be true. She didn't think her mother intended to outright lie to Sophie—she wouldn't do that. But maybe something else was going on. Maybe she'd been so in love with Jenna's dad, her imagination had turned him into a movie star. Or maybe she was inserting herself into some movie she'd watched or some book she'd read, maybe the plot had made such an impression that she now believed she was the heroine. Whatever the case, it was wrong to let her daughter stay so wrapped up in the story. Especially since now, her friends were getting involved too.

"Soph, I know I already said this, but I don't think you should get your hopes up about this movie star," she said. "You're young to have to deal with this, but your grandmother may not be remembering things exactly as they happened. There are diseases—or conditions—that can affect people's memories when they get older. They call it dementia, or there's something called Alzheimer's disease…"

She paused and looked over at Sophie, who was looking at her paper and not listening. She was going to have to be firmer. "Honey, I know that when she was telling you this story, it sounded realistic," she said as she pulled into the driveway. "And I know, too, that it's kind of exciting, this whole mystery about a movie star. But the doctors are concerned about Sweet's memory, and we need to pay attention to them. I know she called it her unfinished work to tell you the story, and I know how important that sounds, but that doesn't mean that—"

"Look!" Sophie squealed. "Mo!"

She pointed at the Jasons' lawn, where Mo was curled up in a ball, his leash tied loosely to the banister by the front steps.

And near him was a man in a dark green shirt and gray slacks, who looked up from his garden hose and smiled, a beautiful, slightly lopsided smile.

CHAPTER EIGHT

She would have recognized that smile anywhere. And his build looked the same, too. He was still slim, his chest flat and toned beneath his shirt. Clothes had always been so nicely roomy on him—tee shirts and sweatpants, but especially tailored clothes like he was wearing now. Steven and the twins had always dressed slapdash, in running shorts with faded logos or tee shirts that looked as though they'd been scooped out of the laundry hamper. But Troy dressed like a grown-up, in button-down shirts and nice slacks, especially as he got older. Probably because he was often going to or coming from work, either at Mr. Miller's dry-cleaning shop or the resort. He'd always seemed older than his age.

Except that now, holding the garden hose as he stood on the front lawn of his childhood house, he hadn't aged. He was just as she remembered.

"Mo!" Sophie called out the car window again, and Mo pulled himself onto all fours and stood alert, his tail whipping back and forth so fast, it was just a blur. Before Jenna had even come to a stop, Sophie opened the car door and bounded over to Troy's yard. Jenna watched as Sophie knelt and Mo climbed up her body until he was standing on his hind legs, his front paws on Sophie's shoulders. She scratched his ears and rubbed his sides, and then untied the leash and picked him up. When Jenna got out of the car, Mo's tail started up again, and he fought to get out of Sophie's arms. Back on the ground, he scampered over to Jenna, his ears perked up and his tail high, his eyes beseeching.

Recognizing that look, Jenna laughed and rubbed the top of his head. He was hungry—what a relief! Only last week, she'd struggled to get him to eat.

She looked at Troy, who was standing with the garden hose at his side. He gave a wave, and she waved back. She knew she had to go over to talk to him. But she was nervous. She thought it might make things easier if Sophie and Mo were around, but she didn't want Sophie to sense any tension and start asking questions she wasn't prepared to answer. "Honey, he's ready for dinner," she said, handing Sophie the house keys. "I stacked his food by the back door—why don't you open a can for him and give him a little?"

"Want some dinner, Mo? Want some dinner?" Sophie said, clapping her hands. She dashed to the house, Mo scampering behind her. "Thanks for taking care of him, Troy!" she called over her shoulder as she went inside.

Jenna kept her eyes on the front door, needing to summon her courage. She couldn't believe how nervous she was. It didn't make sense. It was so long ago, they were so young the last time they were together. So much had happened since that late-August night, and she found herself reviewing all the decisions she'd made since then, as though she might need to defend them. How had she ended up in such an unhappy marriage? How had she found herself in a position where she wanted nothing more than to pack up and move back here, ready to put all remnants of her life in Rye behind her?

Finally, she turned back. Troy was rolling the garden hose around its spool on a nearby cart. He'd rolled up his sleeves, just as he used to when he came home after working the late shift at the resort, on those muggy August nights before the night of the storm, when she'd watch for him through her bedroom window. He'd get out of the car he'd bought with Steven—a used Chevy Malibu. He'd toss his keys in the air and sometimes whistle a pop tune as he waited for her to climb down the twisted oak and through the garden. She'd wonder what the people who dropped their cars off with him at the resort thought about him, if they thought he was smart or clever or impressive. She was lucky, because she actually knew him. Because he actually liked her.

She walked around her car and he dropped the end of the hose and met her on his lawn. "Jenna," he said. She remembered he'd always had a way of saying her name when he saw her. Just saying it. And letting the sound linger before saying anything else.

"Hi, T.J.," she answered, then shook her head, embarrassed. "Troy."

"Yeah. I haven't been T.J. in a while," he said, and she saw again that slightly lopsided smile, his lips on one side lifting a bit more, opening to show a tiny bit more of his teeth, than the other side. It was something that most people probably didn't pay attention to, but she saw it, because she'd studied everything about him that summer. And she found herself studying everything now, too—the slightly leathery texture of his face, the shallow lines at the sides of his eyes, the two distinct grooves that curved from the sides of his nose to the edge of his so-square jaw, the tiny cleft in his chin. His hair was short now, much shorter than when they were young, with gray filtered into the rich graphite color. That night at the lake, she'd loved his long hair, how the ends in the back lay on his collar, and ruffled so gently as the breeze kicked up. A few days later, she had seen his hair ruffle again, but seeing him then had been heartbreaking.

She stayed an arm's length away now, not sure if she was supposed to hug him or embrace him or give him some kind of casual kiss. He swung his arms slightly, as though he didn't know what to do either.

"How's your mom?" he asked. His tone was a mix of concern, warmth, and formality. It was a combination she recognized from long ago. When she was young—eleven, twelve, thirteen—he struck her as so serious. He seemed to always disapprove of her and Steven. He'd barely spoken to her as he bandaged up her knee after she ran her bike into the building, and as he walked her home. And she'd stayed quiet, too, thinking that was what he wanted. Even though he'd done such a nice thing for her.

"She's okay—no broken bones or anything," Jenna said. "Although they still want to watch her. They're keeping her one more night."

He put his hands in his pockets. "Well, you know doctors. They like to cover all their bases."

"That's true. It could have been a lot worse."

"Absolutely. It was a pretty big spill she took."

"It was. We're lucky." She nodded, not sure what to say next. She wanted to tell him more—that she was worried about her mom, that she was concerned by the warning that her mom should no longer live alone, that she feared Chloe would insist on moving her mother away. But it seemed wrong to go into all that. Yes, there were a few days that summer when she thought he had the answers to all her questions. But that was a long time ago.

Then she shook her head as she realized that instead of wallowing in her own thoughts and memories, she should be thanking him. "Oh, hey—I can't believe I haven't said this yet," she said. "Thank you for everything you did. I know that you're the one who called 911. And you took Sophie to the hospital, and you took care of Mo, too. Honestly, Troy, I don't know what would have happened without you."

He shrugged. "I didn't do anything anyone else wouldn't have done. Anyone can call 911."

"I know, but…" She paused. They were talking like strangers, or casual acquaintances, and it left her with a sense of loss. "You know, it's funny," she said, trying to make a connection with the past. "I had no idea who this guy Troy was, this guy the nurse at the hospital was talking about. I had no idea you came back. And when she said Troy took the dog, I didn't know it was… you."

He nodded. "It's been a long time."

"And she kept saying Mo would be fine, he's a vet. And I had no idea that's what you became, and then when…" She stopped. She was about to say *when Mrs. Pearl called you,* but she didn't want him to know they'd been talking about him that afternoon, that she knew he'd been living in Philadelphia. On the other hand, it felt wrong not to let on what she knew. And it felt strange not to talk about what had brought him back to Lake Summers. Wasn't that a question someone would ask of an old friend? She watched him kick at a stone on the grass and decided not to bring up the topic. She didn't want to put him on the spot. She knew how it felt to not be ready to open up. She had been doing her grocery shopping in Rye late at night for months now, to avoid running into other moms from around town and being asked how she was doing, since Matt had moved out.

"I hope Mo wasn't too much trouble," she said. "I know Sophie told you he'd been sick and all."

"He was great," he said. "I had some dog food that was good for a guy getting over pancreatitis. And I topped it with some ground beef to make it more appealing. I boiled and drained off the fat so his stomach could handle it."

She felt her eyes widen. "You *boiled* beef for him?"

"It wasn't a big deal. I had it in the fridge. I was going to grill a couple of hamburgers for myself."

"You gave him your dinner? And then you took him to work?"

"It was a slow day. My tech was glad for the company."

"I don't even know what to say—"

"It wasn't a big deal," he repeated.

She felt herself shrink back a bit. There it was—that edge she'd sensed all those years ago. It was the harshness that had made her ask Steven so often, "What's up with your brother? Doesn't he ever *laugh?*" For most of her life, she hadn't understood what he was up against, how he struggled, how torn he was between what he wanted and what he thought he should do.

"So, how are your brothers?" she asked.

"They're good," he said, nodding. "Steven's a surgeon, if you can believe it."

"A surgeon? I had no idea he wanted to be a doctor."

"Surprised us all. He and his wife live in Connecticut, Joanna's an interior designer. They have three kids. And Cal and Clay are both out on the West Coast, Cal in Seattle and Clay in San Francisco. Both working in tech, both married with two kids each. Cal's wife is expecting another baby soon."

"Wow," she said. "I can't even imagine Cal and Clay married. I still think of them as five years old."

"I know," Troy said. "So what about your family? I was sorry to hear from your mom that your dad passed away. How's Chloe doing? Living on Long Island?"

Jenna nodded. "She and her husband own a furniture store. And your sister-in-law is an interior designer? We should get them together one day."

"I guess so," Troy said. "I guess they'd have a lot in common." He looked over toward his house. "I should finish the watering," he said. "Nice to see you, Jenna. Glad your mom's doing okay and is coming home tomorrow."

She smiled and turned back toward her car, feeling the same way she'd often felt around him when he was young, the same way she felt when he bandaged her knee. She'd only wanted to catch up, and yes, he'd been polite and pleasant, but he'd also pushed her away, just as he'd done after the storm. It was as though he both wanted to see her and didn't, both glad he could help but also determined not to be drawn further into her life.

She popped the trunk and pulled her groceries out of the car. It would have been nice to invite him over for dinner. She had picked up a tray of pasta primavera that looked delicious in the display case, along with fixings for a big salad and some crusty rolls. Why shouldn't she be able to do something to thank him? She had spent much of the afternoon talking with Mrs. Pearl about him, thinking about him and the brick wall, and then going to the footpath and thinking about him even more. It was wrong of him to act as though they didn't have a history. As though they were nothing more than kids who grew up next door.

She closed the trunk, then looked over at him. He was fiddling again with the hose, turning the lever to wind it back onto its spool. Then he started to unscrew the sprayer, but there was still some water flowing through, and a stray spurt shot up into his face. He stumbled back, propelled by the water and probably the surprise as well, dropping the sprayer and nearly losing his balance, his arms flailing to his sides before he caught his balance and righted himself. She looked away, not wanting him to see her laugh. She didn't want to laugh at him. But there was something so comical about the moment, and so boyish in his shocked expression. Something so sweet and heartbreaking about a guy who tries to appear in control but nearly falls on his butt.

She walked into the house just as Sophie flew out of the kitchen. "Mo's eating," she called as she dashed by. "I'm going to look!"

"Soph, can you set the table?" Jenna said. But her daughter was already on her way down the basement stairs. She hadn't paid a drop of attention to what Jenna had said in the car. Jenna started to call downstairs to tell Sophie to calm down and let this go, but she didn't want to start a fight. She went to prepare the salad. With any luck, Sophie would forget about the whole thing in a day or two. Maybe there'd be something going on at camp that would distract her. And Chloe was coming soon, that would be a distraction too…

"Mom!" Sophie shrieked. "*Mom!*"

Jenna dropped the lettuce into the bowl and ran down to the basement. Sophie was standing there, past all the furniture, jumping up and down. "Look! Look! Look! *Look!*" she said. She was pointing at the closet against the back wall. And sure enough, there was a small square chip in the paint near the top of the door.

"Mom! This is it!" she said, still jumping, her arms twirling at her sides as though she were jumping rope. "There's the chip! The chip!" She ran over and grasped Jenna's arm. "Why would you think all that about her memory? Her memory is fine! This is exactly the closet she was going to when she fell!" She went to the door and twisted the doorknob. When the door didn't budge, she pulled on it, leaning back so far that Jenna feared she'd be launched clear across the room if she actually succeeded in opening it.

"It's locked! It's locked!" she screamed. "She locked it because the movie star's inside!"

"The movie star's *inside?*" Jenna asked.

"You know what I mean! The stuff she wanted me to see!" She let go of the doorknob and looked around the room, spinning herself in a circle. "Mom, where's the key, where's the key, find the key!"

Jenna surveyed the furniture, then went to the desk alongside the closet. Her father had always been very organized, and sure enough, a silver key lay in the front of the top drawer. She picked it up, and Sophie grabbed it from her hand. She unlocked the door and though it stuck a bit, eventually she got it open.

The two of them gasped.

The closet was small and tightly packed with shelves all the way from the floor to the ceiling. And each shelf held boxes. Shoeboxes, gift boxes, moving boxes. There had to be close to fifty.

"We found it!" Sophie said, pulling a stack of gift boxes off a middle shelf. The weight of them made her reel backward, and the top two slid precariously sideways.

Jenna grasped them with one hand and steadied her daughter with the other. "Oh, Soph," she said. "Do you know how long it would take us to search through these? Your grandfather was an accountant—he kept every piece of paper he ever touched. It's probably old bills and stuff that should have been thrown away long ago."

"I don't care," Sophie said, putting the first stack down on the floor and running back for more. "I have nothing else to do. She came down to get these boxes, and now I found them! I found the closet with the chip. The stuff about the story is in here somewhere. His name is somewhere in these boxes! This is what she wanted, Mom. Her unfinished work!"

"But…" Jenna started, then stopped herself, as Sophie dashed back and forth between the closet and the stack of boxes she was building on the floor. Her mother had mentioned a chip, and there was definitely a chip in the paint of the door, no doubt about that. She must have had something specific in mind when she came downstairs. So maybe… Jenna had to admit it… maybe there really was a lost love. Maybe her mom had seen her seventy-sixth birthday approaching, and maybe she'd decided she was running out of time. Maybe she really did have a story for Sophie, and maybe she did feel that letting this story live on was her life's unfinished work. If she had something in mind that she wanted to tell Sophie, then how could Jenna assign no importance to these boxes? After all, she'd spent much of this afternoon thinking about Troy—and just now, she'd been aching for him to acknowledge the relationship they once had. The past was powerful. Everyone wanted to know that the things they most cared about when they were young still made a difference.

"Come on, Soph, help me with dinner," she said. "Tonight we can start to pull the boxes out. And tomorrow," Jenna added, "when your grandmother's home, we can start going through them and search for her story."

CHAPTER NINE

"Do we dare?" Chloe said, holding up her large plastic cup, filled to the brim with a thick, magenta-colored mixture, the surface dotted with tiny yellow flecks.

"Of course," Jenna said. "Stan promised it's not too sour."

"Why do I let him do this to me? I always come here knowing what I want, and they always talk me into trying something new."

"It's good to try new things. I bet it'll be delicious. Give it a go. Here, I'll go first."

They were sitting on the patio of the Smoothie Dudes, both of them with a large-size July Fourth special, a lemon-cranberry-green-apple smoothie with a spray of lemon zest on top. Jenna had taken Sophie to camp this morning and then gone food shopping, picking up Portuguese rolls and gooey chocolate-chip cookies from Pearl's, and a rotisserie chicken, wild rice, fresh grilled peaches, and the chopped salad her mother loved from the market, so she could prepare a special homecoming dinner. Back at the house, she'd put fresh linens on her mother's bed and opened the windows wide to let in the sweet scent of the garden. She also put fresh sheets on the bed in the third bedroom for Chloe, figuring she'd sleep on the extra bed in Sophie's room for as long as Chloe stayed. Chloe showed up at eleven, right on time. They agreed to go to the smoothie shop and have a talk before heading to the hospital.

Jenna inserted her straw in the drink and took a sip. It was tangy and refreshing, just as she'd expected, although she wondered if maybe her good mood was influencing her taste buds. She was proud of herself, proud that she'd spoken up to Chloe, that she'd come up with a reasonable plan that took both her own determination and Chloe's concerns into account. After they had ordered and sat down to wait for their smoothies, she'd proposed that Chloe give her six weeks—until their mother's birthday, on August 15th—to prove that she could make a go of things. "If everything is fine when you come up for her birthday, then I'll finalize my plans to move here," she'd said. "And if it doesn't seem that I have things under control and Mom is safe and happy, then we'll start making plans to move her to Long Island. And maybe Sophie and me, too. Can that be our deal?"

Chloe had sat back in her chair and folded her arms, her jaw as tight as her short brown curls. Then she tapped her lips with her fingers, a sure-fire sign that she was thinking things through. "You sound like you think you can handle this," she'd said.

"I do," Jenna said. "Because I know it's best for her. Good for her, for Sophie and for me, too. But absolutely the best thing for her."

Chloe lifted her palms. "Okay, until her birthday," she'd said. "If you're sure you want this, we'll give it a shot."

Jenna took another sip of her smoothie and watched as Chloe took a tentative taste. Just then the shop's co-owners, Trey and Stan, came out to the patio, Trey going to wipe down some tables while Stan squatted to collect an empty cup that had blown onto the ground. He looked over at them, his large belly resting on his knees. "What do you think?" he said. "We have to remind ourselves each year to tone it down. Remember a couple of years ago, when we used Tabasco to give it a fireworks-ish kick? Boy, did we get complaints about that."

"It's delicious," Jenna said. "Nice and tangy."

"It's quite good," Chloe agreed.

Stan carried over a chair over and placed it backward against the table, then straddled the seat and folded his arms across the frame. "We just now heard about your mom," he said, resting his chin on his hands, his bushy salt-and-pepper beard grazing his fingers. "How is she?"

Jenna smiled. Word got around fast in a small town. "She's okay. We're bringing her home this afternoon."

"Fantastic!" Trey said, coming to join them. He was as slim and neatly coiffed as Stan was stout and hairy. "Tell her we need her. We're making a new smoothie in honor of the historical exhibit at the resort, and she's one of our favorite early tasters."

"Have you heard about that yet?" Stan said. "Art Grayson thought it up. It's going to be the highlight of the summer."

"We're calling it the Lake Summers Fizz-storical Smoothie," Trey said. "Kind of a fruity, icy, carbonated concoction—tell your mom we'll give her a taste the next time she's here."

"I don't know if it's ready for tasting," Stan told him, as the two went back into the shop. "I say we go back to the drawing board. There's something not right about a fizzy smoothie…"

Chloe chuckled as she watched the two of them go inside. "They never get tired of doing this, do they?"

"Or of each other," Jenna said. "Such sweet guys."

"Remember when they were making personalized smoothies?" Chloe said. "When they found out I had been Dorothy in *The Wizard of Oz,* they made me the Over the Rainbow Smoothie. It had a million layers of sherbet—blueberry, raspberry, lemon, tangerine… Of course when I put the straw in, all the layers blended together so it looked like mud. But it's the thought that counts, right?"

Jenna nodded. "I remember that show. You were so good. Nobody knew you had such a pretty voice."

"The only reason I auditioned was because of your paddle-board lessons."

"What? What did my lessons have to do with your show?"

"It was the day before the audition, and Mom told me to go to the lake to find you after your first paddle-boarding lesson," Chloe said. "I was thirteen that year, so you must have been nine—younger than all the other kids there, and you having the hardest time of it. All the other kids were paddling toward the middle of the lake, and you kept falling off and coughing up water, and one time the board smacked you in the face. But you kept trying. I found that inspiring. That gave me the boost I needed to go through with the audition."

Jenna sat still for a moment, letting her sister's words hang in the air. Even now, a compliment from her sister could make her feel so proud. "Wow, Chloe," she finally said. "I love that you felt that way."

She took another sip of smoothie. This time, when she looked up, Chloe was no longer smiling. Instead she was shaking her head, an elbow on the table and her cheek pressed into her hand.

"Oh, no," Jenna said. "What's wrong now?"

"I'm sorry, but the more I think about it, the more I'm sure this whole thing with Mom is a disaster in the making," Chloe said. "Be honest, Jenna. You've got too much else going on right now."

Jenna sighed loudly. "We're back to this again? I thought we settled this. I know you think my life's a mess, but getting a divorce isn't easy. And I'm pulling everything together now. I can do that here, that's why I want to move here—"

"But this isn't only about just the divorce," Chloe said. "You and her—you were both always like this, running around and following your whims and leaving all this debris for the rest of us to clean up. Yes, she started this theatrical thing, and yes, everyone thought she was amazing and the town wouldn't be nearly so wonderful without her. But what about when I needed help hemming a skirt or cleaning a stain off my blouse, or there was no food in the refrigerator? What about when Dad wanted a real dinner at a regular time, not a pizza that sat in her car for an hour while she stopped at Village Hall to see one more person, arrange one more thing—"

"She is who she is. She wasn't like other moms. That's what I loved about her—"

"And that's what I resented. She always relied on me. I had to babysit, I had to run after you, she was always asking if I knew where you were, and it was so hard in the summer because you were such a pain, you were always flying around with Steven…"

She stopped, pressing her lips together in a straight line for a moment. "I don't mean that," she said. "I love her, and I love you, too. I'm just so mad that you're in this situation. And I feel bad that I didn't protect you. And I see you suffering, and I see her getting older, and you both won't listen and…" She rolled her eyes and let out a laugh. "You both won't shut up and do what I say!"

Jenna laughed too, glad Chloe saw the humor in her tenacity. But she was also moved by Chloe's concern. "What happened with Matt and me—you couldn't have prevented it," she said. "It happened, and it's hard. But with Mom, it's different. I can take care of her. Wait until you see her with Sophie, they're so cute together. Mom's telling her this story about running away and going to Hollywood and falling in love with some secret movie star, and Sophie's trying to fill in the pieces that are missing—"

"Going to Hollywood?" Chloe paused for a second. "This is what I mean about her needing help—she says things that don't make sense. You don't believe it, do you?"

"I don't know. I honestly don't. It sounded unrealistic to me, too, at first. But you know what? It doesn't even matter. There's something she wants Sophie to know, and it's bringing them together, and if you make Mom move to Long Island, then all that closeness is lost. Even Dr. Roberts, the one I told you about, he agrees with that. He said it'll help her heal faster, being in her own home with us."

"Oh, come on, Jenna. That's like believing in fairy tales. I could find a million doctors who'd say she'd be safer in a place like Ocean Vistas."

"Safer but not happier."

"Happier because she'd be safer! No matter how much you deny it, you're doing this for yourself, not for her. You're running away from a life you can't take anymore."

Jenna put her elbows on the table and rubbed her forehead with her fingertips. Chloe knew just how to push her buttons. This notion that she was running away, that she couldn't handle her life, that she was hopelessly irresponsible, went right to her core. She checked the time on her phone. It was after noon already. She hated the thought of their mom just sitting there in the hospital, waiting for them to come for her. But she had to make Chloe feel more comfortable with their plan first. She tried to bolster her confidence by repeating in her head what Mrs. Pearl had said yesterday: *You weren't just a whirling dervish. You were smart, too. And you thought things out.* "Look, she shouldn't be moved around that much while she's recovering from the bruised rib. And I can always get an aide to come over a few hours a week and help out. Mom deserves a few weeks at home to heal, and then, like I said, we'll reassess—"

"Jenna, stop," Chloe said. She took a deep, loud breath, looking up at the sky. "Oh, God, Jenns. There's something else, too, something you don't even know about…"

"What?" Jenna said. "Something else with Mom?"

"No, not about Mom." Chloe reached into her shoulder bag, which was hooked on the back of the chair. "When I stopped by your house to grab some extra clothes for you and Sophie, and to pick up your mail—well, this magazine was the first thing I saw beneath the mail slot."

She handed it to Jenna. It was the July issue of *Suburban Best Living.* The cover had a huge headline that read, "The Heiress

Takes a Groom." And right below it was a photo of Matt and Felicity, whom she recognized from past Christmas parties Matt's company had thrown. They were on the steps of the Metropolitan Museum of Art in New York City, him in a tuxedo and her in a sparkly gown, clearly about to enter some lavish gala.

"Oh no," Jenna said. It wasn't so much that she was surprised. She'd known she would have to come face-to-face with Matt's new life at some point. But she'd thought it would happen after he'd finally worked up the courage to tell Sophie about his engagement. She'd never expected that the first time she'd see Matt and the woman he'd chosen over her, she'd be in Lake Summers drinking smoothies with Chloe. It stung that it had to happen here, in a place where she'd always felt safe, at a time when she was finally pulling her life together. Although maybe it was for the best. At least now, her first glance of the two of them together was behind her.

"I'm sorry to show you this, Jenns, but you should probably see the whole thing," Chloe continued, then reached over to show her an inside photo spread of the Connecticut mansion where Matt and his new family were living. Jenna scanned the pictures, taking in the massive sunken living room adorned with baroque-style paintings, the movie theater and state-of-the-art gym in the basement, and the infinity pool in the backyard that looked out over a beguiling view of the Connecticut River. A box off to the side showed a thumbnail photo of Felicity's family's Cape Cod estate, where the 300-guest wedding was planned for next summer. Jenna skimmed the accompanying interview with Felicity. There was no mention that Matt had been previously married, and not a word about his eleven-year-old daughter.

"Maybe he wants to embarrass you," Chloe said. "Or maybe he's too clueless to even care."

"It's not even about me," Jenna said. "I'm more worried about Sophie. He hasn't even told her about Felicity yet. Didn't he think she might see this? Didn't he think about how it would make her feel, to learn about her dad's new family this way?"

Chloe put the magazine back in her bag. "I know. That's what I'm trying to get at. I can't control your ex-husband. But if you live near me, at least I can help make sure it doesn't destroy you or Sophie."

Jenna paused, repeating in her head what Mrs. Pearl had said about her yesterday: *You were smart, too. And you thought things out.* "I appreciate that, but it's not your job to make sure this doesn't destroy me or my daughter," she said. "It's mine. So let's keep things as we agreed. Let's go bring Mom home. Okay? That's what we need to take care of right now."

She squeezed Chloe's hand, then grabbed her smoothie, waved to Stan and Trey through the shop's window, and headed to the car, glad to see that Chloe was following her. She knew she had sounded confident about her path forward. Like it was a piece of cake.

She wondered if it would actually be that easy.

*

"Ready?" Sophie called from the basement that night. "Coming up with a big one!"

"We're ready!" Jenna called back as she brought three mugs of tea into the living room and handed one to her mother. Sweet was sitting on her favorite armchair, a Queen Anne-style with a muted floral pattern on a tea stain fabric, and was wearing one of her favorite dresses, blue with a placket collar and pleated skirt. The scene looked so normal that if Jenna hadn't lived through the last two days, she might not have believed they were anything other than a bad dream. The only telltale sign was a black cane resting against the stone fireplace, which Sweet had vowed to put into the trash by the end of next week.

Jenna handed Chloe a mug and sat down beside her on the cream-colored sofa. Looking at her mother, whose eyes were focused on the hallway in anticipation of Sophie's entrance, she knew she had done the right thing by bringing her home. If there was one silver lining to the last two days, it was that they had spurred her to move to Lake Summers even sooner than September and to offer up to Chloe a specific, workable plan. She was especially grateful for the vote of confidence she received from Dr. Roberts, whom she'd seen at the nurses' station while she was waiting for her mother's discharge instructions.

"I'm so glad to see you," she'd said. "I wanted to tell you that I'm staying here with my daughter as you suggested. We're bringing my mom back home today."

"That's excellent," he'd said. "Although I hear the nurses are sorry to see their most popular patient leave. But I'm proud of you, Jenna. You're doing the best thing."

"Would you like to say goodbye to her?" Jenna said. "I'm sure she'd like to see you."

"I wish I could, but I'm on my way to a meeting," he said. "She wouldn't recognize me, anyway, I saw her only briefly in the emergency room. Take care, and good luck. Call me once in a while to let me know how things are going."

She'd nodded and watched him proceed down the hall, glad that he wanted to hear from her. She didn't want to lose touch with him. He was warm and reassuring, and reminded her of her father.

Picking up her mug, she called again to Sophie. "Honey, you okay?" she said. "Need any help?"

"Help with what?" Chloe asked. "What's she doing?"

"Bringing up a box from the basement," Jenna told her. "We've started going through the closet down there. It has a ton of boxes you and I never even knew about. Mom says she was going to find something there, and that's when she fell down the stairs."

"What was she going to find—wait, is this about the secret boyfriend?" Chloe said. She looked hard at Jenna, as though to emphasize that she'd just been proven right, their mother was confused and concocting some memory that never, ever could have happened.

Jenna noticed her expression—and so did their mom. "Chloe, dear, I'll thank you not to mock me," she said. "No matter what you may think, my life didn't begin the moment you were born. I'd never deny you your memories, so please don't deny me mine."

"I'm sorry, Mom," Chloe said, looking down. "I didn't mean to make you think I was mocking you… it's only that I've noticed sometimes—"

"There are tons of boxes down there," Jenna said, cutting Chloe off. She didn't want Chloe to continue with this topic. She wanted things to be relaxed and peaceful for her mom, especially on her first night home. "Who knows what we'll find?" she said. "I think it's going to be fun to go through them. Last night Sophie opened a couple of boxes up and we found a bunch of old stuff Dad saved. Maybe we'll find something of Mom's tonight."

Chloe shrugged, and Jenna took another sip of tea. She still didn't know what to believe about the story. Last night's stash hadn't been very promising; although she'd tried to put a good spin on it, the shoeboxes Sophie had opened contained nothing but old paystubs and benefits statements, service contracts for appliances long since trashed, and supporting worksheets for decades-old tax forms. Still, there was something intriguing about the way her mother had chided Chloe just now, insisting that Chloe couldn't possibly know everything there was to know about her life. At the same time, it was wonderful watching Sophie grow closer to her grandmother as she hunted so diligently for evidence of the long-lost love. Jenna only hoped that Sophie would start finding more interesting mementos, whether they had something to do with the story or not. Her daughter's engagement in the closet would surely wane if she never found anything but tax statements and appliance manuals.

"Here I come," Sophie said as she entered the room, Mo right at her heels. She was carrying a gift box that had likely once held a couple of shirts or sweaters but had been repurposed for storage. Mo curled up by Jenna's feet as Sophie put the box on the square cherrywood coffee table and sat down on her knees. She lifted the lid, revealing layers of blue tissue paper covering a pile of old photographs. She shuffled through them and then held up one, a photo of a little boy with blond curls who was dressed in a cowboy costume. "Cute!" she said. "Mom, who's this?"

Jenna studied the picture. "That's Cal, Troy's little brother. Cal or Clay, they're identical twins and looked exactly alike. I wonder if they still do. Chloe, can you tell which one this is?"

Chloe put on her glasses and took the picture from Sophie. "I can't tell either," she said. "Only Mrs. Jason could tell them apart."

"Bev was amazing," their mom agreed. "And such a good friend. Why don't we see them anymore?"

"Mom, Mrs. Jason died a long time ago," Chloe said, giving Jenna another knowing look.

"She did? Oh, my, I never even said anything to Troy. I must tell him how sorry I am."

"Mom, Troy hasn't been here for years—" Chloe said.

"Of course he has!"

"No, Mom. They moved—"

"No, actually, she's right," Jenna said. "I didn't get around to telling you yet, Chlo, but Troy moved back. He's working at the animal clinic. He helps Mom a lot around the house."

"But they sold that old house, they moved out after Mrs. Jason died—"

"Oh no!" Sophie shouted. "Is this you guys?"

Jenna looked over Sophie's shoulder at a picture of her and Chloe, standing in the bluebell garden, leaning against the twisted oak tree that used to be just outside her bedroom window. They both had on oversized button-down blouses with huge shoulder pads, and their long hair was punctuated by masses of high curls on the tops of their heads.

"That's us," Jenna said. "I must have been around twelve, and Chloe would have been sixteen."

"Look at your hair!" Sophie exclaimed. "You look like poodles!"

Jenna stretched out her legs and tickled Sophie's armpits with her toes. "No making fun of your mom!" she said.

Then Sophie scooped out handfuls of photos, and Jenna pointed to one of a teenage boy with dark, shaggy hair that grazed the collar of his tee shirt. "Can you guess who that is?" she asked.

Sophie studied the picture. "No idea."

"You don't recognize him? That's Troy."

"That's *Troy?*" Sophie looked more closely at the picture. "With all that hair and those weird baggy pants? Didn't any of you own mirrors?"

"Oh, you!" Jenna said, as she leaned down and pushed Sophie's shoulder. "He was actually very good-looking."

"Yes, he was," Chloe said. "He was a year younger than I was, so I thought that made him way too young for me. But I never understood why your mom wasn't interested. The only one she had eyes for was the wild child of the family, that crazy Steven—"

Just then Mo jumped off the chair and gave a few quick barks as he ran toward the front door. "He has to go out," Jenna said, getting up after him. "Sophie, when you're done making fun of us, can you put all the pictures back? And take the box back downstairs. Let's at least try to keep this place organized."

She took Mo's leash from the hook in the closet and brought him out through the front door. The rain forecasted for the evening hadn't materialized yet, but the air was thick and humid, and the night was darker than it usually was at seven thirty, thanks to the ceiling of clouds blocking the stars. Jenna led Mo to the curb, glad he'd given her a reason to leave the house. There was still so much her family didn't know, so much she'd never been able to admit to them about what happened with Troy. She walked Mo down the block, past Troy's house and a few more beyond it, then noticed him starting to limp as they turned back toward home. His arthritis worsened in damp weather. She picked him up to carry him the rest of the way. Suddenly he let out a loud yap, and before she knew what was happening, he jumped out of her arms and went scampering ahead, his leash dragging along the ground.

That's when she noticed Troy standing on the driveway of his house.

He was dressed in gym shorts and a tee shirt, and was drinking from a large water bottle, evidently having just come back from a run. Mo stood in front of him and yapped some more.

"Hey, my man," he said as he squatted down and gave Mo a scratch behind the ears. "How are you doing? How's the stomach?"

"He sure wanted to say hello to you," Jenna said, coming up beside them and picking the end of the leash off the ground. "He noticed you all the way down the block."

Troy finished Mo off with a quick rub on the scruff of his neck, and then stood back up. "Is your mom home?" he asked.

She nodded. "We brought her back this afternoon."

"How's she feeling?"

"Good. She's got a bunch of bruises, but they'll heal." She nodded and then her eyes met Troy's. She hadn't planned to look at him. She had intended to look at the dog, down the street, at the trees, anywhere. But now, her eyes were locked with his, because he was looking into her eyes, too. And just like that, she didn't want to see anything else. She held her breath, hoping nothing would interfere with the fragile moment. Though the night was foggy, the streetlight across the road lit up his face. She'd forgotten how beautiful his eyes were, how the color was more amber than brown, how the warmth of that color belied his normally stoic expression. And it was not just his eyes that held her in place; it was his expression—his lips pressed together in a subtle smile, his chin slightly lowered, his head slightly tilted—that seemed to say he was so glad she'd come back, that everything in his world looked better with her in it.

Finally, she shifted her gaze, thinking that if they stayed that way any longer, they'd have to say something about that storm long ago, the way they'd looked at each other that night, too, and she didn't think either of them was ready for that. She fluffed the hair at the back of her head. "You know, Chloe's here," she said, turning to look at her house. "Would you like to come in and say hello? We're looking at old pictures. There was one of you that Sophie didn't even recognize."

"No kidding?" Troy gave a quick laugh, then dropped his eyes, his hands on his waist, the arch of one foot planted against the curb. "Maybe another time, okay? I've got a schnauzer puppy in the house, he's on some strong medication and I wanted to keep an eye on him overnight. Pretty lively little guy. I just left to go on a short run. I don't know what kind of trouble he'll get into if I don't get back inside soon."

"Sure," Jenna said. "Puppies, they can get into a lot of trouble." She pushed her hair behind her ears. Why was this so hard? There was a time when she and Troy couldn't stop talking to each other. Nights when they'd sit on this very curb, their talks so intense that the hours felt like seconds.

"Goodnight," he said. "Say hi to your mom. Chloe, too."

He started up his front walk, and Jenna watched, her hands clenched together in front of her chest. She was desperate to say something that would buy her a little more time with him. She worried that if she let him leave like this, it would be their pattern: passing each other by with waves and hollow greetings. Maybe looking at each other again, maybe the same way, maybe with less intensity as time went on. And she didn't want to let that happen. They had meant something to each other, even though it was so long ago. It wasn't a dream, it wasn't a wish, it wasn't a hope or a mere thought. It was real, and it mattered to her, and she wanted to know that it mattered to him, too.

But then he was back inside. She stood still, staring at his closed front door until she realized the rain had started. It was more of a mist than a shower, so she hadn't noticed any raindrops. But all of sudden, her shoulders were wet and the ends of her hair were dripping. She would have preferred real rain. At least that way she'd have known what she was up against. She'd have been able to respond before she ended up drenched.

She let Mo pull her back to her house.

CHAPTER TEN

Leaving Jenna behind, Troy went inside to the kitchen. He flipped the light switch, and although the ceiling fixture lit up, the room didn't become all that much brighter. It was that strange phenomenon, the summer twilight, when the inside lights seemed weak and insignificant well into the evening. It happened when the weather was clear and also on evenings like tonight, when the grayness outside seeped through the windows, and the appliances and table and chairs took on hazy, indistinct outlines. Now he understood why his mother always loved winter. It was a good memory, walking into the house at five o'clock after basketball practice or his shift at the dry cleaner when he got older. The aroma of his mom's garlicky baked chicken or sweet basil meatloaf saturated the air. The high hats blazed, and the whole first floor looked brilliant and white, a stark contrast to the blackness through the windowpanes.

He put his hands in his pockets and rocked on the balls of his feet, the only sound the creak of the wood saddle that separated the hallway from the kitchen. There was no schnauzer puppy; he'd needed an excuse when Jenna invited him in, and that was the first idea that came to mind. And it could have been true. He often brought sick pets home with him when he thought they needed to be observed. But tonight there was no sick pet. He'd had only a few vaccinations to do today, and one ear infection that needed a prescription. The problem was, he didn't want to go inside with Jenna. He didn't know what happened to him out on the curb, how he looked at her and couldn't stop. There was something so powerful about being face to face with her, on the very spot where they had spent those five indescribable nights. He liked that she was back in town, much more than he wanted to. He liked knowing that she was right next door, and he liked thinking that she might stay for good—he couldn't help it, he didn't want to feel that way, but he did.

And now he was thinking about her, about how pretty she looked, even prettier than when she was young. Her appearance was somehow more mellow. He didn't know why. Was it her hair? It was smoother and a little shorter, just reaching the very tops of her shoulders. And a little lighter, too—still brown but with streaks the color of something warm and sweet, apple cider, maybe, or a cinnamon stick. She brushed it away from her face now, so it was easier to see her eyes, that translucent shade of dusty blue, tonight aglow by the light of the streetlamp across the road. Her features were softer, her face less angled, although she still had that wide smile and square chin that exuded intention and determination. Sweet had said that the divorce had all but destroyed Jenna. Thrown her into a tailspin, that's what she'd said. And he hated that that had happened to her. He wanted to make that part of her life go away, because she didn't deserve it. He felt he owed her something, a fix, because he had made such bad decisions that August night. But he didn't want to get involved with her. When he let down his guard, he made things worse.

He turned on the oven and leaned back against the adjacent countertop, waiting for it to preheat. Now he wished there really was a schnauzer around. He supposed he should be grateful for the peace and quiet; by August, he'd have one or two dogs in the house constantly, as people went off on their summer vacations and entrusted him with their pets. The clinic was set up to board dogs, but Troy never left them there. He was happy to bring them home. He enjoyed their company. He never charged for this, although people often gave him something anyway, a box of fancy cookies or chocolates from wherever they'd vacationed, a gift card to a nice restaurant, like the fancy Italian place, Sogni di Lago, on the other side of the lake. He usually brought the food to the office. He never used the gift cards. He had a half-dozen Sogni gift cards in the kitchen, in the drawer his sister-in-law had designed for postage stamps and extra keys and other things people kept but rarely needed.

Maybe he should get his own dog, he thought as he opened the fridge and took out the uncooked tin of chicken parm he'd picked up from the market on his way home before his run. He shoved it into the oven and went upstairs to take a shower. He'd always liked having a dog. There was Callie when he was growing up, and then Tick and Tock, the dachshunds he and Stacia had adopted after they'd settled in the old row house in northern Philadelphia. They were senior dogs, ten years old, and inseparable, curled up together in a ball when he and Stacia first saw them at the shelter. Troy would load them into the back seat of the car each morning, and they would sit alongside the reception desk at the animal hospital all day like a pair of maître d's, pulling themselves onto all fours and wagging their tails in unison whenever another animal came in. They lessened the tension in the waiting area for both animals and humans. He and Stacia had had a good run with those two characters.

Back downstairs in a brown tee shirt and a pair of gray sweatpants with University of Pennsylvania printed down one leg, he went to pull a beer out of the refrigerator when he noticed his phone lit up on the countertop. The screen showed that he'd missed a call from Steven. He listened to the voicemail: "*Hey, Troy, I got some big news. This guy who saw the house last fall called and put in a bid today. Look, I know you've settled in there, but I think you'll agree it's too good to pass up. Cal and Clay think so, too, as long as you're okay with it. Call me back, and I'll fill you in more.*"

Troy put the phone down and took the beer out of the fridge, then opened the back door. The rain had moved on, so he went out on the deck and wiped a lounge chair dry with a napkin. He sat down, his knees bent and his bare feet planted on the still-damp mesh fabric.

He took a few swallows, then put the bottle on the side table. Steven's call was the second one he wished he hadn't received that day. The first was from Art, who had called first thing that morning to ask him to come to a planning meeting for the historical exhibit. "But you said all you needed was for me to lend my name," Troy had said.

"And I didn't break my word, you still don't have to *do* anything," Art responded. "But the town trustee who's overseeing the thing wants to meet you, put a face with the name. What's the big deal? Let me buy you a nice lunch at the resort, we'll have a chat, and that's it. You're done and what's more, your stomach is full." It seemed a simple request, and Troy hadn't felt right saying no. But he didn't like at all being pulled deeper into the project.

He brought the bottle to his lips again. Sure, Art was right— what was the big deal about having a lunch? Steven was right, too—it made sense to sell the house now, when the market was hot and they had a good offer. But it was not so much what they were saying, it was what it all signaled: that things were changing without his input. And he was losing control of his life. He didn't want to connect with anyone. He liked having people in town who were pleasant and kind and friendly but didn't encroach beyond the boundaries he'd set.

And he wasn't supposed to be dealing with any of this right now—not Art, not Steven, not Jenna, not anyone. He was supposed to be at Steven's cabin this week. And Jenna was supposed to have left before he returned. Instead, he had stayed, and now Jenna was living next door for who knew how long. In a few short days, his life had been turned upside down. And he knew it didn't make sense, but he was sure Jenna was the catalyst: everything had been steady, but now she was back and the universe was shifting, the planets colliding. She was affecting him in ways he didn't understand and couldn't reverse. Just as she had years ago.

He gazed across the yard and noticed the side of Sweet's house alongside the bluebell garden, now in full bloom. The house used to be blocked from sight by the old twisted oak, but Sweet had had to take it down last fall. She'd told him about it a few weeks ago, as he fixed a loose hinge on her back door. She'd said the leaves had started thinning out, and the ones that remained were developing ominous black spots, and her landscaper had warned that the tree was so diseased, a light storm could send it toppling through her roof. She said it nearly broke her heart to hear the grinding of the buzz saw and see the heavy limbs drop to the grass, one by one. To see only a small brown circle left behind, where the grass, she assumed, would forever refuse to grow.

"I didn't want to watch, but I had to," she'd said. "That tree was a member of my family. I had to give it the dignity of a proper goodbye."

She'd wiped her eyes with a corner of the light blue scarf draped around her shoulders, and he'd nodded and held his hammer still, giving her a quiet moment with her memories. What she didn't know was that the tree had been a part of his life, too.

Because what happened that summer with Jenna long ago could never have happened if there'd been no twisted oak.

He went inside to grab his dinner from the oven, although he wasn't hungry after all. Taking it outside, he put it on the side table. That August, the weather had been just like it was tonight, he remembered. Weeks of brilliant sunshine and comfortably warm temperatures had given way to thick humidity, wet winds, and motionless gray clouds from the moment July ended. Nobody could remember such a hot, wet month, and everyone was on edge. Steven was mad because he liked a girl who was dating someone else. Chloe was mad because all her friends from college had rented a house on the Jersey Shore but her father refused to let her join them. And Troy was mad, too. He remembered storming into the kitchen one morning for an apple to take on his way to his job at the dry cleaner, ignoring his mother's offer to make him French toast. He stopped to glare at the course catalog for the community college on the kitchen table before heading through the hallway to the front door, nearly running over Sweet, who was coming inside to return his mother's ceramic bowl.

"I don't know what's gotten into him," he heard his mother say to Sweet. "I thought he wanted to go to college. This weather is making everyone so crabby! Here, let me take that—did you all enjoy the chilled peach soup?"

He walked outside and paused to take a breath, his eyes downward, his hands on his waist. He didn't like snapping at his mom, but she didn't understand him at all. He wanted to go to college, he just didn't want to go to *that* one. He could feel the sweat beading on the back of his neck and under his tee shirt. It was going to be brutal at the dry cleaner's today. Mr. Miller couldn't afford to install air conditioning, and the presses made the shop unbearable. Lifting his head, he saw Jenna standing on the curb, in shorts and tee shirt, her hair in a ponytail. Their eyes locked for a moment, and she smiled and waved. Then the screen door slammed behind him, and Steven ran past, twirling the key ring with the key to the used Malibu convertible they had bought together with a loan from their dad.

"Hey, slow down, for Christ's sake!" Troy called. "Where the hell are you taking the car?"

"What does it matter to you?" Steven said. "You walk to work."

"You're supposed to tie up the newspapers for recycling."

"I'll get to it later."

"You're supposed to do it this morning."

"I'll get to it when I get to it. What the hell's your problem?"

"My problem is you just got your damn license and you don't know how to handle the car," Troy said. "You go too fast and you're screwing up the brakes."

"Fuck you," Steven said. "Get in," he told Jenna, and she looked at Troy again before she followed Steven's order.

He watched Steven back out of the driveway way too fast, the car bouncing like a rubber ball as it traveled along the gravel. Then the brakes squealed as Steven shifted to drive and took off down the road.

He hated Steven that summer. He hated how Steven had gotten into the habit of driving Jenna to and from her job at the concession stand at the lake, just so he could show off the car to the girl he liked. He hated how Steven worked the dinnertime shift clearing tables at the Grill, so he could be a lazy jerk for most of the day. He hated how Steven never helped out around the house, so their dad was always getting mad. Even when he tried to cover for Steven by mowing the lawn or tying up the papers or oiling the hinges on the garage door, Dad always figured it out and then got mad at him, too. And he hated the way Steven ran down the stairs every morning. He'd just grab the car key off the hallway table, and tear outside, letting the screen door slam behind him so sharply Dad would explode when he came home and saw the wood splintering.

But most of all, Troy hated how Steven was still such good friends with Jenna.

Suddenly that summer, Troy couldn't get Jenna out of his mind. There was something so easy and light about her. So cooling, like the lake, or the stars back in July when the nights were clear. It had something to do with her wide smile, which seemed to just relax and spread across her face like it had all the room in the world. And the way the edges of her smile led to the point of her chin in a near-perfect triangle. She calmed him, because she was so unruffled. He wanted nothing more than to be in the vicinity of that smile.

And he didn't trust Steven. Not with the car, not with Jenna either. He was reckless, and Jenna was… trusting. Naive. He still remembered that time five or six years ago, when she rode her bike right into the Public Works Building, because she wanted to fly down the hill as Steven had. Steven was older and more rebellious now; who knew what risks he'd take with a car instead of a bike under his control? Walking to the curb, Troy watched the Malibu travel down the street, the brake lights illuminating for less than a second before Steven rounded the corner and drove out of sight. Then he continued walking to town. He must have looked enraged because Mrs. Pearl called to him as he passed her shop and brought him a cup of lemonade.

It was late that afternoon, while he was working the register at Mr. Miller's, that Steven went too far. Troy saw the whole thing through the shop's plate glass window. Driving toward town from the direction of the lake, Steven made a way too sharp turn at the corner of Main and Maple. The car banked to the right as it zoomed past the dry cleaner, balanced on two wheels for several hundred feet, then landed back on all fours just before it smashed into a row of metal trash cans lined along the curb. The boom enveloped the block; the dry cleaner's windows rattled before Troy's eyes.

Troy ran out of the shop, leaving behind two customers and an unattended cash register, and raced down the street to where Jenna and Steven were getting out of the car, unhurt. Mr. Brand, the guy who owned the card store directly in front of the crash, also came running out—and when he opened the door to his shop, his little terrier, Pauley, came dashing out as well. The dog leaped around the trash cans and ran into the street, right into the path of an oncoming car. The front tire struck Pauley before the driver could stop. He fell to his side and lay there, motionless.

Troy watched Mr. Brand run into the street, then sink to his knees next to the dog and bury his face in his hands. He followed him, wanting to make sure the old guy didn't get struck as well. He squatted down and put his hand on Mr. Brand's shoulder and saw the tears splash down from Mr. Brand's eyes. Everyone knew that Mr. Brand's wife had died that year, and the only thing keeping him going was Pauley. Troy didn't know how Mr. Brand would ever survive Pauley's death.

Except that Pauley wasn't dead. He was breathing, his furry chest expanding and contracting ever so slightly. Troy scooped up the little guy and held him as he and Mr. Brand got into the car that had struck Pauley and let the driver take them to the clinic.

Later, when the driver dropped Troy off at his house, it was after dark. The neighborhood was lit only by streetlights that formed pale yellow pools on the asphalt. It was thanks to one of these glowing pools that he noticed Jenna, sitting on the curb in front of her house, still wearing the same tee shirt and shorts she'd had on this morning. He didn't know why she'd be sitting there all alone.

"You okay?" he called over.

She got up and walked to him. "Oh my God," she said, and he realized she was looking at his pants soaked with Pauley's blood.

"How's Pauley?" she asked.

He nodded. "He'll be okay. A few nights in the clinic. It wasn't as bad as it looked."

"And Mr. Brand?"

He chuckled. "He's okay, too."

She clasped her hands and pressed them against the front of her shirt. "You saved that dog. He would have died if you weren't there."

"No, the vet saved him."

"No," she said. "It was you." She looked up, and by the glow of the streetlight across the road, he saw a tear drip down her cheek.

"You're always there for us," she said.

He smiled. "Somebody has to be."

"But why? It's like… we don't have to watch out for ourselves, nobody has to watch out for themselves because… you're there. And you just do it."

He shrugged. "He's my brother. You're my… neighbor." He didn't know what else to call her. Although she was much, much more than that.

"But…" she started.

"Come on," he said, and touched her shoulder. Shook it a bit, like a teasing thing, because he couldn't bear her crying. If he had to watch another tear run down her cheek, he would have to leave, just turn around and run, because otherwise he'd melt right to the ground. She nodded and looked away, and he looked at her, at how the front of her hair had come loose from her ponytail and draped across her face, at how the blue stone at the end of her necklace sat in the dip between her collarbones. He didn't know why she'd been waiting for him, what she was trying to tell him.

He looked down and ground the toe of his shoe into the grass. From his house, he could hear his father yelling and his mother yelling back, in that half yelling, half crying way of hers. He couldn't make out the words, but the cadence of their argument was familiar. His father must have had another bad doctor's visit today, and he was saying that he hated the tasteless food she cooked for him now, and she was saying that she loved him and didn't want to be a widow and if he didn't care about himself, he should at least care about her and their four sons. Troy wanted to get in the car, which was now parked in the driveway, which probably was all scratched up in the front from the collision with the trash cans. He wanted to take off and drive, all night maybe. He didn't even need to change out of the jeans he was wearing, stained and stiff with Pauley's dried blood.

"Come on," he repeated. "Pauley's okay. It's all okay. Okay?"

But Jenna wasn't letting it go. "You went into the street and you held Mr. Brand as he cried. And then you picked up the dog. And just seeing that… seeing you… I don't know how to explain it." She sniffled and then let out a jagged breath. "Seeing you there carrying Pauley… seeing you…" She pressed the back of her wrist against her mouth.

"I know," he said. And then he lifted his hand to do something to lighten the mood, maybe to tap her shoulder again, or this time tug her hair, except that what he ended up doing was stroking her cheek with his thumb, and then leaning down to kiss her on the mouth. It was a short kiss, more of a touch, a moment of contact. He wanted to stay there, stay like that forever, but he didn't trust himself, didn't know where his fingers, his mouth, his feelings would take him, and he didn't want to let them loose.

He'd pulled back and watched her open her eyes. She looked surprised, and he could see her chest rise and fall as she breathed.

"Troy," she'd whispered. And then she turned around and ran to the side of her house, and climbed up the twisted oak and into her bedroom window. And he saw she was barefoot, and he marveled at how strong she was. He realized that her parents probably didn't know she'd been out so late. That she'd snuck out of the house so she could wait for him.

He walked toward his front door, expecting to be fired from both of his jobs—from the dry cleaner for leaving the cash register unattended, and from the resort for missing his shift. But by the next day, all of Lake Summers knew how he'd saved Pauley. The *Lake Summers Press* called his house to arrange an interview for a front-page article, and Mr. Miller promised a lifetime of free dry cleaning for him and his family. The manager of the resort threw a party for him when he showed up at work that evening.

But he didn't care about any of it. All he cared about was that he'd kissed Jenna. And he hoped when he got home that night, she'd be waiting on the curb for him again.

He polished off his beer, shaking off the memory. It was dark now, and he was pulling himself off the chair, his chicken parm untouched, when he noticed Sweet's outdoor lights switch on, illuminating the patio. A moment later Sophie emerged, carrying a tray, Mo trotting behind her. Then Jenna and Chloe came out, and Sweet followed, walking pretty well, even though she was leaning on a cane. Jenna went to the barbecue grill at the corner of the patio and turned it on. The flame rose up, and the three of them stood near the grill, each with an arm outstretched. They were toasting marshmallows, maybe making s'mores. He heard Jenna tell Sophie to be careful, as she pulled her a few steps back from the flame.

He turned away and went back into the house, listening to the sound of laughter from next door. That feeling he'd had ever since he walked through the door—unsettled? Lonely? Restless?—was ridiculous. He wasn't a love-struck kid anymore. He wasn't the kid who kissed Jenna on the curb under the streetlights outside their houses.

But no matter what he'd thought earlier about wanting to be alone, to keep everyone at arm's length, to live the life he had made for himself here in Lake Summer, the truth was he was a lonely guy in an empty house. And suddenly he didn't want to be that guy anymore. He envied them, that they were together. A family. Yes, there was a time long ago when being part of a family had been almost too difficult to bear. Taking care of his brothers after their parents died had been excruciating—the fear he felt for them, the guilt, the responsibility that weighed so heavy, it sometimes seemed like he couldn't breathe. He never wanted to feel that way again. But being alone was hard, too. The joy, the ease, that his brothers felt as family men with wives and children—he saw it when they all gathered together at Steven's each year on Thanksgiving. It practically radiated out from all of them. Was it possible that being alone wasn't the only way for him to live? And considering that the person he'd loved more than anyone else in his entire life was right next door now—wasn't it worthwhile to at least make a gesture toward her and see what might happen?

He thought about how he could reverse the damage he'd done when he'd walked away from Jenna so abruptly, brushing aside her invitation to come into the house and look through old photos. And then he had an idea. He didn't want to knock on the door or walk over there and disturb them. Not to mention that he'd told Jenna he was taking care of a puppy. The best way would be to text her, but he didn't have her number. So he found a sheet of paper and pen, and wrote another note to leave at her door:

Jenna,

I know you have a lot going on, with your mom just home. I can take Mo to work with me for the next couple of weeks, to make it easier to get your mother settled. He had a good time the other day. I leave for work at eight thirty, just meet me outside. It's no trouble. I'm happy to do this for you. I'd like to help.

Troy

He rolled up the paper and went outside to place it on her doorknob. Although the rain had stopped earlier, the grass was still wet, and the moisture pooled inside his shoes. He didn't know if Jenna would be glad for his offer or think it unnecessary. There was no way to know. All he could do was see if she showed up on Monday morning.

It was the same way he felt after their first kiss. Wondering if she'd show up again.

CHAPTER ELEVEN

"I'm sorry, Aunt Chloe, but you did look like poodles," Sophie said as she set the patio table for breakfast. "And those tops! How did you get your shoulders like that?"

"They were shoulder pads. All the tops came with them."

"Like, sewn in?"

"Or Velcro."

"To your skin?"

"No, silly! To the inside of the shirt."

"How was that even comfortable? Looking like football players!" She hunched up her shoulders.

"It wasn't like that. We thought it was a pretty silhouette. Broad shoulders made your waist look smaller—"

"What? That is so crazy! I can't believe—"

"Enough about our bad fashion choices," Jenna said as she came through the open patio doorway, carrying a platter of muffins and scones, Mo scampering alongside her. She had gone out with Mo that morning while everyone else was still asleep, tying him to the bench as she ran into Mrs. Pearl's to pick up some treats for breakfast. She came home to find fresh coffee in the carafe of the coffee maker and Chloe's specialty, blueberry pancakes, sitting on a platter on the countertop, covered in foil to keep warm. Outside, Chloe was setting out strawberry jam and maple syrup on the patio table and chatting with Sophie, who was still in her pajamas, sitting cross-legged on a lounge chair as she teased her aunt. Jenna couldn't help but think it so appropriate that it was the last weekend in June, and next week was the start of July. A fresh new month, a fresh new beginning.

"Mo-sey!" Sophie called and came running over. She scooped up the dog, then carried him over to her grandmother, who was sitting on a cushioned patio chair, her legs resting on the matching ottoman. "Look, Sweet! Mo wants to say hi!"

Jenna watched her mom scratch Mo's ear, finding just the right spot so Mo would tilt his head toward her hand and drink in her affection. She was wearing a sleeveless white jersey dress decorated with tiny copper paisleys, with a butter-yellow sweater over her shoulders. She had on her straw sun hat.

"Hi, Mom," Jenna said. "How'd you sleep?"

"Like a baby. I'm telling you girls, I will never spend another night in the hospital."

"I'm for that," Chloe said. "But seeing as that's your plan, then I wish you'd let us rent you a hospital bed for downstairs. The staircase here is as steep as the basement ones."

"Oh, Chloe! Everyone slips now and then. I'm not going to spend the rest of my life listening to you carry on about my fall. And I'm certainly not going to live banished from the second story of my own house."

"Of course you're not, Mom," Jenna said, to stave off any more bickering. "Come on, let's have breakfast. I'll bring out the pancakes Chloe made, they smell amazing. Soph, can you finish setting the table?"

A few minutes later they were all seated. But no sooner had they started to eat than Chloe's cell phone rang. She looked at the screen and then took in a deep breath. "It's Ed again," she said. "I'll take this inside."

Jenna looked at her mom after Chloe left the table. "What's going on?"

"Ed's anxious about the store," her mother answered. "He's not used to managing it without her."

"He keeps calling," Sophie said. "He called twice when you were out, Mom."

"He misses her," Jenna said. "He's not used to being without her. I don't remember the last time Aunt Chloe went somewhere without Uncle Ed."

"But isn't that annoying?" Sophie asked. "To have someone call you so much?" She looked at her grandmother. "Was that how it was with you and the movie star? Did he call you three times every morning?"

Sweet smiled. "No, we were both very busy during the day, if I remember correctly. But we saw each other every night. Every single night when I was there."

"*Every* night? Didn't you get sick of him?"

"Not at all!" Sweet said. "It was so much fun, learning all about him. Every day was a new adventure. Who gets sick of a new adventure?"

"But every day's not a new adventure for Aunt Chloe," Sophie said. "She's been married to Uncle Ed forever. There's nothing else to learn."

"Oh, Sophie. There's always more to learn," Sweet said. "There are many ways to be in love. So many ways to give your heart."

Jenna watched as her mother reached across the table and patted Sophie's chin. She enjoyed hearing the two of them talk about love. Her mother had given such warm and playful answers to Sophie's questions. But it stung that Sophie hadn't asked *her* any questions. She supposed it made sense. Sophie probably had no desire just yet to face the sad fact of her parents' failed marriage. She knew Sophie spoke with Matt on her phone from time to time, although Sophie never mentioned those conversations to her. She assumed Matt hadn't yet told Sophie about Felicity, because she thought Sophie would say something if he did. It seemed the best approach was not to press Sophie into talking. At least she had a grandmother who had wonderful memories about love to share.

Chloe returned to the table. "I'm going to have to leave," she said. "The July Fourth sale is starting and all the new outdoor furniture is on promotion, and Ed needs me back. I knew it was tricky to leave him alone this weekend."

"I'm sorry," Jenna said. "I thought you'd be here at least a few days." She meant it. Although she'd been dreading a confrontation with Chloe for weeks now, the conversation yesterday had gone well. She'd enjoyed having her sister here. They'd all had such a good time last night, looking through those old pictures and then making s'mores for dessert. It was nice having all the girls in the family together, three generations, laughing and having fun. She couldn't remember the last time she'd gotten along so well with Chloe, and she couldn't help but think it was because she had finally stood up to her, as Mrs. Pearl had suggested. She'd never had the courage before, but somehow the importance of keeping her mother home had emboldened her. And Chloe had listened and respected her. It was as though their whole relationship had been reset.

"We have a lot riding on this month's sales, and a lot of salespeople who'll be out of work if we don't meet our numbers," she said. "It's hard running the store on a sale weekend. I don't think I have a choice. I'm sorry," she said, turning to her mother. "I'd planned to stay and help you."

"Don't be silly, honey," her mother said. "Of course you belong with your husband. Go on, now. That's exactly where you ought to be."

They finished breakfast quickly, and Chloe went upstairs to pack her clothes. She came back to the patio a few minutes later. "Bye, Mom," she said, kissing her cheek. "I'll be back with Ed for your birthday. We'll have a little party. Please be careful until then, okay?"

"Bye, sweetheart," her mother said, stroking Chloe's cheek. "Drive carefully. Give Ed our best."

"Bye, Soph," Chloe said, turning to her niece. "Let me know what other bizarre things you find in those boxes, okay? Don't forget."

"I won't." Sophie got up from her chair and reached out to hug Chloe. "It was fun last night."

Jenna walked her sister through the house and out onto the driveway. She unlatched the trunk of Chloe's car and put Chloe's suitcase inside.

Chloe slammed the trunk shut. "Funny, huh?" she said. "You packed for two nights and now you're staying for weeks, and I packed for a week and ended up staying just one night. What do you think that says about us? That we're always on the wrong page?"

Jenna shook her head. "I think it's just a reminder that life is unpredictable."

"Same difference. Although maybe not. I guess it's all about how you look at it." She leaned against the car. "You'll call me if you need anything, right, Jenns? If you change your mind in these six weeks, if things get hard—if Mom gets more confused or Sophie pushes this story too far—you'll call me, right?"

Jenna nodded.

"If you need me to come back, just call. I'll find a way to do it. Once we get through this week, Ed will have a much easier time on his own. The summer slows down after the Fourth—"

"We'll be fine." Jenna reached out and hugged Chloe. "We'll see you back here for Mom's birthday. You'll see, she'll look even better than she does now. We all will."

"Stay in touch," Chloe said. She opened the car door and slipped behind the wheel. "Take care of her, Jenna. Take care of yourself, too."

Jenna nodded and closed Chloe's door, then followed the car down to the end of the driveway. She waved as Chloe drove down the street, then watched as the brake lights glowed red and

Chloe turned and drove out of sight. It had been comforting to have Chloe here, but at the same time, she was excited to be in charge and begin her new life.

She was walking back to the house when she noticed a small white cylinder beneath the hyacinth bushes. Getting down on her knees, she stretched her arm out on the soil until she was able to grasp it. It was a rolled-up sheet of paper, just like the one Troy had left to tell her he had Mo. She unrolled it and sure enough, it was another note. She figured he must have threaded it through the door handle, and the wind blew it down. It was an invitation to take care of Mo again.

She rolled the note back up and grasped it with both hands. The animal clinic probably was a good place for Mo. She was sure Troy was right, that Mo had enjoyed being there. He'd always been friendly, and he probably did enjoy seeing the other animals.

She reread Troy's note. It seemed to be about more than Mo. There was something almost pleading in the tone. She couldn't put her finger on the words that made her think so, but she could tell he wanted to do this for her, almost more than she needed him to do it. Mrs. Pearl had said he'd agreed right away to come back to Lake Summers when she called, and Jenna recognized—related to—that desire to return to a familiar place. She wondered what had made him reach out to her, after pushing her off when she saw him.

*

Sophie went to meet some friends at the lake that afternoon, while Sweet relaxed on the patio with one of her old novels and Jenna did some cooking for the coming week. That night, Sophie brought up another department store box. She picked at the tape that held the top in place. It was so old that at first it started to flake, but eventually she grasped an end and unwound the whole strip. It was filled inside with papers, which turned out to be receipts—restaurant receipts, store receipts, gasoline receipts, and even receipts for musicals and concerts at the Lake Summers Playhouse, which had been turned into a movie theater years ago.

"No way!" Sophie exclaimed, looking at a sheet of paper. "How was a hamburger platter in 1983 only three dollars and eighty cents? At the Grill! What is it now?"

"Twelve dollars? Thirteen?" Jenna said.

"That's wild! And all these receipts were written by hand—like, written in pen by an actual person. That's wild, too! Boy, Daddy complains so much now about how slow they are at the Grill. Can you imagine what it would be like if they had to write out all the prices and do the math themselves? What if they made a mistake? What if they didn't add right?"

"We always double-checked," Sweet said.

"You checked the math? Did you bring paper and a pencil everywhere?"

"No, silly," Sweet said. "We'd do it in our heads. Just a quick estimate to make sure they added right."

"No way! You had to do all that math in your head every time you ate out? I am so glad I didn't live back then!"

She dug deeper into the box, then pulled out a thin, hardcover book. "What is this doing here?" she said. "A book? Sweet, why did you put a book in here?"

"I was never one to sit around sorting things," Sweet said. "Your grandfather, he was the sorter. Me, I just threw things wherever there was room. I figured it would be a sorry day when I had time enough to bother adhering to some overcomplicated organizing system."

Sophie looked at the cover. "*The Autobiography of Carlo Alley?* Who was that? Somebody famous?"

"Not at all," Sweet said. "I don't read about famous people."

"That's true," Jenna added. "You always told me you didn't like reading about people everyone wants to know about. I remember going to the bookstore with you when I was growing up. You went straight past the famous autobiographies in the front and looked for the obscure ones nobody else wanted in the back. The books about people who had big dreams but not all that much success."

"Why do you like people who never get what they want?" Sophie asked.

"The people who get everything—they don't interest me," Sweet said. "The people who just miss have a better story to tell."

Sophie got up and balanced on her knees on the arm of Sweet's chair, sitting back on her heels. "When do you think we're going to find the box with the movie star stuff?" she said. "I want to find out about him so badly! We found the closet, right? It's the one you meant, right? We're getting close to the box where everything is, aren't we?"

Sweet patted Sophie's knee. "Of course you are," she said. "You're getting so close… how do they put it? Warm, warmer, no, you're hot! That's all I'm going to say. Now do me a favor, pretty girl, and bring my teacup back to the kitchen, so I can start to head upstairs to bed. What a busy day we've had. I can barely keep my eyes open."

"Okay," Sophie said and kissed her grandmother, then picked up the teacup. "See, Mom? We're hot! Sweet says we're hot. Maybe we shouldn't stop at one box a night. Maybe we should open another. Or three or four…"

"But then you won't have as much fun," Jenna said. "You probably wouldn't look as closely because you'd have so much more to look through. You wouldn't hear about all the pictures…" But Sophie was already in the kitchen.

"That's my daughter," Jenna said, more to herself than to her mother. "Why do I even talk? She never stops for long enough to hear what I have to say."

"Just like her mom," Sweet said with a wink. Then she shook her head. "Oh, but Jenna, she is just adorable," she said. "Sweet and smart… I so enjoy having her around." She scooted to the edge of the seat cushion, then pressed heavily on the arms of her chair until she was able to rise to her feet. Jenna winced, watching how hard her mother had to work just to stand up.

"Mom, can I help you?" she said, getting up from her chair.

"No, you stay right where you are!" she said. "My goodness, you and your sister act as though I fell out of a plane or something. You both fell a million times when you were babies. If I made a big deal about every one of those, you'd never have learned to ride a bike or swim or sail or do any of the things that children do."

She slowly walked to the fireplace to get her cane and then made her way across the room. Her mother was right; she was doing very well. Though she still had pain, it was remarkable that she could move around as much as she did. But it was the other concern, the confusion, that kept nagging at her. Her mom had such a way with people. She had evaded Sophie's questions about the boxes so skillfully right now, getting Sophie to drop the conversation and run off with the teacup. Did she really believe Sophie was getting warmer? Or was she trying to cover for how little she remembered? On the one hand, it didn't matter. Sophie and her grandmother were having a wonderful time together, bonding in a way they'd never had the time to do before. But if the story about the movie star was never revealed, would her mother feel sad and embarrassed? And how would that affect Sophie? Would she think that her summer had been wasted? Was it the only thing that made her want to stay in Lake Summers?

The doctor had said that her mother's confusion was something to keep an eye on. But Jenna dreaded ever having to admit that her mother's memory was truly failing.

She turned off the lamps in the living room, then started to make her way up to the bedroom, but stopped at the hallway table. She had left Troy's note there earlier today. Now she unrolled it and read it through for a second time, stopping at the last two sentences. *I'm happy to do this for you. I'd like to help.* It was just like Troy to do this, the Troy she knew from way back. And she wanted that person back in her life, no matter whether Mo needed to be out of the house or not. It would be nice to see him every morning when she handed off Mo and every evening when he brought Mo back. He was the guy she'd fallen in love with years ago. She'd felt good that summer just being around him, and she wanted that again.

Suddenly she didn't feel so alone.

CHAPTER TWELVE

On Monday when Jenna took Mo for his walk, the whole town had a new energy. When she got to Pearl's, the line for coffee stretched out the door and onto the sidewalk, making it hard to see the menu with the day's muffin choices. The summer season was now in full swing, and there was a sense of intention in the air, as though everyone was glad this time had arrived and wanted to make it the best summer yet. "Say hi to your mom!" Mrs. Pearl called out from behind the counter when Jenna's turn came, too busy brewing fresh coffee to come around the counter for a chat. She used her wrist to push a stray strand of hair away from her face. "Tell her I can't wait to see her here!"

Back home, Jenna fixed a breakfast of eggs and fruit to go with the apple spice muffins she'd selected, and she, Sophie, and her mom ate breakfast on the patio. Then Jenna cleared the table, and Sophie went upstairs to get ready for camp.

At eight thirty Jenna hooked Mo's leash to his collar and brought him outside. Troy was just leaving his house. She watched as he locked the front door, then halted when he realized she was there. He smiled, so she did, too, and they met at the end of her driveway. She loved how he looked, neat and professional in a white button-down shirt with thin blue stripes and a pair of charcoal-gray slacks, although the deep-gray backpack slung over one shoulder added a boyish touch. But more than his look, his whole bearing was so calming to her. There was something so pulled together about him as he walked down his front steps, a quietness, a sense that he knew where he was going—not just today but tomorrow and the next day. It was so different from how Matt always looked in the mornings—anxious and peeved at his boss, a colleague, a client, or whomever he felt had most recently wronged him. He'd tell her what was going on, and it never seemed to her that anyone intended to slight him. It was always easier for Matt to play the victim than to take responsibility for his disappointments.

"Hey, boy," Troy said as he knelt to give Mo a neck rub. "How are you feeling today?" He turned his shoulder to display his backpack. "I remembered to bring more of your favorite beef for lunch. And if you play your cards right, Zoe may go up to the storage room to see if she can find you a toy."

He stood and faced Jenna, hoisting the backpack more securely on his shoulder. "Guess you got my note," he said.

"I did," she told him. "Mo was thrilled."

"How's your mom today?"

"She's good. I think she likes having us around. Especially Sophie. And she likes Mo, too."

"Oh? Well, hey, if she likes having the dog around, then maybe you should keep him. I only thought if it could help—"

"No, it is a help. Because she still has to get more stable, so the more he won't be underfoot, the better…" She nodded, hoping for Troy to respond, to say something more personal, not about Mo and her mother, but about her and him. She wondered if Troy was feeling what she was—a kind of loss, even now, when he was right in front of her. A sad disconnect between the kindred spirits they once were and the neighbors they'd become. She hesitated, trying to think of something else to say, and the more she thought, the worse she felt. That summer long ago, she was never at a loss of for words. Before she knew it, it was two or three in the morning.

"I wish there was something you'd let us do to thank you," she finally said. "Would you like to come over for dinner one night?

We could eat on the patio, it's beautiful out there in the evenings. We've been going through all these old boxes my mother saved. There's some funny stuff in there…"

"Sure, that sounds nice," Troy said. "Maybe in a couple of weeks or so. It's kind of busy now, with all the summer people coming back to town with their pets… and Art Grayson, remember him? He has me working on some big local history thing, I don't know how I let him rope me into it, but hey, I did… But we'll do it soon, okay?"

"Of course," Jenna said. "Whenever you'd like."

"I should get going," he said, but then continued speaking, as though he didn't want to leave her yet. "It takes longer when I walk, but I think this guy here would prefer that. And it's a full morning. I have an infected paw to clean out, a couple of cats that need vaccinations, and I've already had a call this morning about a puppy with a bad cough. We have our work cut out for us today, don't we, pal?"

Mo looked up at him and wagged his tail.

"I should get going," he repeated.

Jenna handed over the leash. "It does sound like a busy day. Call me if he gets in the way, and I'll come right over to get him. But he really likes you, Troy. Thanks again. See you later."

He nodded and headed toward the road. She wished he'd agreed to have dinner with her. But she supposed all he wanted was to help out a neighbor. She started back up the walk when she heard him call her.

"Jenna?"

She turned.

"I wanted to say…" He looked down. "I want you to know I'm glad you're here. You and Sophie. It's good. Makes it feel like summer again." He paused, then continued down the street, Mo trotting alongside him.

She continued to watch him, wondering if he'd turn again to say more, but knowing full well that he wouldn't. Now she was more confused than ever. He was glad she was back in town, but he wouldn't come over for dinner? It was like he was wrestling with her, and she couldn't figure out what the battle stations were. She wondered what she had done wrong. Or what he was afraid of. She half wondered if she was going crazy. If all her memories of him were a dream.

*

An hour later, after dropping Sophie off at camp and making sure her mom was comfortable on the patio with a tall glass of iced tea and a copy of the *Lake Summers Press*, Jenna pushed all thoughts of Troy aside. She knew she had to get to work making the arrangements for the next six weeks. The new agenda she'd created for herself was intimidating. A week ago, she'd assumed she'd be back in Rye by now, cleaning out the house and waiting for brokers to start bringing potential buyers around. Staying in Lake Summers until mid-August meant much less time to pull off the big move. But she couldn't let the prospect of juggling so much later throw her off her game. She'd work it out. The important thing was she was here now, in the one place she felt strong and capable. After all, she had once crashed into a brick wall right in this very town and lived to tell the tale. There was little you couldn't do if you were strong enough to hit a brick wall and walk away with nothing worse than a scraped knee.

Sitting in the living room at her mother's cherry writing desk, looking out onto the prairie grass and bayberry bushes at the back of the house, she got started on the phone. It took nearly all morning, and a lot of patience, to get advice from the hospital social worker and then work through the insurance bureaucracy, but finally, she got the approvals for a part-time home health aide. Remembering that Dr. Roberts had invited her to call with any questions, she found his business card in her bag and dialed him next to see if he had any recommendations for where to find that kind of help. He mentioned that his granddaughter, Sherry, had recently moved to town and was staying with him, and hoped to earn some money while she pursued a graduate degree in nursing.

"She was working the last few years as a registered nurse, and she's terrific," he said. "If you'd like to talk with her about helping your mom a few days a week, I'd be happy to put you two in touch."

Jenna also called the head of the lakeside camp to extend Sophie's enrollment through the middle of August. That would take them right up to her mother's birthday on August 15th, after which she'd reach out to Lake Summers Middle School and begin the enrollment process for Sophie. She knew she needed to run this all by her daughter, who seemed happy to stay for now and explore the boxes in the basement but might need convincing to move for good. And she also needed to let Matt know her plans. But every time she started to call him, she changed her mind. She didn't know how to explain herself without sounding as though she were fleeing from the mess she'd left behind. How could she make him see that she wasn't running away from her life, but *to* it? There was a time when he had understood her, when he had been open to her feelings. But that had all ended in the months before he left. "You changed, Jenna," he had said the night he told her he was leaving to move in with Felicity. "You don't care about me or our marriage. You haven't for a long time." She'd been surprised to learn there was someone else, but not to hear that he was unhappy and wanted out. She'd known that for a while. She'd wanted to protest that she cared very much, about both him and their marriage. But she knew it was pointless. His mind was made up. His new life awaited.

Finally, she decided to send a short text: *We decided to stay in Lake Summers through the middle of August. My mother needs me. Sophie is very happy and enjoying camp. You're welcome to come visit whenever you want.*

The last thing she did was call Samantha, the no-nonsense editor-in-chief of the *Lake Summers Press*, and ask if she might take on some assignments this month. She wasn't supposed to start her job until September, but since she was staying here for now—and since, with any luck, Dr. Roberts' granddaughter would be coming over to help out—it would do her good to leave the house, meet new people, and earn a little money.

"I can't put you on the business desk yet," Samantha said. "I'm not budgeted for that position until after the summer. But I can use a freelancer this month to fill in for reporters taking vacation. I have one news piece to assign right now, and there'll be more down the road. If you're interested, it's yours."

Jenna was definitely interested. She had left the magazine world after Sophie was born, and just making the call reminded her of why she'd chosen to work in magazines in the first place. It had always felt so exciting, so unpredictable, the kind of job that changed every day, as you interviewed different people and discovered what made them tick. She'd been glad to be able to work at home after Sophie was born, writing marketing copy for a mattress manufacturer, but she'd missed the fun of crafting an original story. Now she was glad to be getting back to her roots, back to the person she was before she'd left her reporting job.

"I'd love to freelance this month," Jenna said. "When do you want me to start?"

"This is a slow week, with July Fourth coming up on Friday," Samantha said. "Stop by next Monday morning and we'll get you started on your first piece."

At that point, the calls were done, and by Wednesday, routines for the summer were starting to take shape. Jenna spoke with her mom's regular hairstylist and manicurist, who were happy to come to the house until her mom's ankle and rib were less painful, and she was ready to go back downtown to get her hair and nails done. On Thursday, Sherry came over for breakfast, and Jenna, her mom, and Sophie all immediately fell in love with her. She looked to be in her late twenties and was tall like her grandfather, with long blonde hair pulled into a ponytail. Her coral-color scrubs were both practical and fashionable, as the top had a mandarin-style collar and the bottoms were joggers. She told them that she'd taken theater classes before deciding to go into nursing, and wished the Lake Summers Theatrical was still operating, as she'd have loved to help out with stage managing or set design.

"Sherry, I am very glad you're here," her mom said when they had finished breakfast and Sophie had gone upstairs to get her backpack for camp. "I don't need any help, regardless of what my well-meaning daughter says." She gave Jenna a sideways look. "But the truth is, it's nice to have people around. Oh, it used to be so much fun in the summers, when we were doing the theatricals. Everyone was so busy. Don't get me wrong, life is lovely now, too. But those were fun days, weren't they, Jenna? So much unfinished work."

"Oh, but you haven't met Chloe yet," she added. "Why didn't Chloe come down for breakfast? Jenna, where is she? She's not still sleeping, is she?"

"Mom," Jenna said. "Chloe left last weekend."

"She left? No, she didn't."

"Yes, she did. Don't you remember? She had to go back to Ed. He needed help with the store."

"What? Oh yes, of course," her mother said. "She left for Long Island. Yes, to be with Ed." She laughed. "I guess I miss her so much, I wanted to believe she was still here."

She got up from the table, took her cane, and made her way outside to the patio. Still sitting at the table, Jenna folded her arms across her chest.

"You look worried," Sherry said. "Has this kind of thing happened before?"

"Maybe a bit," Jenna said. "But she's always been kind of absentminded, so I believe that it actually may have slipped her mind that Chloe left. But the doctor at the hospital thought there might be a problem. And my sister has thought so for a while, too."

"If you want to have her checked out at some point I'm sure my grandfather can recommend a good specialist," Sherry said.

"Thanks," Jenna said. "Let's give it some time. Maybe she's still getting over the fall. Maybe all of this will just blow over."

*

Camp was canceled that Friday for July Fourth, and since Sherry was at the house, Jenna took Sophie on a mother-daughter shopping trip. They started at Lake Summers Fashions, which had a nice selection of women's outfits on the first floor and a loft with a large and trendy teen department. Jenna thought they could both use some new clothes, since she was starting her job next week and Sophie was longing for something new to wear to her friend's pre-fireworks party that night. She ended up buying two casual work dresses—a navy-blue sleeveless tank dress in a light jersey fabric, and a white linen sheath dress. She also chose a pair of tan sandals with a delicate ankle strap and a low, stacked heel—dressy enough for work but also comfortable for walking to interviews and meetings. Sophie settled on a pair of jean shorts and a sleeveless white top with eyelet trim around the neckline.

Jenna watched her daughter survey herself in the store's full-length mirror, trying to decide how her hair would look best to go with her new outfit—in a ponytail, in a half-ponytail, or down with a headband. She was delighted to see her daughter so happy. Sophie had become a whole new person since her grandmother came home. She couldn't wait to go to camp each day, and loved opening the boxes at night and then sitting on the arm of her grandmother's chair and pumping her for more tidbits about the elusive love story.

"What did he look like?" she'd asked yesterday evening.

"Oh, he was beautiful. Tall, so tall. Hair the color of honey. Soulful eyes."

"Soulful?"

"Thoughtful. Penetrating. Like he could see right through me."

"And you liked that?"

"I loved it. It meant he understood me like no one else."

"And that's why he told you the two words? Come on, Sweet, you remember them, don't you?"

"Oh, Sophie, they're buried deep inside. I'm trying my best to dig them up."

"But what kind of words are they? Can you remember that? Regular words like good morning, or hi there? Or old words like… thrice or forsook?"

"Forsook? Where on earth did you come up with that? They're regular words, I think that's right. They'll come back to me, just give me time."

Jenna watched as Sophie hugged her grandmother goodnight, then stuffed that night's assortment of papers back into the three shoeboxes she'd opened and took them to the basement. It was more than wonderful, watching her mother and her daughter get along so well. It convinced her even more that she was doing the right thing by moving up here for good.

Leaving the clothing store, they next stopped at the market, where Jenna picked up some hamburgers and fresh summer squash and corn to grill tonight, along with vanilla ice cream and canisters of red and blue sprinkles. It wouldn't be the same as going to the lake for a picnic, which her family had always done when Jenna was growing up. But she knew her mother wouldn't be able to handle the crowds at the lake, not to mention sitting on blankets on the sandy bank. It wasn't a bad alternative, as the porch had a clear view of the fireworks, and Sherry had accepted their invitation to stay and watch with them.

On the way home from shopping, Sophie suggested they stop for a couple of Fourth of July Specials at the Smoothie Dudes. "We refined the recipe since you and Chloe tasted it, Jenna," Trey said as he reached across the counter to hand them their drinks. "So if you don't like it, tell us you do anyway. Because this is the recipe we're selling at the lake tonight, so we can't do a darn thing to change it now."

That evening, Jenna dropped Sophie off at her friend's house, then came back home and cooked up dinner. The weather was cool and clear, and the smell of the food on the grill made Jenna remember her family barbecue dinners every Sunday evening long ago. Her dad had been an avid summertime chef, and he'd loved throwing anything he could on the grill—whole fish, vegetables marinated with balsamic vinegar and herbs, even fruits like peaches and pineapples. They'd often had neighbors over, and Dad wore an oversized navy-blue chef's apron and the chef's hat she and Chloe had bought him one Father's Day. He'd make a show of his barbecue maneuvers, twirling his tongs around his pointer finger, flipping the burgers high off the spatula, and moaning with glee—"Mmmmmmm-mmm!"—as the food sizzled and snapped atop the dancing flame. He'd always get a round of applause when he finished up and took his bow.

While Jenna's grilling style was more subtle, the food was still delicious, and after she'd cleared the table, she turned the patio chairs in the direction of the lake. Then Sherry helped her mom get settled, while Jenna brought out her laptop and turned the volume up high, so they'd be able to hear the streaming audio of the Lake Summers High School Band, which would be performing marches to accompany the fireworks. The show began as soon as the sky darkened, and Jenna watched her mom tap her fists lightly on the arms of her chair in time with the music and gasp happily with each new burst of color. It was hard to pull her eyes away from her mother's childlike smile, which almost made her cry. Her mom's ability to find joy in every moment was one of her most wonderful qualities. Even now—with her life quiet and small compared to the past, she still found it a treat to be alive.

"Isn't it fine!" she exclaimed as a shower of silver lines poured down like a waterfall in the sky. "Oh, my, isn't it grand!"

When the fireworks concluded, Jenna asked Sherry to stay a little longer while she went to pick up Sophie from the lake. She grabbed her car keys and was heading to the car when she noticed the light on above Troy's front door. It sent a beam of light shining directly onto the front step. And below the beam was Troy, nursing a beer.

Jenna let out a breath. She felt bad that Troy was there all alone. She hadn't seen him that afternoon—apparently he'd closed up his office early because of the holiday and had dropped Mo off with Sherry while she and Sophie were shopping. She had assumed he'd have plans tonight, that he'd be meeting friends or work colleagues at the lake for the fireworks. But why had she assumed that? She'd never seen him with anyone since she'd been back. At the least, she should have gone over there to invite him for dinner. Closing the car door, she started toward his house, so she could apologize.

"Jenna," he said as she approached.

"Hey, Troy," she said. She was always uncertain around him. She couldn't tell if he was glad she was there or if he wished she'd go.

"Is there something you needed?"

"No, I…" She breathed in. "I didn't realize you were home. I'm sorry I didn't invite you over. We have a great view of the fireworks. Although I guess you do, too. But it's fun to watch with other people."

"It's okay," he said. "I was thinking of going to the lake. But I decided not to." He twirled the neck of his beer bottle between his palms, then shifted over on the step and gestured with his chin at the empty space he'd left.

She sat down next to him. "Did you catch any of the show?" she asked.

"A little," he said.

"They were pretty," she said. "I haven't been here on July Fourth in a long time, but I think they've gotten bigger than they were when we were kids. The sky was completely lit up tonight."

He took a swallow of beer. "I guess," he said. "Hard to remember."

"Oh, I remember it all," she said. "Steven and I would organize the relay races, and then there'd be the fireworks, and then my mom would have the big block party afterward 'til way past midnight. And Chloe would be nervous because she always seemed to be going on a first date on July Fourth, and Cal and Clay would blame each other because their team didn't win any races. And then your dad would come back with all the other volunteer firefighters who'd been watching in case there was an emergency, and everyone would cheer for them. And then your mom would come out and give him this big hug, and everyone would cheer for that…"

She stopped when she saw he'd dropped his chin. "Did I say something wrong?" she asked.

He shook his head. "I was just thinking about my mom," he said. "She hated the Fourth of July. It made her nervous, especially when my dad's heart trouble started. She was always telling him to find something else to volunteer for. But he loved being with the fire department and keeping the town safe."

"He was a nice guy," Jenna said. "They were a very cute couple. I remember those hugs she gave him on July Fourth. So sweet."

She looked past his yard, at her patio. Sherry was helping her mom up from the chair. They went inside, and then the patio light shut off. She didn't want to leave Troy yet. She'd never realized how hard July Fourth must have been for him, how hard it was now. Still, it was getting late.

"I wish I could hang out a little longer, but I have to go get Sophie," she said. "She's waiting with some girlfriends at the lake. Hey, why don't you come with me? Maybe Stan and Trey will have some leftover July Fourth Specials. And even if not, you can come inside and have dessert with us…"

"That's okay," Troy said. "Go ahead, you should get her."

"Are you sure? I got ice cream from the market, it's the really rich kind they make right there in the store—"

"No, I'm okay, Jenna. Don't worry about me. Just tell Mo I'll be there bright and early Monday. Have a good night. Say hi to your mom and Sophie."

He looked at her, and she saw so much in his eyes—sadness, regret. Resignation, nostalgia. He got up first, and then she stood and headed to her car, feeling bad for having bothered him. For being so caught up in her own concerns that she never—not back then and not now, either—realized that July Fourth would be a hard night for him. She wished there was something she could have done or said to make him smile. Mrs. Pearl had mentioned last week that both she and Troy had come back home, sounding as though that linked them in some way, but now Jenna saw how different their homecomings really were.

For her, coming back was all about comfort. And family.

For him, coming back was about emptiness. And loss.

No wonder he didn't want to be with her.

CHAPTER THIRTEEN

"You look like it's the first day of school!" Mrs. Pearl said, waving from the doorway to the kitchen. "All dressed up and ready to go. Jake, give our town's newest crack reporter a cinnamon muffin on the house. The *Lake Summers Press* will win its first Pulitzer once our bluebell girl gets going!"

Jenna laughed as she accepted the muffin, along with her usual iced coffee and a few words of congratulation from the joggers and shopkeepers and young parents with strollers, the early risers of Lake Summers who made Pearl's one of their first morning stops. It was the following Monday, and Mrs. Pearl was right—it did feel as though she was starting a new school year. She'd packed a sandwich and a peach in her shoulder bag for lunch, and also brought the spiral notebook and box of pens she'd bought at Main Street Sundries over the weekend. She knew the office was probably well stocked with supplies, but she'd always been particular about her writing tools, preferring rollerball pens and paper ruled with light-colored, barely perceptible lines. She was wearing the navy-blue dress she bought when she shopped with Sophie on Friday. The leather of her new sandals was soft, and the heels made her feel office-ready.

She waved to Mrs. Pearl and left the shop, enjoying how the warm breeze gently tossed her hair, which she had spent extra time drying this morning so there'd be no flyaway pieces. She was excited to be working in Lake Summers, to be a member of the business community. Main Street looked different to her this morning. Each shop seemed to announce itself, calling out its mission, banking on the back-and-forth between sales staff and customers that would play out when the doors opened. This was the beginning of a new life for her, the life she'd imagined when she arrived in town last month and stopped for something to drink at Pearl's.

Walking up Main Street, she took a bite of the muffin and then a long sip of the deliciously strong coffee. She wondered what stories Samantha would assign her. Were there new businesses opening, new and fascinating residents moving to town, special art installments planned for the lobby of Village Hall? Were there marriages to cover, engagements to announce, outdoor concerts at the lake or the green with guest artists to interview? She wondered if the Italian restaurant across the lake was introducing a new summer menu this month, and if she'd be the lucky reporter assigned to preview the fare. Or if the annual summer issue was in the works, and she'd get to interview the Smoothie Dudes and write up what always turned out to be the most entertaining piece of the year.

Passing Main Street Sundries, she stopped to scan the array of local, regional, and national publications on the metal rack next to the front door. By this time next week, she could have a byline within the pages on this rack. While it had been exciting to work on a big magazine, she'd always imagined it would be fun to be part of a small, local paper. She liked the idea of writing about people she knew, and for people she knew. What a kick it would be for people to stop her on the street to comment on something she'd written: "Great review of last week's jazz concert on the green!" "Loved your piece about the new high-school principal and his thoughts on state testing."

Reaching the white clapboard house where the *Press* was located, she threw her cup and napkin away, then went up to the porch. She checked her reflection in the front window, making sure she had no crumbs on her face, before opening the blue door and stepping inside. The air conditioner in the window to her left rumbled, adding to the homey atmosphere of the place. A tall woman wearing smart black capris and a white button-down blouse, her long dark hair piled up on her head and her tortoiseshell-framed glasses riding low on her nose, was coming down the steps. Although Jenna had never met her in person before, she knew this was Samantha from her picture on the editorial page.

"Samantha, hi," she said, holding out her hand. "Jenna Marsh."

"Oh, Jenna, great to have you here," Samantha said, putting her pencil into her mouth so her right hand was free to shake Jenna's. She removed the pencil and continued talking. "We're a little behind because of July Fourth, so we're firing on all cylinders today. I just emailed out the week's assignments—I used your regular email address, but you'll want to set up your own account here. Grab any computer that's available upstairs and give a shout to Alyssa if you need anything—she's our editorial assistant, over there in the corner. Hey, Dave!" she shouted. "I have to talk to you—wait up!"

Jenna watched Samantha continue through the hallway to a group of reporters in what probably once was the dining room of the house. She was elated that Samantha hadn't felt the need to walk her through her first assignment, but had enough confidence in her to let her fend for herself.

She walked upstairs to an open space filled with about a dozen mismatched desks—some wood, some metal, some a combination. About half were occupied, the reporters barely noticing her because they were typing away. The place had a team feel, and Jenna loved the vibe. She sat down in front of a computer and took out her phone to read the email Samantha had sent. It was an intriguing assignment—to investigate the town's as yet unconfirmed intention to build a bandshell on a piece of unused property adjacent to the lake—and she couldn't wait to get started.

She sat down at the closest available desk and got down to work. First, she searched the newspaper's digital archives and skimmed old articles for relevant information, learning that there had been attempts to use that property in the past, but until now, the town board couldn't agree on a project. She also found out that two years ago, the board polled the community and held a series of focus groups about the land, and "bandshell" had been checked off more than twice as much as any other idea. Many people felt the green was good for jazz and smaller concerts, but the town needed a larger music venue as well.

Jenna called the mayor's office and arranged to speak with him later that afternoon, then left the building to check out the property for herself. Because of everything that had happened so far this summer, she hadn't spent nearly as much time by the lake as she expected to. She got in her car, which she'd left near Pearl's, and drove the short distance, then parked in a spot adjacent to the parcel of property. Getting out of her car, she viewed the space earmarked for the bandshell and then took a moment to soak in the beauty of the lakefront. Although there were people swimming and sunbathing, it still looked vast and uncrowded, and the area felt serene. A few seagulls glided above, their high-pitched calls melodic. Way over by the rocks, she could make out the kids in Sophie's camp starting out in their kayaks and canoes, the boats skimming the water as though it were a sheet of ice. Jenna felt lucky to have a job in town, so she could stop whenever she wanted and take a peek at what her daughter was doing.

She removed her sandals and walked down toward the lake, introducing herself to a few vacationers and asking their opinions on the possibility of a bandshell. They all said it was a wonderful idea but worried about the impact on taxes as well as the character of the lakefront. "They need to get private funding," a man with a weathered complexion said as she recorded his statement on her phone. "And there'd need to be a committee to decide on the types of bands, the hours the music could play, food concessions, and so on. There are a lot of things to consider. But it's time to do something with that land."

She thanked him, then called back to the paper for a photographer to come get a picture of the man as well as some shots of the property, with the blue sky and sparkling lake in the background. While on hold, she decided she'd go back to the archives to see if there were any bandshell sketches she could use. Alyssa, the editorial assistant, came back on the line and said the staff photographer, Jim, was finishing a shoot. She said she'd send him there right away.

Leaning against her car as she waited, Jenna closed her eyes and lifted her face to the sun. It was good to be reporting again. She liked how easily she'd fallen into the rhythm of the work—doing the research, targeting people to interview, and strategizing the perfect photo to drive home the story. But oddly enough, now that she had a moment to herself, she also felt a subtle twinge of guilt. As though she were misbehaving, overstepping the boundaries. She'd felt the same way last spring when she'd emailed Samantha her résumé, but she'd pushed it out of her mind, too busy with her excitement about possibly relocating to give it much thought. But now, with some time on her hands, she paid attention to it, explored it, like she was tasting something familiar and trying to figure out where she'd had it last.

And then she realized what the root of her guilt was. A part of her—a big part—blamed her ambitions for the end of her marriage.

The crazy thing was, it had been a fluke. A silly idea, one of those things you come up with when you're thinking about nothing. Sophie was in second grade, and Matt was working hard in textiles sales, hoping to finally be promoted to sales director. He was on the road a lot, and she filled the quiet nighttime hours after Sophie had gone to bed by taking on writing hangtags for mattresses.

"Do you realize that I think about nothing but beds?" she riffed on the phone to her mother one evening, when Matt was in Cleveland on a sales trip. "Do you know what a crazy thing that is to think about every minute of every day?"

"I think it's a lovely thing to think about," her mother said. "I love my bedroom. I can't think of anywhere I'd rather be, especially now that it's spring and the garden smells delicious at night."

"No, not the bedroom, the bed—the *mattress*," Jenna said. "Springs and coils and padding and foam and edge support and pillowtops and pressure points… It's always there, in the back of my mind, like when you hear a song too many times and you can't get it out of your head. I actually dreamed about beds last night. I dreamed I built one!"

"You did not," her mom said.

"No, I'm not kidding. I dreamed I had one night to make a king-size bed. I worked on it all night, hammering the wood, twisting the coils. I woke up exhausted. My muscles were literally aching!"

"Oh, Jenna, you're a riot," her mother said. "Do you know how funny this sounds? You should write a book about it. People would love it!"

Jenna didn't really think she could write a book. But she was lonely, with Matt working so hard and traveling so much, and the idea of channeling her musings into a new project was irresistible. She mentioned it to her boss at the mattress company, who had a friend at a publishing company specializing in quirky, novelty books, and before she knew it, she had a contract to write *Bed: The Inner World of a Mattress Maniac.* It was small in size, something that could be sold as an impulse buy near the register at a bookstore or gift shop. The text was all fun facts and fanciful Q&As: What did Marie Antoinette sleep on? What did King Henry VIII sleep on? What's the best type of mattress for romance? What's the most expensive bed ever sold? She interviewed historians, mattress makers, sleep experts, and relationship experts for the answers, while her editor engaged a cartoonist who'd done work for the *New Yorker* for the illustrations. Stores marketed it as a stocking stuffer for Christmas, a Valentine's Day accompaniment to flowers and candy, a present that brides could give their bridesmaids. The frenzy lasted a few short months, but during that time, it seemed everyone thought *Bed* was a true sensation.

Everyone, that is, except her husband.

*

When Jim had finished taking pictures, Jenna returned to the office and placed her call to the mayor, who confirmed that the project was on the town board's priority list, that a budget was in development, and that expert analyses of potential problems such as garbage overflow, crowd control, and noise complaints would be released to the public in the next week. He also stressed that the burden on taxpayers would be minimal. "We've reached out to Art Grayson on the local history exhibit going up at the resort," he said. "There's a fundraising element to the grand opening event, and he's agreed to target some of the proceeds to the bandshell project." He also shared that the board was currently taking bids from contractors for the work, and would be fielding questions about cost at the next town meeting, which residents were welcome to attend. Jenna wrote up the story and submitted it to Samantha in plenty of time to head back to the lake to pick up Sophie.

That evening after Troy dropped Mo off, Sophie carried up a carton that was so big, it nearly blocked her vision. "This one's heavy," she said as she brought it to the living room and placed it on the coffee table. She ripped the masking tape off and tipped it over, and a huge stack of magazines came pouring out.

"What are those?" Jenna said, getting up from the sofa and sinking down onto her knees next to Sophie. Then she gasped as she recognized them—issue upon issue of *Ultimate Bride,* the magazine where she'd worked after she'd graduated from college. She hadn't seen them in years.

"Mom, you kept all these?" she asked. She could hardly believe that Sophie had brought up this box on the very day that she'd returned to publishing.

"It was your first writing job," her mother said. "You were so young and so busy that I knew you'd never think about saving these. But I suspected one day you'd have a daughter. I wanted to make sure she could see how amazing her mother's always been."

Jenna found the oldest issue and opened it to the masthead, which had a picture of her in the lobby of the magazine's office. She remembered feeling very grown up when that picture was taken, but now she thought she looked more like a little girl playing dress-up. *"A big welcome to Jenna Clayton, our new editorial assistant!"* the caption read. *"Jenna graduated from New York University last year with a degree in journalism, and we are over the moon to have her here."* Meanwhile, Sophie was paging through later ones. "Look it!" she said, holding up an issue. The spread had a photograph of a floral sofa alongside a stone fireplace with a fire roaring. "'Turn Your Apartment into an Irresistible Love Nest,'" Sophie said, reading the article's title. "Love nest? Who talks like that?"

"Come on, that's the kind of magazine it was," Jenna said. They both looked through a few more issues, and then Sophie pushed another spread her way.

"It's you, Mom," she said, and Jenna looked at a picture of herself in her wedding gown. She'd adored that gown, with the seed pearls across the bodice and the layers of tulle that draped to the floor. "Listen to this," Sophie said, reading the text below the photo. "Congratulate our senior editor Jenna Clayton Marsh, who was married at the Lake Summers Resort in the Adirondack Mountains on December 2nd. The couple is going to St. Martin on their honeymoon, and Jenna says she's never been happier. We wish the bride and groom a long, happy life together."

Sophie lowered the magazine onto her lap and the room was quiet for a moment. "Wow, Mom," Sophie finally said. "You were really into marriage back then."

Yes, she was, she thought as she watched Sophie and her mom go upstairs a little while later, then went into the kitchen to turn on the dishwasher. And if she hadn't written that silly little book, she might still be into marriage, and still be with Matt. But writing the book was like tipping over a large bottle of glitter from one of Sophie's old arts-and-crafts kits. It was impossible to contain the fallout. Within a couple of weeks, she was feeling like her old self again, independent and outgoing. She enjoyed traveling to bookstores and reading aloud from her book. Meanwhile, Matt was begging for ten minutes with potential clients and being passed over for promotions.

From that point on, their marriage was never the same. And her bed, once a source of inspiration and humor, soon became a sad and lonely place. Lying way over on her side of the mattress, she'd sometimes wonder what if. That was the problem with her mother's worldview—that life was a series of unplanned projects still to be completed, unfinished work still to be done. It didn't fit with Matt's view of how their marriage should be. Predictable and fixed when he needed it to be so. That's what he'd meant the night he told her he was leaving. "You changed, Jenna," he'd said. "I can't be married anymore to the person you are now." But he'd been wrong. She'd never changed from the person she saw this evening in that picture in the magazine, the new editorial assistant of *Ultimate Bride*, smiling so joyfully as she posed in the lobby of her office building. Jumping on the idea to write that mattress book, she'd been true to herself, following the instincts she'd always followed, embracing an opportunity to be creative and have fun. She'd never changed from the person he'd married. The problem was that he was so angry about his own stalled dreams, he no longer wanted to be with her.

She returned to the living room and put all the magazines back in the box, then pressed down on the tape to seal it. But the tape wasn't sticky anymore. She'd have to remember to buy some more masking tape tomorrow. She picked Mo up from the rug where he'd been sleeping and started to take him upstairs when her phone buzzed. She took it out of her pocket. It was an email from Samantha.

Hi Jenna,

Great job on the bandshell article. Good research, well written. You still have your journalism chops! I have another assignment for you, a related one, actually. You know the local history exhibit you mentioned in your piece, the one Art Grayson is organizing? We just got a press release on it, and it's going to be a big deal. I'd like you to get in there as soon as you can and write up a preview of it. There's a guy you should reach out to, he's the honorary chair according to Art. I don't know him, but apparently he grew up here, and his dad was some kind of local hero. You can reach him at the animal clinic. His name is Troy Jason.

Sinking down on a step with Mo on her lap, she pressed the back of her head against the banister. She supposed she could say no to the assignment, but she didn't want to cause problems during her first week on the job. Yet she was nervous. Would she be emptying another full bottle of glitter, making a new mess that could never be cleaned up?

CHAPTER FOURTEEN

"So it's moving like clockwork, right on target for an August 8th opening," Art said. "We have a perfect space in the newer wing of the resort, the area that was rebuilt after the big fire—it's set off from the main part of the building but still connected, so people can walk from the lobby to the exhibit and back again. And the wall space, perfect for large prints. We're dividing the area into four or five galleries—still working that out. And the exhibit will move chronologically, from one hundred years ago to today."

Troy looked across the table at Victoria Connor, to whom he'd just been introduced. A thin woman with long, gray hair held back with a blue ribbon, she was a town trustee and head of the Arts Council, and right now her head was bowed as she took copious notes on a yellow legal pad. The three of them were having lunch on the rooftop patio of the resort, one of the most beautiful spots in all of Lake Summers, with its expansive view of the lake and, in the distance, Mount Marcy, the highest peak in the Adirondacks. But no matter how fancy the napkins or pretty the view, Troy still didn't know what he was doing here. Art had said it was a simple lunch, but Victoria didn't look particularly casual, so furiously was she writing everything down.

"It's thrilling," Victoria said as she put down her pen and cut into a slice of mozzarella cheese on her caprese salad. "I don't know why we've never had a local history exhibit before. This could be a first step toward a formal historical society with a town historian, which is something our community sorely needs. I spoke with the mayor this morning, and you've got his full support. We want to make this the event of the summer, the event of the whole year, in fact. Art, it's so important that we can depend on visionary business leaders like yourself."

"Absolutely," Art said. "It's good for the town and it's good for business, too. As I've been telling my friend Troy here, I've got a headache over just north of Lyons Hill, a couple of big hotel chains going up. They see how popular the region is and they want a piece of the action. And not only are they after our guests, they're after my staff, too! One of my best front desk supervisors, a guy I took straight from college because I knew he was management material, he just took a job over there because he thinks he can swing a transfer to New York, which is where he wants to be. As I was telling Troy, I can't make a go of this place without an energized and dedicated staff. We need to make our young people want to stay in this town. We have to give them a reason to be with us and grow with us."

"And the bigger this event is, the more money we can raise, which can help fund the new bandshell by the lake," Victoria said. "Can you imagine lakeside concerts all summer long? Troy, have you heard about the bandshell?"

Troy nodded. "I read about it in the paper this morning," he said. He'd been surprised to see that Jenna had written it. He'd had no idea she'd taken a job as a reporter.

"Well, I know the mayor is very interested in bringing the whole community out for a grand opening celebration. Now tell me, Art, have you given that event much thought?"

"I'm thinking big," Art said. "A Saturday event, afternoon straight into the evening. Food trucks with regional cuisine, games for the kids, some old-fashioned carnival rides. A silent auction, raffles, maybe sell some sponsorships, that kind of thing. I'm thinking part of the proceeds can also go toward a local charity—maybe the Mountainside Rescue. That's who you've been working with, right, Troy? I hear you're finishing up a very successful pledge drive. Your name holds a lot of weight in this community."

"It's not me," Troy said. "Claire and Zoe have been doing the work."

"And Mayor Peterson was hoping to add a second charity, too," Victoria said. "Maybe the county food bank or the Kids Club recreational program in New Manorsville. We want this to be an inspiring day, and people come out for these things when they believe their money will be well spent. What do you think, Troy? Any additional charity you feel strongly about?"

Troy looked at his watch, and then polished off the remainder of his burger. He really, *really* didn't know why he was here. It was a nice lunch, as Art had promised. Certainly a welcome change from his usual turkey club sandwich from the market or meat-eater's special from Lonny's Hot Dogs, which had the best hot dog platters in the region, maybe even in the world. But as he'd said when Art first came to his office, he had no interest in getting involved with the town. That was his dad's role, his dad's passion. All he wanted to do was run his practice each day and sit home alone with a beer at night. That was the plan when Mrs. Pearl called him and he said yes, he'd come back.

"Hey, Art, thanks for lunch," he said, lifting his napkin from his lap and placing it on the table alongside his plate. This lunch was miles outside his comfort zone. "And Victoria, very nice to meet you. I've got plenty of pets to see this afternoon, and I left my car at work and walked here, so it's going to take me a little while to get back. And my tech is there alone now. I need to get back to the office so she can take her lunch break—"

"Hold on, hold on," Art said. "I wanted to bring you up to speed, but I haven't even gotten to the best part." He held up his hand to wave to one of his servers, who nodded and ran to the kitchen. "Victoria and I had a quick call with Peterson last week," he continued. "And while he's leaving the details up to us, he did emphasize that what really gets a community charged up is an award. And Troy—he's proposed creating a new honor—the Lake Summers Citizen of the Year Award. He wants to present it at the opening of the historical exhibit. And he wants you to be the first recipient, on behalf of your family."

"What?" Troy said, nearly knocking his water glass over as he reached his hands out in surprise. He righted the glass and patted the wet tablecloth with his napkin, just as the server returned with three crystal flutes and a bottle of champagne. "No, I'm just lending my name for the posters, that's what we agreed," he said, even though neither Art nor Victoria was looking at him. Instead they were watching the server pop the cork.

"It's just my name you wanted," he repeated when the server finished his task. "I wasn't supposed to receive any award. That's what you said, just lend my name—isn't that what we agreed?"

"At first, that's what I thought, yes," Art said. "But this can be even bigger than I envisioned. We can raise a lot of money, Troy, and put it to good use. We can do a lot of good."

"You're certainly worthy, Troy," Victoria said. "I've heard your family's name mentioned around town for years. You've added a lot to our community."

"If we're going to do this, we have to do it right," Art said. "And from your point of view—hey, who doesn't like being publicly thanked? All you have to do is stand still on stage while the mayor thanks you on behalf of the town. Maybe say a little speech, nothing too fancy, just a memory of your dad or something. Then you can drink in all the adoration."

Troy felt his heart race. This was not what Art had proposed, and he was not going through with it. No matter how many hotel chains moved into the region. No matter how many junior managers at the resort got lured away to greener pastures. "There's no reason for the community to thank me," Troy said. "I haven't done anything. There's got to be someone else more… I don't know, more deserving."

"More deserving?" Art said. "But your family has a history of making this town a better place. Hell, your dad sacrificed his life that night of the big storm. Your family gave a lot to us all, Troy. We've got a special space in the exhibit devoted entirely to your family."

"We're still waiting on those prints," Victoria said. "They'll be the last ones installed."

"But it isn't me," Troy said. "My dad's the hero."

"As are you, my friend, as are you," Art said. "You came back home to stop the local animal clinic from closing down. You left a big, impressive practice in Philadelphia because Connie Pearl called and asked you. You're raising money like gangbusters. Peterson read me the press release the rescue sent out—your clinic is one of the top five veterinary practices in the region when it comes to donations made this year. And you're competing with some mighty big practices."

"But I told you, that's my colleagues, not me," Troy said. "If you want a hero, pick Claire. She took over the practice when Dr. Munoz died, and she's been working like crazy through her whole pregnancy."

He got up from his chair, the force of his movement causing the table to shake and the glasses to wobble. He caught his water glass and righted it again. He was sorry for jumping up so aggressively, but he couldn't stay another minute, or he feared giving them hope that he'd relent. But he was not going to be the center of attention at this over-the-top event Art was planning. He was not going to stand on a platform and listen to the mayor reel off gibberish about his contributions to the community. No way would he stand still on a stage and, as Art said, drink in the adoration.

"I appreciate the thought and the lunch, and the champagne and everything," he said. "But pick someone else. I'm happy to be the honorary chair like we discussed, but for the rest, pick someone else."

He crossed the restaurant and took the elevator down to the first floor, then marched across the lobby and left the building. He continued on down the long, sloped driveway, then turned onto Main Street and headed back to his office. It wasn't that warm a day, but he felt like he was burning up, like the air he was breathing was lighting his chest on fire. All he wanted to do was get back to his office and treat the pets coming in for care. He wanted to forget that lunch at the resort had ever even taken place.

But as soon as he walked in, he knew the subject was far from closed.

"Congratulations!" Zoe said, clapping her hands. On her desk was a chocolate cake decorated with fondant in the shape of their building. On the floor beside the desk, Mo looked at him, his tail waving wildly.

"Mrs. Pearl made the cake special," Zoe said. "How was lunch? Art let us in on everything, and we're so excited for you. Claire wanted to be here, but the doctor just put her on bed rest." She paused. "What's the matter? You don't look happy."

"I didn't send those fundraising letters. You and Claire did. Why did you tell them I was the one who did the rescue fundraising?"

"I didn't say that. But we did it as a practice. And your name is the one on the letterhead. Troy, why are you mad?"

"I'm not mad. I just don't deserve this."

"Are you kidding?" Zoe said. "There's nobody more deserving! You're like every kid's role model. They still have your picture up at the dry cleaner. They named a club after you at the high school that helps out at the animal shelter in New Manorsville. I joined that club when I was a freshman. The Troy Jason Shelter Club."

"It's a small town. Everyone has a club named after them."

"Of course you'd say that. But that's so not true." She raised her palms upward. "We thought you'd be happy. How did we get it so wrong?"

Troy cupped his hands behind his head and walked away from the desk, stopping to look out the front window. Zoe was a sweet kid, and he felt bad for making her think he was angry. He wasn't angry with her. He wasn't angry with anyone. It was his own fault this had happened. He'd made a mistake by letting Art talk him into being the honorary chair in the first place. He should have realized things could snowball. The words "honorary chair" said it all. It was an honor that Art was handing to him, and that wasn't a word to take lightly. But what was done, was done. Zoe was right, there'd been a misunderstanding. And he needed to correct it.

He turned back around. "Okay, I messed up," he said. "I should have been clearer. I didn't come back to town to win any honors. I came back for myself. Not for the town. For myself."

Zoe poked a finger up under her glasses and wiped her eye. "I'm sorry, Troy," she said. "I feel horrible for telling Art about the rescue and getting Mrs. Pearl to bake the cake and all. I didn't mean it as a bad thing."

He took a tissue from the box on her desk and handed it to her. "I know that. It was nice of you to talk to him. And the cake looks great. I mean, we can still eat it, right?" He smiled, and was relieved when she smiled back. "Is there anyone in the examining room?"

"Mrs. Franklin. Whiskers has been coughing. She thinks he may be sick."

"Did you get out for your lunch break yet?"

"No. Don't worry about it."

"No, go ahead, it's a nice day, you should get some fresh air. I'll go see Whiskers and take care of everything here."

"Okay," she said. She grabbed Mo's leash and hooked it to his collar, then led him outside. Troy watched them start down Main Street, then closed the door.

He sighed. He had vowed not to get involved with anyone. And yet here he was. Letting people down again.

*

When his appointments were over, Troy drove home with Mo beside him, his front paws on the armrest as he watched the world pass by his window. He still felt bad about making Zoe cry and rushing out of the resort like some kind of lunatic. Art and Victoria had the best of intentions, and now he felt responsible.

He slowed for a red light. It was the time of day when nearly every car in town converged on Main Street, with people coming back from the lake, driving home from work, or looking to park for the evening, and he knew the ride home would be full of starts and stops. Lake Summers was far more crowded than when he was growing up. He usually didn't care about the traffic, but today it rattled him. The light turned green, and the driver behind him leaned on her horn, evidently because he didn't accelerate fast enough. What was he doing here, anyway? He'd left Philly to get away from memories, away from people, to lead a quiet, private life. So why was he living in a town where everyone knew everything about him and his family? He should have turned Mrs. Pearl down, and not come back to Lake Summers. He should have known the legacy his father left would never stop haunting him. The clinic wouldn't have closed. They'd have found another vet.

Back home, he took Mo out of the car and walked him over to Sweet's house. He knocked on the door, and when Jenna opened it, Mo trotted inside. Jenna stooped down to unhook his leash. "Sophie's making your dinner, go ahead!" she said, and they both watched him scamper toward the kitchen.

She stood back up and looked at him, the leash still in her hands. "What a lucky boy," she said. "Do you have any idea how much he loves you? He watches out the window for you in the mornings and then rushes to the front door the minute he sees you. He can't get to you fast enough."

Troy looked down, feeling his cheeks get warm. It was ridiculous; he wasn't the kind of person to get embarrassed. But there he was, looking down at the ground and willing his face to stop simmering. He was embarrassed at how good it felt to hear that Jenna admired him. Suddenly all his frustration with Art felt overblown. Irrelevant. Of course he didn't wish he'd never come back home. There was no place he'd rather be than right here, right at Jenna's doorstep, hearing her celebrate his place in her life.

"He's a good boy," he said, looking up and squinting in her direction, hoping she'd attribute any lingering redness on his face to the heat of the descending sun. He knew she was expecting him to say goodbye and head home, but he wasn't ready to leave her yet.

"How's your mom doing today?" he said, hoping she'd understood that it wasn't just Mo he cared about. He cared about Sweet and Sophie. He cared about her, too. He wanted her to know that he was relieved her mother was okay. He knew how close they were. He was glad she'd gotten a job at the paper. He was glad she was settling in.

"She's good," Jenna answered. "She went into town today with Sherry—she's our home health aide. She got her hair done and bought a new dress. I met them for lunch at the Grill. She knows so many people. Everyone welcomed her back to town."

"That's great." He nodded. "Oh, by the way, nice article in the paper. I didn't know you were working there."

"I just started. That was my first piece."

"It was good. Congratulations."

"Thanks." She pressed her lips together. "Would you like to come in? We're about to have dinner. Sherry stayed late tonight and is making lasagna. It smells amazing."

"No, no, but thanks," he said. "It was a long day. Maybe another time."

"Later this week?" she said. "How about Friday? We can celebrate Mo's last day with you. Two weeks, right? That went fast."

"I can keep him longer if you want…"

"We've imposed too much on you already. Anyway, Sherry says it'll be good for my mom to have him home now. You know, pet therapy and all."

"Yeah," he said. "Dogs are a… help…" He put his hands in his pockets. "Well, have a nice night," he said, forcing himself to walk away. "See you tomorrow—"

"Troy?" she said.

He turned around.

"I have another newspaper assignment coming up, about this historical exhibit at the resort. They want me to write a preview before the opening. They gave me your name as the chair. Would you possibly be able to show me around?"

He rubbed the back of his neck. The last thing he needed right now was more talk about the historical exhibit. After all, he'd told them he couldn't be a part of it anymore. But then he looked up at Jenna, standing by the door in gray sweatpants and a white sleeveless tee shirt and blue running shoes, her hair pulled back in a ponytail. He could almost imagine that she was seventeen again, back when he couldn't get enough of her warmth and her candor, of her total embrace of who she was and what she felt. He'd been so bottled up back then, and he couldn't figure out how anyone could be as open and unchained as she was. He'd have saved a thousand dogs a day, been covered in blood from head to toe, if that's what it took to find her waiting for him at night. But he hadn't needed to do that. She'd showed up anyway on those five August nights.

He nodded, thinking there was no reason not to. As of now, he was still the honorary chair of the project. "Sure," he said. "When did you want to stop by?"

"I need to do a little background research first. So would Friday work? Ten o'clock?"

"Sure," he repeated.

"Good, thanks." She was starting to close the door when he realized he had a question for her, one that he couldn't stop himself from finally asking.

"Hey, Jenna?" he called.

She pulled the door open, standing with one hand on the doorknob and the other on the doorjamb.

"Why did you move back?"

She looked at him as though she didn't think she'd heard correctly. "Why did I what?"

"Why did you move back to Lake Summers?"

"Why did I move back?" she asked. "I'm not really sure I have. Moved back for good, I mean. It's still not quite settled. But I guess it's because my mother needed me. Chloe wanted her to move out, and I didn't want her to have to do that."

"And that's it? The only reason?" he asked.

"Yes." She paused. "No. No, it's not." She looked toward the hallway and then turned back to him. "It's because I love it here," she said. "I never wanted to be any place else. It was good here. Even when it was sad, it was good here. Wasn't it?"

He nodded.

"And the bad stuff back in Rye—I've known for a while that things don't seem so bad when I'm here. I used to think it was because of the distance. But now I think it's me. I think I'm better here. I like myself better here."

She looked down and shook her head, the way he remembered she used to when she was making fun of herself. Sometimes she'd do it with the top of her head leaning against his chest. "Okay, that sounds ridiculous. I know."

"No, it doesn't," he said.

"It is. It's silly."

"No, I'm glad you said it," he replied. He looked directly in her eyes, wanting to reinforce what he'd said. She looked back at him, and he held her gaze, not wanting to say another word. Wanting only to let her know that he'd missed her all those years and felt lucky she was in his life again.

Suddenly Sophie called from inside. "Mom? Sherry says dinner is ready!"

"I have to go," she said. "So, Friday? You're sure it's no problem?"

"I'll see you then," he said.

He waited for the door to shut, then walked slowly back toward his house, the orange sun shining low from across the street, the twilight approaching. He liked what Jenna said about being better here. About liking herself better here. Maybe that's why he had come back, too. He thought about Zoe and what she'd said this afternoon, how everyone knew his family's legacy, how his picture was still up at the dry-cleaning shop, how there was a club at the high school named after him. And then he remembered what Art had said when he'd first stopped by the clinic, how Troy reminded him of the candidate for Congress who so inspired his son.

It was true—he was the best person he'd ever been when he was in Lake Summers. So maybe he'd been playing this all wrong. Maybe he didn't have to be the guy haunted by memories. Maybe he could be the guy who stepped up whenever he was needed. The guy who wasn't always pulling away.

And maybe, like Jenna, he would like himself more.

He pulled out his phone and wrote a quick email to Art:

I overreacted. I wasn't expecting that conversation. But I do want to do my part for this town. And if you think I can make a difference, then I accept. Count me in.

CHAPTER FIFTEEN

On Friday morning, Jenna steered her car up the winding driveway that led to Lake Summers Resort. She'd always loved the place, with its elegant stone facade and romantic, rounded gables atop the covered front patio. She'd spent much of her childhood on the resort's grounds, mostly on the trails behind the building, where she and Steven would hike and climb trees and splash around in the burbling brook. One time she stubbed her toe against a sharp rock as she chased him up the bank from the water, and when she got home, her toenail was almost all the way off. Her mother rushed her to the doctor, who bandaged her up and told her to keep the toe covered as much as possible and take it easy for a full two weeks, or she could develop an infection and maybe even lose the toe. Still, she unwrapped her foot every morning, putting a bandage back when she got home before her mother could see. And she never got an infection. It was just the way things were back then.

Circling a garden of orange daylilies and lavender peonies, she drove over to the parking lot, then walked up the paved hill to the entrance of the hotel. The place had seemed like a palace to her when she was young, and she would imagine living there like a princess, hosting dinners for men in waistcoats with pocket watches, and women in silky pastel gowns, their hair adorned with diamond chips that sparkled as they moved. One summer Chloe was invited to a Sweet Sixteen on the outdoor terrace that looked out over the lake, and Jenna had been so jealous that she'd corralled Steven to spy on the party from the grassy hill at the top of the hiking trail.

"God, those poor jerks!" Steven had said, pointing to the guys looking hot and sweaty in their dress shirts and long pants. "What normal guy goes to a Sweet Sixteen anyway?"

Jenna had scowled, annoyed with Steven for not understanding that the guys *wanted* to be there because the girls were there. That's what happened when guys got older, they wanted to go to parties, they wanted to dress up. She spotted Chloe, with her strapless dress and moussed hair and platform sandals, and was so jealous that she felt as though someone was squeezing her chest. There'd been plenty of times when she'd wanted things she couldn't have—a new ten-speed bike; permission to stay out with her friends past nine at night; the ability to make the bluebells in the garden stay in bloom all summer long. But this was the first time she'd wanted something she couldn't put her finger on. It wasn't about Chloe's clothes or shoes or her friends. It was about Steven, and not wanting to be his sidekick anymore.

She stopped at the front desk and explained who she was, and a receptionist invited her to have a seat. She was excited to see the exhibit with Troy, to spend more time with him than the minute it took each morning to hand him Mo's leash. There was something almost heartbreaking about the way he'd asked her the other night why she had returned to Lake Summers. He was struggling. Trying to figure out where he belonged and how he should live his life. He reminded her of the boy he once was, who also was searching for answers and a path forward. They'd spent five nights together after their first kiss, five nights of talking on the front curb until the early hours of the morning. Seeing him in the twilight the other evening when he asked her why she came back, she remembered how wonderful his kisses felt, how close she'd felt to him, how well they complemented each other.

A moment later the receptionist came out from behind the desk. "I reached him on his phone, he's coming over right now from the clinic," she said. "He asked me to take you down there, and he'll join you in a couple of minutes."

Jenna nodded and followed her down a winding staircase to a set of doors at the end of the hallway, with LAKE SUMMERS: THE STORIES OF OUR LIVES imprinted on the glass. Ignoring the PRIVATE—NO ENTRY sign, the woman unlocked the door, then pulled it open and turned on the lights. "Just lock it up and drop this off with us on your way out, if you wouldn't mind," she said, handing the key to Jenna. "Go ahead and enjoy. It's spectacular."

Jenna thanked her and walked inside. The area was set up like a museum, with small galleries lined with mounted, poster-size prints. They dated as far back as a century ago, and came from the archives of the *Lake Summers Press* in addition to private collections, according to the introductory sign near the doorway. She reached into her bag for a notebook, then changed her mind, deciding that she'd prefer to drink in all the images. She was glad to be alone for a few moments in the silent space, her footsteps inaudible on the plush carpet. It was kind of thrilling, like watching a movie about time travel, but she also felt a deep poignancy. Just as her mother chose books about people who never became famous, she also used to love trying to decipher the stories about people she'd seen in magazine photographs—not the central people, but the ones in the background. Now Jenna wondered about all the ordinary people she saw upon these walls, anonymous people caught by the lens of a camera. What stories did they want to tell her? What stories would she and her mother have discerned?

She studied the first picture on her left, a black-and-white photo picturing the Lake Summers Fire Department, circa 1922, according to the caption. The building was small and flat-roofed, and about a dozen firefighters stood before it in a semicircle, all dressed in double-breasted coats. She suspected her mother would have been most interested in the young man on the end of the line, probably still a teenager, the one with the self-conscious half-smile and the twinkling eyes. She studied him the way her mother would have done, and decided that his name was Anthony, although everyone called him Tony, and that he lived with his mother and older sister, his father having passed away not too long ago. She imagined his eyes were twinkling because he was thinking about his girlfriend. Maybe her name was Sheila or Lainey. He was going to take her out to a movie that night. He was saving up his salary for an engagement ring.

The next poster showed the Lake Summers train station, circa 1935. There was a small station house with a bench positioned just outside of it, where two women in heavy coats and hats were sitting. And there was a little girl, maybe eight or nine, on the train platform, looking in the direction from which the train would be coming. She was wearing a hip-length coat with a pleated skirt sticking out beneath it, and thick stockings with lace-up shoes, and a flat-topped hat with a ribbon around the base, and she had one knee bent, as though she were hopping or twirling. She probably had a romantic name, Jenna thought: Gabriella, maybe, or Sasha. And the women on the bench were her mother and grandmother, and they were taking her somewhere special. Like New York City. Maybe she was going to see the Rockettes and the big Christmas tree in Rockefeller Center. And maybe her mom would buy her a hot pretzel or roasted chestnuts from one of the street vendors before they came home.

Jenna studied the picture some more. It made her think about her mother, and the trip across the country Sweet had told Sophie she'd taken. If she'd taken a train, it would have left from the very same station where the little girl was. Of course, her mother would have been older than this girl—seventeen, that's what Sophie said. And it would have been the early 1960s, not 1935. Her mother probably would have been in bell-bottoms or a miniskirt. And she wouldn't have been dancing or hopping. Maybe she was scared, since she was running away. But she had to push ahead. The effort was worth the risk of getting caught.

Still, what was her mother trying to accomplish, if the story was true? What was so bad at home that she had to leave? Was it to fall in love—or had that happened by accident? What was her endgame? Jenna wished there was a picture here of her mother, that some photographer had passed the station that morning and thought her mom was interesting enough to capture. At least then she'd have proof that the story actually happened, and a clue about what her mother was hoping they'd discover in the basement. Had there actually been a man with honey-colored hair and soulful eyes? Could her mother have had a first love—a love nobody knew about, a love she'd never gotten over? Maybe the Lake Summers Theatrical had always been a diversion from a life her mom had never chosen and didn't like. A life she'd resigned herself to, because she had two daughters she loved. But if all that was true, why would she want to tell the story to Sophie? What message about life was she trying to convey to her young and impressionable granddaughter?

She looked toward the space on the wall between the pictures of the firefighter and the little girl. Wouldn't it be amazing, she thought, if there really were a picture of her mother there? So she could look in her mother's eyes, study her mother's stance, get some clues into what was going on at that very moment in her mother's mind. Or what if there were some interesting pictures from her own past?

Like a picture of her and Troy on the night they met on the footpath.

What if there were such a photograph? she thought. And what if that image wound up on some wall in a historical exhibit several decades from now, long after she and Troy were gone? What would a visitor think about the way he touched her face, about the way she lifted her chin? Would it have seemed that they were truly in love, that they were completely committed to carrying out their plan? Would a visitor guess that they'd spend their lives together from that point on? Here was another way that she and her mother were alike—they both had stories locked deep within them, stories they wanted to explore. Just like her mother, she was looking for someone to tell her story to, someone who knew that it mattered, someone who could help her unearth all the meaning the story held.

She needed Troy to talk with her. And not just about Mo or her mother. Like the ghosts on the walls surrounding her now, there were ghosts inside of her and him, the ghosts of the boy and girl they once were. And with Troy living next door, it was becoming way too hard for her to keep her ghost inside.

The sudden clang of a door shutting made her jump.

"Jenna," a voice said. "Sorry. Didn't mean to scare you."

Troy walked toward her, and she felt her face redden. She was embarrassed that she'd been thinking about him, even though he had no way of knowing she'd been doing that.

"No problem." She gave a little smile. It was crazy; she saw him every day when he came to pick up and drop off Mo. She'd seen him just this morning for that very purpose. But being near him was still so disarming. She loved how he looked, still so much like the boy she'd fallen in love with.

"Did you design all this?" she said. "Did you pick the photos?"

He shook his head. "My role is pretty minor, despite the big title," he said. "Or at least, I thought it would be. It's my first time here. What do you think of it so far?"

"I love it," she said. "I haven't gotten very far, but what I've seen is amazing. I mean, thinking about all these people who once lived here, maybe stood in the very same spot we're standing before

the resort was even built, who had families and kids and lives…"
She looked around the room. "My mother taught me to look at
old pictures and think about what the people were like," she said.
"How their lives might have been different from ours, but in the
end, they simply wanted to smile and laugh and be loved, to be
surprised and delighted, to have passion and be remembered…"
She shrugged. "I know this must sound so silly to you."

"Jenna," he said. "You never used to worry that I'd think you
were silly."

She looked up at him and held his eyes for a beat. It was the
first time since she'd been back that he'd acknowledged, even
subtly, that they'd once shared a past.

She turned away, self-conscious. "Okay, then. Look at this
guy," she said, pointing to the firefighter. "I think his name is
Anthony, and he's feeling nervous because tonight's the night he
asks his beautiful girlfriend to marry him. And he's so in love
with her, and they're going to live in a house on the lake and
have lots of children and grandchildren. And this little boy…"
She walked toward a photo on the opposite wall, which showed
a small section of the lake where a handful of kids in hats and
heavy coats were ice skating. "The small one with the cap. His
name is Sam, and he wants to be a speed skater when he grows
up. He's going to skate in the Olympics. He's going to marry a
figure skater."

Troy laughed. "So basically, everyone who grows up in Lake
Summers has a happy story to tell?" he asked.

She lifted her shoulders. "I don't know, maybe," she said. "I
guess in my world they do."

She walked to the next gallery and circled the perimeter,
looking at the posters as the decades flew by. There was a photo
of an early Lake Summers schoolhouse, a small wooden structure
with bicycles parked alongside the steps to the entrance dating
back to 1943, and a similar structure labeled LAKE SUMMERS

POST OFFICE from 1948, with a mail carrier with a big black mustache standing on the step. There was a picture of Main Street from 1952, before all the private homes were converted into shops and eateries, and a photo of a sandwich shop from 1965. There was a picture of the opening of Pearl's Café, back when Mrs. Pearl's father owned the store. A thin, bald man, he stood outside the entrance with his arms folded proudly across his chest.

"Now, here's one you'll want to see," Troy said from across the gallery, and he waved her over.

"Oh, look at that!" Jenna said. It was a photo of a large stage under construction on the green, with the caption LAKE SUMMERS THEATRICAL, FIRST SHOW, 1987. People were scattered all around the area, a blend of kids and grown-ups, some painting the backdrop, some laying the flooring, some hanging the curtain. And there, in the middle of it all, was her mother. She was standing on the grass, her head tilted upward, pointing toward two men who were balanced on scaffolding, installing stage lights. She looked so young, in jean shorts and a gray Lake Summers sweatshirt, and sunglasses, her shoulder-length hair pushed behind her ears.

"I remember that show," Jenna said. "*The Wizard of Oz*, right? I was just talking about this with Chloe. See, they're putting down the yellow brick road. Steven and I got into so much trouble that summer. My mother said we could help with the set, but when she wasn't looking, we climbed on that scaffolding so we could walk along that crossbar at the top. He went first and got pretty high but then he lost his balance and fell, and then I lost my balance and I fell, too."

Troy nodded. "You both got banged up. You were lucky it wasn't worse."

"My mom put us in charge of publicity after that. Which meant that all we were allowed to do was stand on the sidewalk and hand out flyers. Chloe was Dorothy."

"And the twins were Munchkins," Troy said. "And your mom made me stage manager, in charge of a bunch of little kids who wanted to move the scenery around. I was only, like, twelve or something. I don't know why she thought they'd listen to me."

"She loved you. She said you were the most responsible of all of us."

"I wasn't always that responsible."

"No, you were. Serious and responsible."

"I don't know." He put his hands in his pockets and looked down. "I remember being sometimes… not so… responsible."

She started to protest, then stopped herself. She knew what he was thinking about. Going to the footpath the night of the storm. She suspected he saw himself as incredibly irresponsible that night. They both had been. But what happened afterward had been catastrophic for him, not her.

His cell phone rang. "It's my office," he said, looking at the number. "I'm going to have to take this upstairs, they told me at the front desk the cell service is pretty bad down here. I'll be right back."

Jenna watched him walk toward the entrance to the exhibit. Then she rubbed her forehead with her fingertips. Now it made sense, why he'd been so hesitant to spend any real time with her since she'd been back, why he wouldn't come into the house to have dinner or even just to see Chloe. He blamed himself for what happened to his father on the night of the storm, and he probably blamed her, too. Or if not blamed her, then associated her with the evening, and with the decisions he made leading up to it. But it was wrong to look at the evening that way. Nobody could have predicted what would happen. They were young and following their hearts. They never imagined things would turn out as they did.

A moment later he returned. "I'm sorry, there's a dog at the clinic that probably has a broken leg," he said. "Zoe's made him comfortable, but I should get back. Do you mind if I leave you here?"

"No, that's fine," she said. "I have a photographer coming in a few minutes. I'll wait for him. And then I'll take off."

"Did you get everything you needed?"

"I think so."

"So what will you write?"

"I'm not sure," she said. "I think something like what we were talking about. How the people in these photos are so much like us. How they remind us of what's good about Lake Summers and why we want to be here." She paused. "Because I believe that, Troy," she said. "I truly do." There was an edge to her voice, but she couldn't help it. She didn't want him to chalk up what had happened that night merely to bad judgment. It was so much more than that.

"Sounds like another good piece," he said, evidently not hearing anything amiss in her tone. "Do you have any idea what he'll photograph?"

"I don't know, he'll take a look at the lighting and see what he thinks will show up well," she said. "I'd like him to take some of the early photos. Like maybe the firefighters. Or the train station. Or the skating on the lake."

She wandered back to that picture. "I would have liked to skate there, but we were never here in the winter. Did you ever get to do it?"

"No, they stopped it before I was old enough. A girl broke through the ice one year. She wasn't hurt, but that was the end. They built a rink behind the high school after that."

"That's too bad," Jenna said. "It looks like it would have been fun. Don't you wish you got to skate on the lake just once?"

He paused. "You know something? Yes," he said. "I would have liked that. Even just once. I would have liked that a lot."

He walked out. This time the clang of the door sounded like a bell. Or a set of cymbals.

She could almost imagine it sounded like music.

CHAPTER SIXTEEN

She watched through the glass doors as he walked down the hall and turned onto the steps. She didn't know exactly why she suddenly felt hopeful. But there was something light and playful in the way Troy had talked about skating on the lake. It made her remember how he'd been during that week in August long ago, how open he'd been, and how he'd told her things she'd never imagined were on his mind. She didn't think she'd ever truly gotten over how suddenly and sadly everything had ended.

Jim showed up, and she gave him her suggestions for which photos to shoot, then handed him the key to lock up when he was through and went back to the office to begin working on the story. It was nice to have a workplace to go to, and colleagues to see, after working alone at the kitchen table for so many years. She waved to Samantha and a few other reporters as she entered the workspace, and then found a computer. Since she hadn't taken notes, she wanted to get straight to work, while the images and impressions were fresh on her mind.

But as soon as she sat down at the computer, she realized it was going to be hard to concentrate. Every time she tried to remember her thoughts as she walked through the space, her mind went directly to the moments she'd spent with Troy. She'd liked how it felt to walk next to him, to hear his laughter. And even when the conversation veered toward the terrible consequences of the night they'd met on the footpath, there was a piece of her that felt so relieved that he'd finally shown he might trust her again.

Just as he had trusted her enough to kiss her, that night on the curb when she'd waited for him to come home after saving Pauley. She'd never before felt anything like she'd felt when she stood on the curb outside the card store, watching Troy hold Mr. Brand's shoulder as he sobbed. And then watching him scoop Pauley into his arms. Suddenly everything changed, and he was no longer just Steven's older brother.

She'd had crushes before, lots of them, but this hadn't felt like a crush. It was a revelation, an answer to a question she didn't even know she'd been asking. And then when he'd stroked her face with his thumb and leaned down to kiss her, it was more than she could handle. She climbed up the tree and into her bedroom because she needed to separate from the moment. When she got into bed, she found herself wondering if she had imagined the whole thing. Because what she'd experienced outside that night didn't seem real. It was more like a breeze, like a breath. Like something you sensed but couldn't hang onto.

She never told anyone what had happened. Somehow she knew it should stay a secret. In a few weeks, she would be leaving town and starting her senior year at high school. She'd be writing college applications and hoping to attend New York University the following fall. And Troy would be attending some classes at community college and starting to take over his father's printing business, preparing himself to eventually settle down with one of the local girls from high school. She was sure that neither the Jasons nor her parents would have objected to a relationship between her and Troy. It wouldn't have been forbidden or frowned upon. But the families would have found it unexpected and confusing. And she didn't want to have to justify herself to anyone.

The next night after her family was asleep, Jenna watched through her bedroom window for Troy to come home. When he pulled into his driveway, she climbed down the twisted oak tree, then motioned to him to follow her. She led him behind the tree and to the back of the bluebell garden, close against the house, where no one could see them. He started to ask, "Hey, what are you—" but that was as far as he got. Because before he was able to finish the question, she grasped his head and kissed him. He picked her up and spun her around.

"I was hoping all day that you'd be here," he said.

And that was the beginning of their nights together, five glorious nights. She'd climb down the tree and run into his arms, and they'd sit on the curb and talk. And mostly it was Troy who talked, because he was older and had more decisions to make, and had never had anybody to talk to. He told her how he felt about his father's heart trouble, how the doctor was telling him to pull back from work, and how he was dead set on having Troy take over the store as soon as possible. She had known these things, Steven had told them to her, but she hadn't known what they meant to Troy.

"I love my dad," Troy told her one night. "But he thinks I want to live the same life that he has. And I don't. I can't."

He told her he wanted to go to the state university at Binghamton, a real city, four hours west. He wanted to get a college degree, maybe go on to graduate school, maybe be a doctor or something really important. "I was good in high school," he said. "I can do something important with my life." He told her he'd already missed the application deadline, but he was going to drive to the university and talk to the admissions office and see if there was some way he could enroll this year. Even auditing classes, he'd do it, just to get his foot in the door.

"I'll get a part-time job and rent an apartment and do whatever I have to do to make this work," he said. "Then I'll come back when everything's in place and explain it to my parents."

"You're going there first?" Jenna said. "Not even talk to them? Just go?"

"Maybe I'll leave a note to tell them not to worry," he said. "But I can't tell them what I'm doing, or they'll talk me out of it. My dad will get all hurt and my mom will cry, and I'll never be able to go through with it. No, I have to go there and arrange everything and come back when it's a done deal. And then they'll have to accept it because there'll be no turning back."

She took his hand and threaded her fingers around his. "I love that you're doing this," she said.

He laughed. "You love that I'm destroying my parents?"

"No, I love that you're going after what you want, and you're not letting them hold you back. I love that you're being true to your heart. I mean it, Troy. I think that's so great."

"Can I come with you?" she said.

"What?" he asked. "No. You have your own life. You have to finish high school."

"I don't mean to stay. I mean to get it all set up. I want to help you."

"I can't ask you to do that—"

"No, I want to. I want to see where you're going to school and where you'll live. I want to help you find an apartment. I want to be there when they tell you you're in."

"They may not say that," he said. "And anyway, Jenna, this isn't a fun-and-games trip. I'm leaving at night, so my parents won't know I'm gone until the next morning. My parents are going to be upset. This is a big mess I'm making."

"Then I can be there for you if you start to have doubts."

"But it's going to take a couple of days. What about your parents?"

"I'll leave them a note."

"You can't tell them where you're going. Because then they'll tell my parents."

"That's okay. I'll just tell them not to worry."

"But what will they say when they find out where you were? That you went away for a few days with a guy?"

"You're not just a guy," she said. "You're Troy, and they love you. And I know they'll understand. It may be hard for you to believe this, but when I tell my mom I did this to help you go to college like you wanted, I think she's going to be proud of me."

He put his arm around her shoulders and pulled her close and kissed her. And then he told her exactly how he was going to do it.

They both should have known better, she thought now, as she drove home from the office a few hours later, having gotten almost nothing written. He was almost twenty, and she was seventeen. He should have been able to stand up for himself, to tell his father what he wanted to do, and she should have encouraged him to do exactly that. It was crazy that they thought their best option was to sneak off in the middle of the night. Not to mention how absurd it was to think that Troy could convince some admissions officer to enroll him, even though the application deadline had passed months earlier and acceptances had been sent out long before the summer had even begun. They both knew how colleges worked—he'd seen the application with his own eyes, and she'd watched Chloe go through the whole process.

Still, there was something so tantalizingly innocent about the way the two of them worked it out. Being together and carrying out their plan had been almost more important than actually getting Troy enrolled. She'd been so infatuated with him, and so giddy that he felt the same way. And there was a piece of her, a small but significant piece, that believed they'd never go through with it. Maybe they'd rethink their approach, or maybe Troy would decide to speak to his parents after all, or maybe one set of parents or the other would find out ahead of time and stop them, or maybe any of a million other things would happen. It wasn't the running away that she wanted; it was the intimacy she adored, the way their secret drew them together and set them apart from everyone else on the planet. Troy was the guy she had dreamed of rescuing, back when she used to run down the staircase of her home, holding up her pretend princess dress. She wanted to show him she could save him. She wanted him to know her sole desire that summer was to help him with what he so deeply believed he had to do.

*

That night, Sophie carried up two sweater-size boxes from the basement and set them on the coffee table. Jenna followed her into the living room, placing her mother's cup of tea on the side table next to her chair and then sitting on the sofa. Her mother looked lovely in the new buttercup-yellow dress she had bought when she'd gone shopping with Sherry. It was astonishing how much progress she'd made. She no longer used a cane when she moved within the house or went out onto the patio. Dr. Roberts had been right about bringing her home. Though Sherry said she gave him updates about how Sweet was doing, Jenna vowed to visit him at the hospital sometime soon and thank him in person.

Sophie opened up both boxes and tipped one box over, pouring the contents onto the table. There were pictures of Sophie from the time she was a baby until a few years ago: running around in only a diaper across the kitchen floor; splashing in the lake when she was a toddler; marching in her second-grade Halloween parade in a homemade lion costume; riding her first two-wheeler…

Jenna nudged Mo off her lap and reached out for the bicycle picture. "Oh, Sophie, do you remember this bike?"

Sophie nodded. "Misty."

"That's right, you named her Misty! You were fast friends. You used to pretend she was a lion, and a witch put an evil spell on her that turned her into a bicycle. And you were the only one who knew what she said. Do you remember that? You were always translating for her. Misty says she wants to go back to the jungle.

Misty says she misses her friends the elephant and the giraffes. Oh, you were so cute. Remember, Soph?"

Sophie emptied the second box. This time when she shuffled the pictures around, she found a sealed light blue envelope.

"Sweet, look," she said, holding it out. It was addressed "To You," and there was a small number one with a circle drawn around it.

"What's this?" Sophie said. "Can I open it?"

Sweet was quiet for a moment, her mouth open slightly. She looked stunned, as though she couldn't even formulate an answer. Then she smiled and sat up taller and tapped her clenched fists on the arms of her chair. "Of course!" she said. "The blue envelope. I wrote that letter. It's my story!"

"Your story?" Jenna said. "Mom… *The* story?"

"Go ahead, Sophie!" Sweet said. "Open it up!"

Sophie brought the letter closer to her chest and grasped it with both hands, as though she was scared that if she moved it at all, it would disappear into thin air. Then with a sharp gasp, she ripped the flap and took out a single sheet of light blue paper.

"It *is* a letter," she said, her voice almost a whisper. "It's your handwriting, Sweet." She put it on the table, flattening the fold with her hands, and then started to read. '*Dear BG*'—Wait, who's BG?"

"BG?" Sweet said. She put her hand to her lips. "BG? Is that what it says? I don't know. Isn't that silly? I don't remember."

"Maybe it will say later," Jenna said, not wanting her mother to feel bad for forgetting. "Go on, honey, read it," she said to Sophie.

Sophie looked back at the letter and continued reading. "*Dear BG…*"

My father had a friend in the Navy who taught him a valuable lesson. He said that sometimes when a ship wants to reach a destination, the best strategy is to veer to the side. He said that often looking straight at a target is the worst thing you can do.

I never knew why my father repeated this all the time. But now I've decided it makes so much sense.

I'd been looking straight ahead, searching for my grown-up life. And I just couldn't figure out how I could make sure I'd be happy. Until I planned to veer off. To go to California.

I went to the Lake Summers train station early that summer morning. I couldn't believe I was doing it. I was so scared. But then I realized I was more scared of not going, of having Dad find me before the train came and make me come home and "forget all this nonsense." Which is what he would say.

But shouldn't a person have at least one great adventure in her life? I knew I needed one. I felt it in my whole entire body. There were nights I couldn't even fall asleep.

Anything could happen—and that was scary.

But anything could happen—and that was wonderful, too.

Did you ever feel like you didn't even know who you were? Did you ever worry that you could be pushed to become someone you wouldn't even recognize?

Will you be proud of me?

"Who were you writing to?" Sophie looked up to ask.

"I don't know," Sweet said. "I know it was someone important. Someone I loved…" She shook her head.

"But you never sent this letter."

"No, I suppose I didn't."

"Why would you write a letter and never send it?"

"I don't know."

"But how could you—"

"Honey, let's keep reading," Jenna said. She didn't blame her daughter for being curious, for not even noticing her grandmother's anguish at not being able to answer her questions. But Jenna saw it, and she had to make it stop. "Let's hear more."

Sophie turned the page over and continued.

I knew where I was staying—there was a girl from Lake Summers who went to college in Los Angeles. I had written her a letter and asked if I could stay with her and she said yes.

But I had no idea where I was truly going. I was lost. And in the process of finding myself. And I had to do that, because if I never found myself, how would anybody ever know me? I wanted to be known not just as anyone. I wanted to be known for the person I was meant to be. What if nobody ever knew that person?

"That's where it ends," Sophie said. She picked up the envelope. "There's nothing else inside." She pushed around the photos on the table. "Is this the only letter? Did you write more?"

Jenna looked at her mom, who was tapping her fingers against her lips, the same way Chloe did when she was thinking hard about something. How strange it must be to hear your own words—from what, sixty years ago—being read to you by your granddaughter. How strange to find the words, the letter, to see a familiar envelope, maybe to remember placing the letter inside and sealing it up, but not to remember who you were writing to or why you never sent it. She replayed in her mind the sentence from the letter that had affected her most: *I wanted to be known for the person I was meant to be. What if nobody ever knew that person?* It was a question Jenna had asked herself many times in her life. Many times this year. She didn't want to be known as the poor woman that Matthew Marsh walked out on. It was the reason she had come to Lake Summers this summer—to find the person she was meant to be. Just as her mother had gone searching, too, so many years ago.

"So what happened next?" Sophie said. "How did you meet the guy?"

"Come on, Soph," Jenna said, pulling herself up from the rug. She didn't want to subject her mother to more of Sophie's questions. "I think that's enough for tonight. Sweet is tired, and so are you. Let's go up and get ready for bed. Mom, I'll come down in a little while to say goodnight."

A few minutes later, Sophie was under her coverlet, and Jenna sat down on the side of the mattress. The golden glow from the small bedside lamp made the room feel secluded, like a cave.

Sophie drew her knees to her chest. "Mom, why did I like Misty so much?" she asked.

Jenna was startled. She had expected questions about her mother and the letter, but she hadn't expected a question about that old kid's bike. She stroked the outline of Sophie's foot, the coverlet separating her skin from Sophie's. She imagined that her daughter had a lot to process. She wanted to let Sophie take the lead. "Some kids have an invisible friend, and you had a bicycle one," she said. "You washed her, and you dried her, and you asked her if she was tired if you'd been out a long time. You sometimes took a blanket and covered her at night. You once asked me for a Band-Aid when she got a scratch on her fender. I think she was like a little sister to you."

"Did Sweet have any brother or sisters?"

"No," Jenna said. "You would have known them if she did. They'd be your great-aunts and great-uncles."

"Do you think Sweet was lonely?"

"I don't know. Why?"

"She sounded lonely in the letter. Like she didn't have anyone to talk to. Like her parents didn't understand her. She only had this person to write to, and she doesn't even remember who that was now… Mom?" she said. "Did you and Daddy ever want to have another baby?"

"What? Where did that come from?"

"I just want to know."

Jenna paused. Getting pregnant with Sophie hadn't been easy. There were trips to the fertility doctor, and different medications, checking her temperature and all those ovulation kits. She felt so lucky when she finally got pregnant and was so grateful when Sophie was born. And she didn't want to tempt fate instead of appreciating the one daughter she had. Still, it was funny how life went. One day you thought you'd have a big, messy family like the Jasons next door, and then when you turned around, you had one daughter and a broken marriage.

"I think we were happy just to have you," she said. "Why? Did you ever want a little brother or sister?"

"Maybe. I think so. It's hard to know because I never had one. I don't even know what it would have been like."

Jenna nodded. It was strange—Sophie was the closest person to her in the world. But this was something that separated them: she knew what it was like to have a sibling, and Sophie didn't. And as much as she loved Sophie, she could never truly know what Sophie experienced as an only child. The realization made her sad, maybe because she was also thinking of how isolated her mother was, with her secret buried deep inside. It seemed that true closeness was an illusion. Nobody ever really knew what someone else was going through.

"You know, I used to pretend I had a younger sister, too," Jenna said.

"But you had a sister."

"Not a younger one. I used to pretend what it would be like to have someone who looked up to me and thought I had all the answers. Who thought I was the coolest because I got to wear lipstick or drive a car or go to parties before she did. Someone who would come to me when she had boy trouble or friend trouble. I think I would have been a good older sister. I think you would have, too."

"Do people always want what they don't have?"

"It looks that way sometimes. Although I don't think it's always a bad thing. If it makes you think about what you need in your life, and how to get it, then maybe it's a good thing. Like if you want to take care of a little sister, and that makes you think you might like to help people when you grow up, like be a doctor or a teacher…"

Sophie shook her head. It seemed that this was way too intense a conversation for late at night. "Get some sleep," she told Sophie and turned off the lamp.

"Mom?" Sophie said to the darkness.

"Yeah?"

"Do you think there are more letters?"

"I hope so."

"I mean, there was a number one on the envelope, did you see? So there could be two, three, four, five others, right? Sweet should know how many more letters."

"Honey, it was a long time ago, and her memory isn't good. It was never that good, but it's getting worse. I told you, that can happen to people as they get older. She wants to answer your questions—but she might not ever remember."

Sophie sighed. "There are only three boxes left in the basement."

"I know."

"I'm scared to open them. What if they don't have more letters? Or anything else we want? We'll never know the story. Or who he was or the two words that were so important to her. I'll feel so bad for her. It's horrible to have something you wanted to tell someone, and never be able to say it."

Jenna nodded, even though Sophie wouldn't be able to see her in the dark.

"Because it's not like what you said, about deciding to be a doctor because you never had a little sister," Sophie said. "If she can't tell us about the movie star and the two words, then that's just the end. I mean, Mom, it's all over. All we'll have is this one letter that sounds kind of excited but kind of makes her sound lonely, too."

"But it's not over yet," Jenna said. "Maybe the other boxes will have something. There are still three more. We'll keep going, okay?"

She kissed Sophie's head and went back downstairs. The living room was empty—her mother must have decided to go to sleep as well. Sophie was right—it had to feel horrible to have something you wanted to share and not be able to share it.

She sat down in her mother's armchair. She could see why her mother loved it so much—it was soft and deep, and the arms curved around and held her like a hug. But no matter how cozy it was, it couldn't erase the fact that the summer she had been looking forward to, the summer she had thought would be her new beginning, the summer she had decided to share here in Lake Summers with her mother and her daughter, could end with an enormous let-down for all of them.

Because Sophie was right: there were just three boxes left and only one letter had been stashed in a box so far. What if that was the only letter they found? What if the last three were filled with papers and photos, as nearly all of the others had been? How was she going to face her mother's disappointment, when the closet was empty and they all had to admit the story was still lost? How was she going to face Sophie's disappointment? By allowing things to unfold as they did, she had set her mother and her daughter up for a fall. And she didn't know if she was strong enough to catch them and put them right again.

She looked up and let her gaze drift over to the window. The sky was clear and full of stars, and the moon looked nearly full. And then she noticed a silhouette moving past her house. It was Troy coming back from his run.

She stood up, and as he headed toward his house, she knew she wanted to speak to him. He would no longer be coming for Mo. She didn't know when she'd have this opportunity again.

She rushed to the door and stepped outside, the grass soft on her bare feet. Just as it had been the night she'd come down to meet him at the footpath, carrying her ballet flats in the front of her dress. She ran down her driveway and past her car, and stood on the curb as he reached for his front door.

"Troy!" she called.

He turned back and walked over to meet her. They were in the same spot they had been the first time he kissed her.

"Hey, what's wrong?" he asked. "Your mom okay?"

She nodded. "I wanted to say thanks again. For taking Mo these last two weeks. It's been so helpful. I appreciate it."

"It was no problem," he said. "He's a good little guy. I'll do it again. Anytime you need."

"Okay," she said. "Oh, and Troy?"

He looked back, eyebrows raised.

"I also wanted to thank you for today. It was great to get in and see the exhibit. I know you have a busy job…"

"It was nice to take a tour myself." He paused. "Anything else?"

"No. No, that's all. Just a bunch of thanks, I guess."

"It's fine," he said. "Goodnight, Jenna."

"Wait, Troy!" she said.

He turned around once more and she hesitated for a moment, then decided to take the plunge. She was upset about her mother and concerned about Sophie, and she thought that if she didn't say it then, when would she ever work up the nerve?

"I've been here for weeks trying to help my mother with a story," she said. "She wants to tell Sophie something about her past, but she can't remember all the details. It's about a movie star that she supposedly once loved, and two lost words that meant the world to her. And it's killing her that she can't remember. And it's killing me, too. Because she has a story she wants to tell with every fiber in her body, and she's terrified we'll never know it.

"And ever since I got here, you and I have talked about Mo and my mother and Lake Summers and even the girl skating on the lake… but it's not enough. We have a past together, Troy, and we have a story, and maybe it was painful, maybe it ended badly, but I can't keep pretending it never happened.

"I'm my mother's daughter, and if I've learned one thing from her this summer, it's how damaging it is to be silenced," she said. "So I'm here to tell you that it mattered, and it meant something. Those five days were the best days of my life."

She turned around and ran back to her house, not even wanting to wait for a response. She didn't know how she felt about what she'd said, and she didn't think she could bear to face him. It was just like the night after he kissed her for the first time, and she'd climbed up the tree and into her bedroom. Like that night, she figured that tomorrow she'd have a better idea of what to do.

CHAPTER SEVENTEEN

Troy arrived at work on Monday to find a huge white banner hanging over the entrance to the clinic, the words "Congratulations!" printed in red bubble letters. Two bouquets of multicolored balloons were tied with blue ribbons to the railings on either side of the steps. Inside, the reception room was jammed with people carrying cake boxes, flowers, and bottles of wine and champagne covered in festive bows. The folders normally on Zoe's desk had been replaced with a huge spread of muffins and bagels, along with coffee in three half-gallon containers that featured the Pearl's Café logo above the bright blue spouts.

He looked at the commotion, stunned. What was going on? Was it Zoe's birthday? Or did she get engaged? He knew she was seeing the manager of the bookstore, but he hadn't realized it was serious. Or no, he thought—it had to be Claire. Of course! She must have given birth over the weekend. After all, Zoe had said she was on bed rest last week. It was early, but not too bad, he thought—the doctor had told her that as long as she lasted through July Fourth, the twins would be fine. But why hadn't she called to tell him? And why were the gifts coming here, instead of to her house? He'd have to make two or three trips to get this stuff into his car and bring it over to her. And why was there so much champagne? Didn't people usually give things like blankets and diaper bags?

Across the room, Zoe was trying to find space on the magazine table to accommodate all the gifts. She looked up and saw him, and raised her index finger to show that she'd be right there, and then wove her way among the crowd until she could get to him.

"Oh, man, Troy!" she said. "Isn't this amazing?"

"So when did it happen? How's she doing?" Troy said, shouting to be heard over the voices in the crowded space.

"Wait, what?" Zoe said.

"How are the babies? Did you speak to her?"

Zoe shook her head like she was trying to shake out Troy's crazy questions. "What are you talking about? This isn't for Claire, it's for you! Hey, look, everyone!" she called. "Troy's here!"

The crowd in the reception room turned almost in unison and soon, like a tidal wave, people were headed his way—people whose dogs and cats he'd treated, merchants from the town center, even some of the nurses from the hospital whose pets he'd cared for in his home while they went on vacation. Troy held up one hand as though he could stop the crowd from approaching, and pulled Zoe into his office with the other, closing the door behind them.

"For me?" he said. "What are you talking about?"

"The Lake Summers Citizen of the Year Award! Art tweeted about it on the weekend, and the trustees tweeted too, and then there were tons of retweets. Didn't you see it? He stopped by this morning and put up the banner. He said you changed your mind and wanted to be honored. He said you'd be expecting people to stop by. Weren't you?"

"Of course not. Not like this!"

"It's not a bad thing, Troy. Everyone's happy for you."

"But I didn't do anything. Doesn't anyone care? My dad was the hero, not me."

"But you told Art you changed your mind. He said you emailed him."

"Yeah, but not to…" He shook his head. This was nuts. He couldn't stand it there any longer. He had to get out of the building. "Do we have any cases this morning?" he asked.

Zoe shook her head. "I pushed everything back to the afternoon. There was too much going on here. I didn't want to freak out all the animals."

"Good," Troy said. "Because I have to get some air. See if you can clear everyone out while I'm gone, okay? I'll be back in a couple of hours."

He opened the office door, pressing his palms forward to nudge people back and murmuring, "Thank you," and "I'll be back," as he made a beeline for the exit. Once outside, he kept his chin down as he strode along Main Street, not wanting to speak with anyone who might have heard the news. There was something so strange about all those people in the office this morning thinking there was a reason to celebrate him. Yes, he had given Art the green light because he felt bad letting him and Victoria and even Zoe down, and he'd thought Jenna had a point about being better, liking herself more, when she was in Lake Summers. He liked himself better here, too. He also thought he could handle life better here. But he hadn't expected his decision would create such a madhouse. He hadn't expected people would care this much.

Was Art right—was he a leader? Was Zoe right—a role model? Or was he nothing but a fraud? Why was it that all his effort to withdraw backfired? It was like two people were fighting inside of him, one that wanted to push people away, and the other who kept yearning for connection. Like the note he had left at Jenna's on Saturday morning.

It was the best five days of my life, too.

Why had he done that? Because he felt sorry about all she was going through? Because he felt guilty for making her think he didn't care about what happened to her?

Or did he admire her ability to stand up for herself, that assertiveness that had always been a hallmark of her personality?

Or was he simply so relieved to finally admit that yes—that week had meant everything to him, too?

He hadn't had a destination when he left the clinic, but now he found himself heading to the resort. He walked up the driveway and entered the building, stopping at the desk for the key before crossing the lobby to the winding staircase and making his way down to the history exhibit. He unlocked the door, then switched on the lights and started wandering through the galleries. He saw the prints of the firefighter and the skater at the lake that Jenna had pointed out. He stopped by the print of *The Wizard of Oz* production.

And then he saw three new posters lining the back wall. They hadn't been up when he was there with Jenna, but now he remembered Victoria saying over lunch that they'd be going up last. He was glad they weren't up when Jenna was there. He wouldn't have wanted to look at them with anyone around. He wasn't even sure he wanted to see them at all. But he thought it would be harder to try to avoid them.

The first was an old picture of Main Street from when he was a little boy. And there it was, right in the middle of the block: Jason Printing, the words in simple block letters, chosen by his dad for their simplicity and practicality. The place now housed the Smoothie Dudes, which Troy found kind of funny—the shop that his salt-of-the-earth dad once owned was now the site of one of the trendiest eateries in town. When they'd first opened, the owners had made smoothies in honor of all the businesses that had once been on the block. Troy wasn't there to see it, but Art told him that the smoothie they'd invented to honor his dad's shop was the Jason Press Smoothie. It was made with cold-pressed juices, Art said, which gave it a strange, pulpy consistency. His father would have hated it. "Smoothie, shmoothie!" he'd have said. "Give me a milkshake any day of the week!" Still, his dad wasn't all rough and tumble. He drove the fire truck around the town every Christmas, sounding the siren and tossing candy canes out of the truck for all the kids who came running.

Even back then, Jason Printing was not long for the world. His dad had never invested in new equipment and could only handle the simplest of jobs. He didn't even make enough in sales to give his boys summer jobs as they got older, which was why Troy worked at the dry cleaner and parked cars at the resort. But his dad was adamant that his oldest son would take over the business. His parents had no interest in sending him to a four-year college, despite the offer from Mr. Brand, Pauley's owner, to pay his first year's tuition. What was the point? Community college at night, if Troy insisted. And even that was delayed a year, as his dad developed angina the year Troy graduated from high school, and the doctor said he should ease himself out of the day-to-day.

"Meet me on the footpath," he'd whispered to Jenna before getting in the car with Bethany, the girl his parents assumed he'd eventually marry, even though they were just friends. "Meet me at ten."

His plan was to take Bethany to the dance at the resort, where they'd go their separate ways as they'd agreed. Then he'd sneak away and rush over to the footpath to meet Jenna. He would tell Jenna that he'd changed his mind about bringing her with him to Binghamton. It wasn't fair to drag her into his mess. He was going to enroll at the university and stay there, and not return until he had his degree. Then he'd come back to patch things up with his parents. And then he'd find her and marry her. He wanted to meet her on the footpath so he could tell her that he loved her. He wanted to kiss her one last time, and ask her to promise to wait for him.

He'd rounded the bend intending to meet her and tell her what he'd decided. But before he could say any of that, the earth seemed to explode. A zigzag of shimmering white light electrified the sky. And a boom that felt like it originated in his very core made the ground tremble beneath their feet.

"We'd better get out of here," he'd said. "Let me take you home." He thought he'd walk her home, and then run back to the resort to get his car. But just then the heavens opened up, and he knew they were in trouble. The rain poured down so hard that he could no longer see the path, and the winds sent pieces of dust and sand into his eyes. There was another lightning strike, and then a tree came down near them. They heard the crack as the trunk snapped in two, and the top half floated down as if in slow motion. He froze, not knowing which way to go. He felt Jenna take him by the hand.

"Come on, Troy!" she screamed, strands of wet hair plastered across her face. "We have to run! Come on!"

The rain was striking his skin like darts, but if she was feeling it too, she didn't seem to mind. Instead, she stayed intent on leading him home, and he marveled at her focus. Apparently, years of riding bikes with Steven had given her an uncanny knowledge of the town's ins and outs, and she led him behind stores and down alleys to make it home quicker. A tree had crashed through Pearl's window; they skirted around fallen wires that sent sparks high into the air.

When they reached his house, his mother was standing outside on the lawn. Her mascara was streaked down her face and her legs were visible beneath her soaking-wet dress. "Troy!" she cried, throwing her arms around his neck. "Oh, thank God, thank God! We didn't know what had happened to you."

"Why?" he said. "What's going on?"

"They evacuated the resort," she said. "The lightning started a fire. Bethany called because she couldn't find you. Your father ran down there to help look."

"He's at the resort?"

"Troy, I'm so worried. He'll run into the building if he thinks you're there!"

He pulled away from his mother and ran to her car in the driveway, while she went inside to get her car keys. She threw them to him, and he started up the car. As he sped away, he saw Jenna climbing back in through her bedroom window. He didn't know if anyone in her house had even noticed she'd been gone.

He drove toward the resort, barely able to see through the windshield because of the rain. He could make out red lights flashing as he approached, and smoke billowing overhead. The driveway was blocked off, so he left the car in the street and went up the slope on foot. Breathless, he sprinted toward the front entrance.

"Sorry, kid, no one's getting in there," a fireman said, pushing him back from the structure.

"But my dad is looking for me. Billy Jason, William Jason—"

"Shit, Billy went inside? Are you sure? Take a look around the lawn, kid, maybe he came back out…"

Troy turned around and scanned the grounds frantically, his hands holding the sides of his head. "Dad!" he screamed out into the rain. "*Dad!*"

And that's when he spied his father, sitting against a tree, weeping. His legs were splayed out. His face was in his hands.

"Dad!" Troy said and ran over to his father, and knelt beside him. "Dad, are you okay?"

"Troy," his father said and crumpled against Troy's chest. It was as though he was the son and Troy was the father. "Troy, I thought you were gone. I thought I lost you. I wouldn't have made it. I swear to God, I wouldn't have been able to live anymore…"

Troy held his father's thick, wet body against his own until the rain stopped. Then he helped him up, and together they stumbled to the car.

He lay in bed later that night, shaken by what had happened, relieved that it had been a close call only. He was home now, and his dad was, too. He wasn't going to the university, not now and not ever. He'd let Jenna know tomorrow that he'd changed his mind.

That's when he noticed red lights circling outside his window. He ran downstairs to see two paramedics wheeling his dad out on a stretcher. "His angina was bad tonight," his mother said. "I thought it best to get him checked out. Stay here with your brothers. I'll call you after I speak to the doctor."

By the next morning, the storm had passed. The air was clear, the sun was out. Troy went outside to pick up the newspaper. He felt a touch of fall in the air.

A short time later, a taxi drove up. It was his mother.

She'd come back alone.

Troy turned his head away from the picture of his father's store. He wondered now, as he'd often wondered in the past, what would have happened if his dad hadn't died. What if the storm had bypassed Lake Summers, or the lightning hadn't struck a transformer and set the resort afire? Would he have gone to Binghamton as planned? Or what if he'd driven his dad straight to the emergency room instead of bringing him home? Would he have stayed in Lake Summers and taken over the store? Would Jenna have stayed with him?

The next poster had the newspaper picture from when he'd saved Pauley, with his mom, dad, and Mr. Brand, who was holding Pauley in his arms. They were standing in a row outside the dry cleaner shop, and Pauley had a cone around his neck so he couldn't bite the stitches on his belly. His parents looked like they couldn't have been prouder.

A few feet away was a photo of the drawbridge dedication. The trees in the background were bare, and he and his brothers were in heavy coats, their hair blown back from their faces by what must have been a strong wind. Troy was standing next to Steven, his hand on Steven's shoulder, and the twins were standing in front of them. A heavyset man with a long red scarf around his neck was facing the brothers and reading from a sheet of paper. A crowd of people was gathered around.

By then, his mother was gone, too.

Only two short months had passed between the time of the newspaper picture and the time of the bridge dedication.

And yet, he'd become a whole different person.

He arrived back at the clinic that afternoon to find the waiting room busy again, this time because of the appointments that had been postponed from the morning. The banner was off the front of the building—he assumed Zoe had done that after he'd reacted so badly to the fanfare in the office. The presents on the magazine table were also gone—Zoe must have found something to do with them, too. He waved to Zoe, who was on the phone, and went into his office to see the afternoon's schedule. First up was Dudley, Mrs. Carson's sheepdog puppy, who needed his rabies vaccine. When he went back out to find Dudley, Zoe was smiling at him, her chin resting on her hand.

"What?" he said.

"I know you're not going to like this," she said. "I know you're going to think it's too much of a fuss and all that. But guess what? The lieutenant governor is coming down for the opening. He is going to give you a proclamation!"

"Who?" Troy said. "What?"

"The lieutenant governor of New York. That was Victoria on the phone. Troy, you're going to be famous! They said you should expect newspapers calling for interviews."

"Wait a minute," Troy said. "Does Art even know?"

"Of course," she said, as the phone on her desk rang. "He's the one who told the mayor to send the press release to the governor's office. Wait, I think this is him now."

She handed him the phone, and he walked a few steps away from the desk. "Art," he said. "What the hell is going on?"

"You're a celebrity, that's what's going on."

"But I didn't—I'm not—"

"You can't run away from your legacy, my friend! It's like I said, it's in your blood. It's a human interest story, the favorite son of Lake Summers comes home and completely transforms the town."

"You and I both know I didn't transform anything—"

"Our timing couldn't have been better. The state has been urging this kind of partnership between the corporate world and town governments since the beginning of the year, and they love that the resort is partnering with the town to honor you. We're being recognized as a model in this effort. I'll be getting applications from grads from all the top business schools. This is big, Troy. I won't forget this.

"Now, look," he continued. "I know the mayor, he's not going to let this pass by without a lot of pomp and circumstance, especially with the lieutenant governor coming. It's only two weeks away, we need to strategize how we're going to handle it. We can't have the ceremony down where the exhibit is, there's not enough room for everyone who'll be coming. We'll do something outside—we'll get my events department involved. Catering, too. And maybe sales—this will sell a lot of business sponsorships. By the way, have you spoken to your brothers? Maybe they can arrange to be here…"

Troy handed Zoe the phone. "Get Dudley ready, okay?" he said, and went into his office. He sat at his desk and dropped his head in his hands. A proclamation from the state? The newspapers would be asking him about his dad again, and the night of the storm. There'd be coverage all over again about his father's heroics when the fire broke out, and the tragedy of his dad's death that very night. They'd make him relive the whole thing.

He looked up and noticed the little space beside Zoe's desk where Mo would sometimes lie and sun himself in the afternoons. This had started that night he'd taken Mo home from the hospital, he thought. The night he was supposed to go to Steven's cabin.

How had he let this get so far?

CHAPTER EIGHTEEN

Back home that evening, he sat out on the deck with some leftover pizza and a beer, watching the sun go down and the stars start to appear. The conversation with Art was still on his mind, but stronger still, on this quiet night, were the pictures from the exhibit. It felt as though he'd been looking at someone else's family. The boy in the pictures, standing alongside Mr. Brand, holding Steven's shoulder—that couldn't be him. He didn't remember what it felt like to be so young. So vulnerable. So capable of such sadness. At some point he had stopped himself from having those feelings.

He picked up his empty beer bottle to bring it inside. That's when he saw Jenna across the yard, sitting on her patio, also alone, also looking at where the sunset had been. That was a feeling he remembered well—how thrilled he'd been to see her those five August nights. How he barely made it through his shifts at the resort, so excited was he to get back home. How every hour of the day was so endless, so brutally slow, but how he wished the time they were together in the dark outside her house could last forever. That's why he'd left her the note on Saturday. He meant what he'd said. That's why he wanted to go see her right now.

He walked down the steps of his deck, through his yard, and past her driveway and around to the back of her house. She looked up when he approached. The light from inside her house spilled onto the patio. Inside, the TV was on, some kids' show he figured Sophie was watching.

"Hey," he said.

She smiled. "Hi."

"You're deep in thought."

She lifted her hand, showing him what she was holding. It was the note he had left for her over the weekend. "I was remembering a lot of things," she said. "I was up to the summer when we came back and you weren't here."

The TV suddenly got louder with the sound of a studio audience laughing. "Do you… want to take a walk?" he asked.

She nodded. "Let me get Sophie into bed," she said. "I'll meet you out front."

He walked around the house and waited for her at the end of her driveway. She opened the front door and came to join him. She was wearing a sleeveless dress, and her hair was down, the breeze making it flutter on her shoulders. Just as it had done the night they'd met on the footpath. Before the wind kicked up and the rains came.

They began walking side by side down the street. "It was so strange, that summer we came back," she said, continuing the conversation they had started on her patio, as though she wanted so badly to tell him how it felt. "I thought about calling or writing you that winter, but I didn't know what to say, after all that happened. I never expected to come back and see new people in your house. Mrs. Pearl told us your mom had died."

He kicked a stone on the road. "I tried to keep us in town, but I couldn't take care of my brothers by myself," he said. "Steven was getting into fights all the time, and then Clay stopped going to school altogether. That's when a social worker from the county showed up. I wanted us to stay together, so I agreed we'd move to Scranton, where my mother's aunt lived. We got a small rental house, and I worked managing a copy shop, which was what stores like my dad's were changing into. I took care of my brothers until they got out on their own. I thought I owed my parents that."

"Mrs. Pearl gave my mom a phone number for you," Jenna said. "But by the time we called, it was disconnected."

"Yeah, we bounced around a little before we settled down," he said. "I might have gotten some letters or calls from people back here, but I couldn't bring myself to deal with it."

"We all felt terrible," she said. "But we didn't know what to do. I wanted so much to find you and be there for you. There were times I thought I could help you get through it all. If only I could find you, I could do something or say something or just sit with you and listen…"

"Hey, come on," he said and nudged her with his elbow, trying to cheer her up. The same way he'd done the night of their first kiss, the night she cried, the night he came home after saving Pauley and found her outside waiting for him. "It was okay," he said. "My aunt lived close by and she did a lot for us. And we had still had Cody, and nobody could be unhappy for long with a big, crazy golden retriever jumping up and licking your face."

He looked at her, glad to see her smile, too. He didn't want to talk about those years. He didn't even like to think about them. Because the truth was, he was lying to her. They were awful. He had lost so much after that storm: his parents and the life he'd loved—and yes, he'd loved it, no matter how much Steven annoyed him, how much he wanted to break free of his father's plans for him. And he had lost his dreams of going to Binghamton, getting his degree, and coming back to reunite with his family and marry Jenna. He still remembered so clearly that winter morning he and his brothers left the house for good and headed to Scranton. Clay had suggested they stop for one last breakfast at Mrs. Pearl's, and Troy had told him no, forget it, they needed to leave, they weren't stopping for anything. He still felt bad, even now, remembering the sound of Clay sniffling in the back seat. They were only thirteen, Cal and Clay. He wished now he'd have let Clay get a stupid muffin. Why was a few minutes such a big deal, if Clay could at least have had something delicious to eat? But back then, he couldn't even consider making a stop. He hated that he had to leave his house and Lake Summers. And he'd been scared that if they stopped at Pearl's, he might not have been able to force himself back into the car.

And that was why he'd never reached out to Jenna either, even though it would have been easy to call her. He couldn't let her know where he was. Seeing her, or even just talking to her on the phone, would have reminded him of everything he'd lost, everything he'd thrown away by being such a fool and arranging to meet her when he knew a big storm was coming. The only way to get through that first miserable year was focus on his sole responsibility—taking care of his brothers. Pushing away all feelings, all regrets, all longings. It was the same way he'd been managing ever since then.

"It all turned out fine in the end," he continued. "This lawyer tracked me down after a few years. Mr. Brand had died, and since he didn't have any kids, he left all his money to me. It paid for my college, and then vet school. It felt like a good way to use the money."

"He left you all his money?" Jenna said. "Because of Pauley? Oh, Troy, the way you saved him—it was the bravest, kindest thing—"

"It wasn't that big a deal. Anyone would have done it."

"That's not true. I didn't do it. Steven didn't. That's why I waited outside for you to come back to your house…" She stopped herself, as though she couldn't bring herself yet to talk about that night. As if she didn't know if she thought they were ready, but she wanted him to know how much it meant to her.

"So after you finished vet school, what then?" she asked. "Did you ever settle down with someone?"

"I lived with someone for a while," he told her. "Stacia. We worked together at the animal hospital in Philly. But I didn't want to get married, and she didn't want to *not* get married. So she moved on." He kicked another stone. "I don't know. I was older when I went to college and older when I went to graduate school—my twenties were mostly a blur. I think I missed the boat on marriage. I think that whole urge to share your life… it passed me by. He was a salesman for one of our equipment suppliers, the guy she left me for. Doug. He was a nice guy."

"I'm sorry," she said.

"No, it's okay," he told her. "They were a good match. It was for the best. Still, it was pretty quiet in that apartment after she left. A couple of months later, Mrs. Pearl called. And I decided to come back."

"And now you're getting an award," she said. "Samantha showed me the press release that came in this morning. I had no idea how much work you've done for the animal rescue, and you've only been back a few months. It said the clinic—"

"Think we should turn back?" he said. "I know you probably don't want to get too far from home." He turned around and without even thinking, he reached for her hand. She put it in his and looked up at him, her eyes pleading, as though she sensed she had said something wrong in bringing up the award, and she didn't understand why that would trouble him. He hadn't intended to make her feel bad. He jiggled her hand.

"So tell me about you," he said as they started to walk back toward their houses, still holding hands, their arms swinging slightly in unison. "What you've been doing all this time…?"

She looked toward the sky. "There's not much to tell," she said. "I made some mistakes and I let my marriage fail. This chance to write a book came out of the blue—it wasn't even the book I cared about, but it was doing something fun and being creative and connecting with people, and… putting myself out there again. I loved it. But Matt hated it. He resented that things were going well for me. And then it was too late. I should have been smarter. I should have seen what a risk I was taking. And I shouldn't have let myself get carried away."

"But you didn't do anything wrong," he said. "You were just being who you are. Full of life. That's the person everyone around here loves. You shouldn't be with someone who wants to tamp you down. I don't know why anyone would want to try to do that to you."

She sighed. "It's different when kids are involved. Sophie suffered so much this year. The last thing she wanted was for us to split up."

"But she seems okay now. She's a good kid, Jenna. You're doing a great job with her. I bet you taught her a lot by being true to yourself."

"Thanks," she said. "That's a nice thing to say."

They walked a few steps more, eventually coming to the start of her front walk. She turned to face him.

"Troy?" she said.

He nodded.

"I don't know if I should say this… I don't know how it's going to sound. But I want you to know that I never saw anything in my life as moving as the expression on your mother's face at your dad's funeral. The pain she was in, it was so sad, but… it was beautiful, too. She looked so young, in a way—I don't know how to explain it, but there was something in her eyes. And I thought to myself that it must be love, that love makes people look younger. And I couldn't help thinking how amazing it was that your mother had such a love. I mean, my parents loved each other too, but that was different. My mother was so strong, and of course she was sad when my dad died, but I knew she was going to be fine. But your mom… I don't know. I just wanted you to know that."

"She had a heart attack six weeks after he did," he said. "I think she couldn't go on living without him."

"She died of a broken heart," Jenna said.

Troy nodded.

She pulled out her house key. "I'd better go inside," she said. "Sophie should be asleep by now, but you never know…" She paused. "Troy, I'm sorry about how everything turned out that night after the storm," she said. "I'm so sorry about what happened to your dad."

"It wasn't your fault, it was mine," he told her. "I shouldn't have asked you to meet me that night. I knew the storm was coming."

"But it wasn't supposed to come that early," she said. "We both weren't thinking. We were kids. We didn't believe bad things could happen. We were too happy being together."

He nodded and leaned down and kissed her cheek. Then, feeling the pull toward her that he'd felt so long ago, he grasped her shoulders and kissed her mouth, and he felt her kiss him back. With his eyes closed, he could almost imagine that he was young again. That when he opened his eyes, he would see her climb the tree back into her house, knowing she'd be waiting for him again tomorrow.

He pulled back slowly and let his hands slide down her arms. She took them in hers and then looked up at him and smiled. "That was incredible," she said. "Even more incredible than before. Maybe because of all that happened. Maybe because of all we went through to get back here." She leaned in toward him and dropped her chin, and he kissed her forehead. Then she squeezed his hands. "See you tomorrow?" she said.

"See you tomorrow," he said and watched as she went inside. He could hear the click of Mo's toenails tapping on the floor as he came to greet her. Then he started back to his house. She was right. They had both been through a lot to get to where they were now. A part of him wished they could go back, but do it all differently this time. He wished they'd had their eyes open. There were so many better ways he could have gotten to Binghamton. He'd been too foolish to see them. And their fate was sealed.

When he got to his door, he turned back to her house and studied it for a moment. She was right in another way, too, he thought.

The kiss had been incredible.

CHAPTER NINETEEN

It was the best kiss of her life. That's what she'd thought that night as she walked into the quiet house and made her way upstairs, Mo at her heels. That's what she'd kept thinking, even now, as she sat at one of the café's inside tables, waiting for Mrs. Pearl to join her for coffee. Maybe it was because of what he'd said about her, that everyone loved the person she was, and nobody should try to change her. It had made her feel so good, to know that's what he thought. He'd made her see that she wasn't to blame for the failure of her marriage. Or maybe it was because he'd opened up about all that happened since he left Lake Summers. She hadn't expected him to kiss her, not after the way he'd been struggling these last few weeks, reaching out to her but then pushing her away. It had been a wonderful surprise, the way he placed his hands on her arms and moved his lips from her cheek to her mouth. She'd leaned into him, wanting to get closer, enjoying so much the warm press of his lips. She hoped that the kiss was a sign that he was ready to put all their ghosts behind them. As she was.

Mrs. Pearl came over with two cups of hot coffee and a plate of cookies on a tray, and sat down on the opposite side of the table. The place was empty, thanks to the rain that had started last night and continued all afternoon. Now it was more of an insidious mist, which Jenna had barely noticed until she walked into the shop and realized she was wet and shivering. Mrs. Pearl had handed her a clean dishcloth to towel off with, and motioned her to the table, and Jenna suspected she was grateful for some company. It wasn't so much the rain itself that kept people away; it was more the gloominess that suffused Main Street on days like today. Even though the overhead pendant fixtures were on full blast, the absence of sunshine pouring through the skylights made the shop dark. The shafts of light aiming down from the long ceiling track above the bread shelves looked grayish-yellow, instead of bright white, as they usually did.

"So what's up at home?" Mrs. Pearl asked. "Anything more about the movie star?"

Jenna updated Mrs. Pearl on the latest boxes they'd opened and the letter they'd found. "So we'll see what happens," she said. "It all comes down to tonight."

"Sounds mysterious," Mrs. Pearl said. "Do you think there'll be something more?"

"I hope so," Jenna said, wiping the last drops of rain from her arm. "Another letter, maybe, talking about how it ended in California, what happened after she came home. Some kind of closure, maybe. Of course, I'm sure Sophie wants something way more dramatic. I think she expects to find the guy's cell phone number and a big sign that says 'Call me!'"

Mrs. Pearl laughed. "Oh, I hope for her sake there's some extra little nugget waiting inside. I would hate for her to be disappointed."

"Me too," Jenna said. "I think I'll be a little disappointed, as well."

"You? Well, that's a turnaround. If I remember correctly, at first you didn't even believe the story was true."

"I know," Jenna said. "At first it was just something fun to keep Sophie occupied. But then we found the closet and it all got so important. I mean, I know my mom gets mixed up sometimes and doesn't always make sense. But this is so different—there's a whole part of her past that she wants Sophie to know. And it's been so much fun, spending all this time together, watching my mom and Sophie grow close. It was my mother's story, but it became our story, too. We've been making our way through it together, the three of us."

"You should be proud of that," Mrs. Pearl said. "You've come so far. There was a time you didn't even think you'd be able to stand up to Chloe and stay here."

Jenna nodded. "I am proud. It was a good idea to stay here. Sophie loves Lake Summers—she made a lot of friends, and she feels at home here. I haven't seen her this happy since before Matt left."

"That's wonderful," Mrs. Pearl said. She picked up their coffee cups. "Here, let me top these off."

She went back behind the counter, and Jenna looked out the window in the direction of the Public Works Building, where she once ran into a brick wall. That was the one part of her life here in Lake Summers that was still uncertain: where she stood with Troy. She hadn't seen him since they kissed on her doorstep, and she didn't know what that meant. She was tempted to talk to Mrs. Pearl about it, but she'd been keeping the secret of their past to herself for so long now that revealing it to anyone seemed an impossible hurdle. Still, she needed help to make sense of what was going on. Before she'd gone inside that night, she'd said to him—no, she'd asked him—"See you tomorrow?" And he'd answered, "See you tomorrow." Yet he hadn't come by. And she hadn't seen him on his deck or out front taking his regular evening run. His house had stayed dark. It didn't even look as though he was home.

"Have you seen Troy Jason lately?" she asked when Mrs. Pearl came back.

"As a matter of fact, I was going to ask you the same thing," Mrs. Pearl said, putting the cups on the table. "He hasn't stopped in for coffee for the last two mornings, which isn't like him at all. And Mrs. Closson told me yesterday there was a message on his machine steering people to Lyons Hill if they needed a vet. So much fuss about this big award, with the lieutenant governor coming and all, that he probably couldn't stomach it. He's not a hoopla kind of guy."

"What are you saying? That he left?"

"His brother Steven owns a little cabin up by the Canadian border. He goes there sometimes to get away. He was supposed to go there the week you came to town. He changed his plans after your mother fell."

"Oh," Jenna said. She looked down at her hands, folded on the table. She hadn't known about Troy postponing his trip. He'd never said anything. He'd been there to take care of her mother. To take care of Mo. To help them all out. Quietly and without fanfare. The way he'd been taking care of everyone all his life.

"Did you get… reacquainted with him this summer?" Mrs. Pearl asked.

Jenna considered the question, not sure how to answer. She looked at her phone. "I need to get Sophie," she said, handing Mrs. Pearl the towel and her empty mug. "Thanks for this. Thanks for listening."

"Take the cookies with you," Mrs. Pearl said and went back behind the counter for a bag. She put the cookies from the table inside of it and folded down the top.

"Have fun this evening," she said. "I hope you and Sophie both find what you're looking for!"

Jenna waved. "I'll let you know."

She left the store and walked up Main Street, stunned at the news that Troy would have gone away without telling her. Why would he do that, after their evening together, after their kiss on her doorstep? She'd thought it meant something, the way he grasped her shoulders, as if he wanted to hold her as close to him as he could. Why did he leave? Was she part of the fuss that Mrs. Pearl said he couldn't stomach?

As she approached the lake, her cell phone rang, and she looked at the screen. She was surprised to see it was Chloe. Her sister hadn't called Jenna's cell phone since she went back to Long Island. She usually called the house phone, so she could speak to their mom, too.

"Hi, everything okay?" Jenna said. "I'll be home in a little while. Did you want to call back so you can speak to Mom?"

"No, I just called the house," Chloe said, her voice clipped and tense. "I spoke to her. We need to talk. I hear you found a letter she wrote about that guy?"

"It was in one of the boxes in the basement," Jenna said. "Why? What's wrong?"

"Look, Jenna," she said. "Tell me the truth. Do you believe that Mom was in love with a movie star?"

"Kind of. More now than I did before we found that letter."

"And she wanted to spend her whole life with him, and would have if Grandpa hadn't dragged her home?"

"I don't know. That's what we're looking to find out."

"Don't open any more boxes, Jenna. Do you hear me?"

"There's only one more left."

"Don't open it, Jenna. Leave it be."

"Why? What is going on?"

"Look, you went back because you were having a hard time with Matt. I get that," she said. "And I was okay when you were trying to cheer Sophie up and distract her by looking through locked closets and digging through boxes. And it was fun, seeing all those old pictures. But now it's getting serious. You're opening a can of worms, Jenna. And I think you may regret it."

Jenna sat down on a bench overlooking the lake. "But Mom wants us to see this stuff. Mom's wanted all summer to tell Sophie her story. Chloe, this is ridiculous. People look through old stuff all the time."

"Yes, pictures and things. People are happy in pictures. But this is different." Jenna could hear her take a big sigh. "I thought it was all innocent, just entertainment. But now I don't know. The letter changes everything. Maybe it did happen. And if it did, do you really want to know about it?"

"Why not?"

"Because, Jenna, it changes our *lives.* How are you going to feel if you learn that she never wanted to marry Daddy? That she never stopped loving this other guy? I mean, she stopped telling Sophie the story right in the middle. Maybe it wasn't falling down the stairs that stopped her. Maybe she changed her mind about telling the whole story."

"That's not how it happened. She was going to the basement to find the boxes with the letters."

"We can go through that last box another time," Chloe said. "Down the road when Mom is gone, and everything settles down. But I'm not sure I want to deal with this right now, and I'm not convinced Mom does."

"Chloe, you've got this all wrong," Jenna said. "I'm trying to give Mom her voice back. She wants to tell this story. She has a right to share it if she wants."

"But there's more to it than that," Chloe said. "Look, I didn't have the greatest relationship with Mom. We weren't the same, like you two were. But one thing I always believed was that Mom loved Daddy, and that made him happy. And if you take that away, I will never forgive you."

She hung up just as Jenna spotted Sophie, waving to her friends as she ran up the grassy slope.

"Tonight's the night!" Sophie said and plopped down on the bench, her hair flying around her face from the wind, her skin glowing from the moisture in the air. "The last box. I decided not to be afraid anymore. We're going to find out everything tonight, right, Mom? Tonight we'll learn how to find Sweet's old boyfriend!"

Her excitement was innocent and genuine and full of heart. She didn't want to quash it, not even a tiny amount.

"I can't wait either!" she said as she put her arm around her daughter.

CHAPTER TWENTY

The rain cleared out late that afternoon, and the evening was beautiful, the sunset warm and orange, the breeze mild and soft. Jenna made a big pasta salad and served it with a loaf of the market's best Italian bread, and Sherry stayed to eat with them out on the patio. As the sun went down, Jenna watched her mother take off her hat and fluff her hair. The soft white waves framed her face, and she couldn't help but think how far her mother had come since that night at the hospital. She looked healthy and strong. The cane she had been using was nowhere to be found. She had gotten rid of it, just as she had vowed to do her first night home. And yet her forgetfulness wasn't going away, as Jenna had hoped it would as more time passed since her fall. That morning she'd gone out to the patio to see if her mother wanted her to put another pot of coffee on, and when she'd brought out the second cup, her mother had looked at her in surprise. "For me? You must be a mind reader! How did you know I was about to come in for a refill?" She had no recollection of asking Jenna for more just minutes earlier.

Sherry left after dinner, and Jenna cleared the table, then rejoined her mother on the patio. It was so warm and comfortable that she decided they should stay out and open the box there. No matter what Chloe's fears were, their mother's desire to share her story had crystallized around this one last box, this one final evening of discovery, and Jenna wasn't going to prevent the process from playing out.

A few minutes later, Sophie bounded upstairs with the final box from the closet, a square box with a logo from a local discount store that had long ago gone out of business. It was all Jenna could do to keep her hands on her lap and let Sophie open it. She had enjoyed hearing her mother's voice, young and adventurous, in the letter from the other night. She hoped there would be another letter tonight. Or more revelations, like what the two words were, the words that proved so life-changing. It was such a good story, romantic and captivating. And she hoped they could wrap it up tonight by finally learning all the details of how her mother's Hollywood trip played out.

Sophie put the box on the patio, then got down on her knees. She pressed her hands on the top, spreading her fingers out. Jenna knew just how she was feeling, wanting to open the box and yet not wanting the whole search to end just yet. Wanting so much to hold onto the feeling that the thing you most wanted might actually come true. And the wonderful thing was, Sophie wasn't hoping for a present for herself, a sweater or a necklace she'd had her eye on and had decided would be a good birthday present. No, she was hoping for something that would make her grandmother feel her voice wasn't lost. Nearly a whole summer of searching and exploring and expecting had come to this.

Sophie closed her eyes and took a breath. Then she opened the box in one sweeping motion, raising the top over her head and settling it down on the patio by her side.

She unfolded a few layers of tissue paper and smoothed them aside, then put both of her hands in the box. They emerged holding a heap of assorted arts and crafts materials—construction paper, pipe cleaners, pom-poms, ribbons, and beads. She put all the materials down, then dug back in and lifted out some more. She sat back on her heels.

Jenna sat down on the patio next to her and moved the objects around. There were pictures of Sophie from when she was in preschool, housed in frames made of popsicle sticks and decorated with dried macaroni. There were homemade cards that said, "Happy Birthday, Grandma!" and "Happy Birthday, Grandpa!" in crayoned letters, with silver sparkly stars affixed to the paper and dried glue peeking out. There was a construction paper booklet tied together with string with a title in marker that read, "Why My Grandparents Are Special." There was a first-grade report card, with comments along the side: *Pays attention; plays well with others; takes responsibility.* There was a certificate for having completed her second-grade summer reading list, and another for being part of the kindergarten soccer league. Jenna didn't even know how her mother had come to possess some of these things.

"It's my old stuff," Sophie said. She looked up at her grand-mother. "Sweet, why did you keep all this?"

"Because she loves you," Jenna said, trying to answer so her mother wouldn't feel compelled to speak up. They'd put Sweet through so much this summer, asking her questions, testing her memory, day after day, every time Sophie had opened a new box up. Her mother had smiled and laughed, but Jenna could sometimes see more in her mother's eyes. Confusion. Even fear. She could only imagine how awful it must feel not to be able to recall where you'd saved the documents and words and written thoughts that defined the most important time of your life; not to be able to remember the story you wanted to share with your granddaughter, so it would inspire her and comfort her and help shape the woman she would become; not to know that even after you were gone, the events that made you who you were would be part of a new generation's story.

"It's all so cute," Jenna continued. "Look, she even has report cards. I must have shown them to her, and she asked to keep them. She wanted to save a piece of the little girl you once were, so—"

"Sophie," Sweet said. "It's the story of the beginning of your life. It's the first part of your story."

"And that means it's important?" Sophie said.

"Of course it is," Sweet said. "It's where you began."

Jenna watched as Sophie walked over to her grandmother, then leaned down and hugged her. She was so proud of her daughter. Sophie may have been angry and hurt this year by the divorce, but she still was full of love. Her heart was as a big as her grandmother's.

"You know what's funny, Sweet?" Sophie said. "All this time we were trying to find your story. But you were making my story. Right from the beginning."

"Yes, I was," said Sweet. "And now you have a story in the boxes, just like me. And you know what else, Soph? I remember now, I thought this was the perfect place to hide another letter. Right with your memories. Look under everything, I bet you'll find it."

Sophie dug deeper into the box and pushed away the tissue paper. A moment later she pulled her hand out and waved a blue envelope in the air.

She got up and sat on the arm of Sweet's patio chair, and pulled the letter out of the envelope. "*Dear BG,*" she read.

Yesterday I met him. I'm going to keep his name to myself, because it's more romantic that way. More private. He's in my heart, and no matter what happens for the rest of my life, he'll always be there, forever mine. All I'll say is that his first name begins with a G and his last name is something long and Italian with too many vowels. That's what he said. But he also said it doesn't matter because he's going to shorten it and make it more American for when his first movie comes out. Because he's going to be a movie star, that's what he said.

And he sure looks like one. He has thick, honey-brown hair that he cuts real short on the sides and little longer in the front. And he has the most lovely brown eyes with sparks of gold and russet. And his smile—how do I describe it? His top lip is long and straight, while his bottom lip isn't straight at all—it has more of a "u" shape beneath his teeth. And it makes him look all hopeful and kind and welcoming. Like a "Gee, I really like you" kind of smile. Because he's kind of folksy and old-fashioned, which makes me laugh, because I thought I was running away from old-fashioned things. But I guess I was just running away from the way things were. And his ears are big, which I guess could be a bad thing to some people, but I think they're really cute.

Carrie, the girl I'm living with, works part-time for a movie studio, and she got me a job there, answering phones. He had a part in a movie there about Abraham Lincoln. And I guess it made a lot of sense because of how tall he is.

Someone at the studio said they heard he was having trouble with the Gettysburg Address, which he had to read for the part. So they were looking for someone to work with him on the speech, and that's how we met.

We sat at a little table in the back corner of a coffee shop, and that's when he told me he wanted to be famous and he was excited about the part because he had run away from his home just like me, except he did it so he could star in movies. I think he lived in Wisconsin or something. Anyway, he laughed because I ordered my coffee extra sweet, and so he started to call me by that nickname, Extra Sweet—like "Hey, Extra Sweet, I got us a table in the back."

Sophie looked up. "*That's* why people call you Sweet? The movie star gave you your nickname?"

Her grandmother nodded. "Oh my, he was so clever."

Jenna watched Sophie lean over and kiss her grandmother's forehead before turning back to the letter. A part of her wanted to get up and get her phone so she could snap a picture of this moment, the two of them sitting so close, their heads leaning in toward the letter. But she didn't want to interrupt the mood or call attention to herself. Instead, she looked at her mother and her daughter together, vowing that she would hold the image in her heart forever.

Sophie continued.

Every night he tells me so much about Abraham Lincoln, because he does a lot of research to help him with the part, so he can get into the character. He told me that Abraham Lincoln met the love of his life even before he went to Washington—that he was in love with a girl, but her father didn't think he was good enough. I bet the man would have changed his tune if he knew he was going to be President—you can't be limited by what people think you are the first time they see you.

Then last night, he told me about being an actor. He said it was about finding the one thought, the one moment, that mattered and making that the character's whole reason for being. And I told him I thought that was what life was about, that's why I came here, I was looking for my moment. And he said you have to believe in that moment with all your heart, and I said that's true of life, too. That's when he stood up and leaned across the table and held my face with his hands and kissed me.

Sophie giggled. "He kissed you, right there in the coffee place!" she said.

And then I told him about the Navy guy and veering off, and he told me he LOVED that idea. And now I'm wondering—was that my moment? The moment of the kiss? And what if it was? What if my moment was over? Was remembering it forever and knowing I had my moment—was that the best there could be? I got back to Carrie's house that night and couldn't sleep at all.

How would I recognize my moment? How would I live with myself if my moment was over?

Sophie turned the page over, then looked back in the envelope. "There's no more," she said. Then she knelt by the box and dug her hands inside. Jenna watched her, wishing she could ease the disappointment that was speeding headlong in Sophie's direction. It seemed certain to her that this was the end of the story, and while she was sorry she wouldn't get the closure she'd told Mrs. Pearl she was hoping for, she felt worse for Sophie. How would her daughter react when she realized she'd never know what the two words were or what happened to the movie star? She'd never even know his name. For a moment Jenna wished she had stuck to her guns from the beginning, that she had squashed the search weeks ago. She'd predicted this moment would happen, and now it was coming true.

But then again, if Sophie hadn't decided to investigate the story, she'd never have spent so much time with her grandmother. They'd never have grown as close as they did. Would Sophie understand that her relationship with her grandmother this summer was worth whatever disappointment she felt? Was she mature enough to see that?

Sophie pulled herself to her feet and sat back on the arm of her grandmother's chair. "I can't believe it's over," she said. "I don't want it to be over."

"I'm sorry, Soph," her grandmother said. "I know you wanted to know his name. I know you thought you could find him. I guess I never wrote it down. I thought it was more romantic that way."

"It's okay," said Sophie. "You wanted to keep his name to yourself. It was private. You didn't know back then you might want to tell people his name later on." She paused, and Jenna saw her running her tongue along the back of her teeth. She seemed to be trying to figure something out.

"It's weird," she finally said. "It's like I don't even care so much about the name anymore. I just don't want it to be over. It was fun going through the boxes. Sweet, do you think we can do it again? Do you think there's another secret story I can find?"

Sweet smiled and squeezed Sophie's hand. "Oh, I think I have a few more stories up my sleeve," she said. "In fact, I have one for you right now that just came to me. You know how all the letters started off with 'Dear BG'? I remember now—the moment on the train when I decided to do that. It stands for Baby Granddaughter. I always suspected I'd have a granddaughter. I just didn't know what her name would be."

"You mean you wrote these letters to me?" Sophie said. "Way before I was born?"

Sweet laughed. "Way, *way* before you were born."

"So you were really saving the story for me? Just like you said when we were at Mrs. Pearl's that day?"

Sweet nodded, and Jenna watched Sophie let that news sink in, enjoying how special it made her daughter feel.

"Wow, Sweet," Sophie said, shaking her head. "Just... wow." She kissed her grandmother's cheek, then looked over at Jenna. "Do you need me to help clean this up, Mom?"

"No, I'll take care of it," Jenna said. "You go on ahead and get ready for bed." She walked over and held Sophie's chin in her hand. "I love you," she said. "I'm proud of you. You made these last few weeks amazing."

Sophie smiled and went into the house, and Jenna pulled a chair over next to her mother's. "I think she must be the only eleven-year-old in the world who thinks that spending every night with her mother and grandmother makes it a great summer," she said. "You're amazing too, Mom."

"I don't know about that," her mother said. "I'm just glad to have you two around."

"So you think you have another story to tell?"

Her mom sighed. "Honestly, sweetheart, I don't think this story is over. I know I wrote more letters. They're somewhere else, somewhere even more secret than the closet. I wanted them good and hidden. I never imagined I'd forget where I put them."

"It doesn't matter," Jenna said. "As long as we get to spend more time with you. I feel that way just like Sophie does."

Her mom pulled herself up off the chair. "I'm exhausted, and there's still a lot to clean up. Let's get started, shall we?"

"Don't worry about it, Mom," Jenna said. "I'll take care of it."

"Are you sure?"

"Yes, it's fine. I have a lot to think about."

"I'll leave you to it, then. Goodnight, my bluebell girl. I love you."

"Goodnight, Mom," Jenna said. "I love you, too."

Her mom went into the house, and Jenna cleared the table and brought the dishes to the kitchen. She put them down on the countertop and then leaned against the sink, feeling like she might cry. There were so many emotions rising inside of her. She was happy that Sophie and her mother had come so far together and were looking forward to more fun evenings in each other's company. But she couldn't help but feel that the ending of the movie star story, the opening of the last box, was not enough of a resolution for her. It had been wonderful to return to Lake Summers, to see her mother recover and Sophie thrive, and it had been wonderful, too, to reconnect with Troy. But that part of her life was still unsettled. Where was he now, and what did his disappearance mean for her? How could she give him her heart when he wasn't around to accept it? How could she move forward when the house next door was empty and dark?

She finished with the dishes, went upstairs to kiss Sophie goodnight, and then came back to the patio. The last box was still outside, its contents strewn over the table, and she supposed she should clean it up in case it rained or the wind kicked up. She put all the things—the popsicle frames, the cards, the papers with the sparkly stars—back into the box. Then she picked up the letter from the ground where it had ended up. She went inside and placed it on the kitchen counter, in case Sophie wanted to read it again. Then she brought the box downstairs. In the basement, Sophie had stacked all the boxes in a corner, so the closet was now empty. Jenna figured she might as well start to put them all away. She opened the closet, thinking it best to work her way up.

And that's when she saw it.

It was a safe, about the size of a jewelry box, near the bottom of the closet. It was attached to the floor and bolted to the left-hand wall, obscured by the shelf above it. She had seen it before, she realized now—it was the place where her father kept the family's most valuable papers and documents. But suddenly she saw it in a whole new way. Her breath grew short, as she focused on a spot—no, not a spot; a chip—on the front of the safe. A chip in the front panel of the safe's black, pebbled surface.

The chip that her mom remembered wasn't the one on the closet door; it was on the door of the safe inside the closet. Her mother must have decided to hide the last, most important letters here, once she'd moved back into the house for good. She must have thought it the perfect hiding space, after Jenna's dad died. A place where no one would discover them until she was ready to reveal them to BG. Her granddaughter.

She knelt and pulled on the door of the safe. Somehow whatever locking mechanism there had once been no longer worked, so the door stuck a bit but then opened right up. A few envelopes and rolled-up folders tumbled out. And behind them were two blue envelopes.

Jenna walked back upstairs into the living room and curled up on her mother's chair. She would have expected to be excited, or even giddy, but instead she felt calm and patient. She thought about waiting until the morning to read the letters with Sophie, but knew she didn't have the willpower to resist them so long.

And besides, she thought, it would be better if she read them by herself first. They were sure to contain something very significant, or her mother wouldn't have hidden them separately from the others. She wanted to have the whole night to process what it was she'd discover. Then she'd be prepared to share the letters with Sophie and answer her questions about whatever they contained.

She opened the first letter, recognized her mother's curvy handwriting and started to read.

Dear BG,

The next night was the most exciting night of all. Because he found it! The moment in Lincoln's speech that made everything make sense. And I was amazed because it's a really serious speech with a lot of old words all about war and dying. But then he pointed to the words he thought were so important: There is still unfinished work.

"Those are the words?" I asked. "I don't get it. Of course he had unfinished work. He had so much left to do."

"It's not about particular work, Sweet. It's a way of living," he said. "It's about not giving up, not giving in. We are all unfinished work, we will always be unfinished work because nothing ever ends. Our stories go on. We're never done. We think we finish something, we think we put something behind us, but everything we do leads to the next thing. We're all stories still being written. All our lives, we're unfinished work."

Honestly, I wasn't sure that night that I even understood. But he was so thrilled with his ideas, and I just knew that those two words were going to stay with me for the rest of my life. And we stayed together all that night, and I never, ever wanted the night to end. I never met anyone like him before, and I never spent a night like that before. His eyes were so open, he just wanted to be filled up with life and meaning and people. He lived life big and grand and so differently from anyone I'd ever met before.

And everything changed after that night. I was someone new, I was different, because I knew him, and knowing him was changing me. I never wanted to be without him. I got through the days at work by knowing that I'd see him at night.

And it was during those too-few days that I came to understand the meaning of the two words he found. Unfinished work. That was the whole point. He was unfinished work, I was unfinished work. As long as you were alive, life was unfinished. Maybe it sounds silly. It sounds a little silly to me now that I'm writing it. But it's everything. Because I think that life is at its worst when we think there's nothing new coming up. That's why I was so unhappy at home, because I thought I had to grow up and be just like my mother. And my mother is a good mother, don't get me wrong. But just knowing, just realizing, that that's not the way I have to be—it was just the most wonderful lesson. I don't have to be like the Navy guy only this once. I can veer off whenever I want. Oh, it doesn't have to be so big as running away across the country. I can veer in little ways. It's up to me, that's the point. The story will always be unfinished. But how I write it is up to me.

Jenna looked up from the page to the clock over the fireplace. It was almost midnight. The sky through the window was black. The whole house was still, even Mo was so sound asleep, he wasn't even snoring. The lamp on the table next to her was the only light on in the house, the only light on in the world, she thought. Here was her mother at seventeen, trying to understand all her feelings, trying to find the meaning of life, trying to figure out, as she stood on the brink of adulthood, how her life was supposed to go. On the one hand, she felt motherly toward this young girl, Sweet, who had so many questions. But on the other hand, she also felt the weight of her mother's wisdom, even as a seventeen-year-old. There they were, the words her mother told Sophie were magical. Unfinished work. That was the lesson her mom had wanted to teach Sophie, during this horrible year when her parents split up. She had written this story for Sophie almost sixty years ago. And she had waited until this summer to tell it to her—the summer when Sophie needed it most.

Jenna turned the page over. And found one more surprise.

When he was having trouble with the Gettysburg Address, he did a lot of research about Lincoln and the Civil War and Washington, D.C. He even went to just about all the flower shops in Los Angeles until he found one that would order him a bouquet of these purple flowers called Virginia bluebells, which he said was an incredibly hearty flower and had grown in Washington, D.C. for centuries. They were pretty, like little clusters of silky bells, and they smelled sweet, a little like lilacs but not as strong. He said Lincoln would have seen them, and it was the closest he'd ever come to seeing something Lincoln saw. And they were just about the prettiest flowers I'd ever seen, and it was amazing to think that Lincoln had seen these very flowers, too. And that's when I started thinking how some things last forever. Like love. And the feeling you get when you hold a beautiful fragrant flower. You know what? If I ever go back home, the first thing I'm going to do is grow a garden of Virginia bluebells right outside my window.

Jenna stayed still for a moment feeling the thin, smooth paper between her fingers. So this was why her mother had created the bluebell garden, this was why they were the bluebell girls. It was a reminder that some things never die. Like the sweetness of a flower. Like the sweetness of love.

She opened the other letter. There was an airline ticket taped to the paper. American Airlines, Flight 238. Los Angeles to New York.

Dear BG,

And before I knew it, I was on an airplane coming home, my dad in the seat next to me, snoring away. The stewardess gave me a Coke and a silver pin shaped like a pair of wings. It was my first-ever airplane ride.

I was alone in the coffee shop when my dad showed up. Just like that. My parents made some calls when they couldn't find me, and one of the calls was to Carrie's parents. So they gave me two weeks and then my dad decided to bring me home. And you know what? When I saw my dad I wasn't even all that surprised. I knew they wouldn't let me go forever. I knew they loved me and would find me eventually. So my dad walked over to my table, and I would have thought he'd be yelling at me, right there in the shop, but it looked like he was crying. And then I felt bad. Because I did love my parents, too. I didn't mean to make them sad. And all he said was, "It's time to come home."

And you know what I did, BG? I nodded and said okay. Because I kind of agreed. I was only seventeen. I was tired and ready for my bed, for my home, for my mother's cooking. I was homesick for the lake and for going into town and having hamburgers at the Grill. There were only a few days of summer left. I was going to be a senior. Next year I'd be in college.

We went back to Carrie's, and I called my boss to tell him I was quitting. And then I gathered up my stuff from Carrie's, and we got a taxi to the airport. I thought about asking Dad if we could stop at the movie studio so I could say goodbye. But then I decided not to. He was filming his big scene in a few hours. I didn't want to distract him.

I guess you'd think I'd be really sad, right? But I wasn't. Because it wasn't over. I was unfinished work, like the words in the speech. I still had a whole story, a lifetime of stories to write.

I wanted to make my own life, not fall in line with someone else's dream.

Although it didn't turn out to be a dream come true for him after all. Carrie wrote to me a couple of days after I left. The studio canceled the movie, she didn't know why. But she said it happened a lot out there.

There was no way I could find him. And I wondered if he even would have wanted me to find him. He was all into moments, and we'd had ours, right? It was time for both of us to find the next one.

So there I was on that plane, on the red-eye, flying overnight, heading to New York. It was three hours later in the day there. So actually I was flying toward the dawn. The new day was coming fast.

There was something wonderful about that.

Jenna read the letter a second time and then held it against her chest as she settled back into her mother's chair. She loved the enthusiastic and passionate seventeen-year-old her mother had been, and she loved that her mother had gone all the way across the country, wanting to understand where she fit into the world. And she loved how her mother had found not just adventure, but love. Deep, crazy, love. And most of all, she loved the way her mother had realized in the end that she didn't have just one chance to invent her life or to fall in love. Just the opposite. She understood that every day, in a sense, she was flying into the dawn. No wonder that phrase, *unfinished work*, stayed with her all these years. If Jenna had stopped to think about it, she'd have recognized weeks ago that these were the two words Sophie had been searching for. She didn't need the final letters to know that these were the words her mother lived by.

But she was glad she'd found it anyway.

Unfinished work. They were words she had adored as a child because they meant you could do anything—crash into a brick wall, climb down a twisted oak tree, or run to the back of the bluebell garden to kiss the boy you loved. They were words she had forgotten all about after she grew up and married Matt. But they were words she understood even better now than she ever had before. Being unfinished was a call to arms, an awakening. It didn't just mean that sometimes she was wrong; it meant there was openness, opportunity. It meant something could change, even the whole world could change. Being unfinished meant that something new, something wonderful, could happen. Being unfinished meant there was something to grasp onto.

Suddenly two shafts of light appeared outside. Stepping over Mo, she went to the window. They seemed to be headlights, and they were coming from Troy's driveway.

She went to the closet and grabbed her sweater. Maybe her mother and Sophie were asleep—but there was someone awake who would want what she'd found. Someone who knew what it was like to be young and in love. Someone who needed to know that he didn't need to be perfect for her, that he could be unfinished.

She left the house, not even bothering to find her sandals. She closed the door softly behind her and ran in bare feet down the front walk.

CHAPTER TWENTY-ONE

The wind was picking up, and Jenna's hair whipped across her face as she made her way over toward Troy's house. His car was backed up into the driveway, his lights on, his trunk open.

Then she saw the light above the front step switch off. Troy came out a moment later, in a half-zip sweatshirt and shorts. She saw him lock the door, then test it to be sure it wouldn't open. Then he strode down toward his car.

"Jenna!" he exclaimed, stopping short when he saw her. "You scared me. What are you doing up?"

"I came to show you…" She extended her arms, showing him the papers. "I found them," she said. "My mother's letters. The story she was trying to show Sophie. She did run away to Hollywood, it was all true. Unfinished work—those were the two words she wanted Sophie to know."

"That's great," he said, though he didn't sound that excited. He continued toward the open trunk. "I know that's what you were wanting. Does Sophie know?"

"Not yet, she's sleeping," she said, following him and standing alongside him next to his car. "I'll show her tomorrow. But I had to tell someone. And your car lights were on, and…" She realized now that there was a duffel over his shoulder. He tossed it in the trunk. She saw two other suitcases already inside. "Where are you going?"

"I'm leaving," he said. "Steven has a cabin by the Canadian border."

"I know, Mrs. Pearl told me. But what do you mean, for a few days, or something?"

"I'm going there for good. I came down for the rest of my clothes."

"What are you talking about? You live here. You have a job here."

"I don't," he said. "I left the clinic."

"But what about all the animals you care for?"

"Claire will take over the practice as soon as she's ready to come back. In the meantime, people can go up to Lyons Hill."

"But what about the award you're getting?"

"Claire can accept that, too."

Jenna couldn't believe what she was hearing. That awful but familiar feeling that she had merely imagined her time with Troy crept up on her again. "But it's you they're honoring. You're the one…"

He didn't respond, but went back to his front step and returned with an insulated bag. "Here," he said, holding it toward her. "Some of the low-fat beef I made for Mo when he was coming into the office. I froze it, and you may as well have it. And there are some cans of his food, too. I was going to leave it for you on your front step. With a note—"

"Leave it? What are you talking about? You live here, people need you—"

"Jenna." He held his palm out, and she stepped back. She felt an ache developing deep beneath her stomach. She didn't want to hear this. She didn't want to hear what he was going to say. Just when everything had changed for the better. How was it that everything was changing yet again?

"I can't do it," he said. "I thought I could. But it was a mistake to come here. I can't stay in town."

"No, wait," she said. "What about the other night? What about the note you left, about the five days we had? What about all we talked about?" She thought of their kiss, the way he'd touched her.

"I know," he said. "And that's the reason I wanted to stay. But I can't make it work."

"That doesn't make sense. What about everyone in town who cares so much for you? What about the people who bring their pets to you? What about… us?"

"That's what I'm saying, Jenna," he said. "I keep getting involved. And I don't want to get involved. I don't want to care."

"But you do care—"

"But I don't want to. I came here to get away from caring. And it was a mistake, to come back to a place where I knew people. And people knew me. Maybe it would have been better if you hadn't even been here. Maybe I could have stayed then."

She took in a sharp breath. "What are you saying? You're leaving because of me?"

"No. I mean, yes." He put his palm on the car and leaned his body weight forward, his other hand on his waist. "You remind me of everything, okay? You remind me of everything I lost by getting too involved. I thought I was doing the right thing that summer when I decided to leave town to go to college. I thought I was doing the right thing when I told you to meet me on the footpath so I could head out that night."

"But it wasn't your fault," she said. "Your dad's heart attack—it was a terrible tragedy, but it wasn't your fault."

He looked up at her, his palms raised. "I know that, okay? I know it wasn't my fault. But I don't want to be responsible for anyone anymore, don't you see? I don't want to be involved."

"But you are involved. You have relationships here. People know you and care about you. Like my family. And me. I don't want to lose you. And I don't think you want to lose us—"

"You're right, I do care. I care about you too much. I care about your mom, I care about Sophie, I care about your dog! And I don't want to. Because you know what, Jenna? I can't bear to lose you again. I can't bear to lose anyone else."

"Oh, God, Troy."

"It's true. So what if you found the damn letters? So what if you know what the two words are? It doesn't matter. It doesn't change anything—"

"It changes everything!" she said. His voice had been getting louder, and now hers was, too. She looked toward her house.

"It matters a lot," she said in a loud whisper, practically spitting out the last word.

"Why? It's not real. It's a story, it's in the past. Okay, maybe it gives you a little entertainment for a few weeks, something to share with Sophie when she's missing her dad. So what, that she once went to Hollywood?"

"So what?"

"What's the point? What does it matter that your mother called this her unfinished work? So now it's finished. What does it matter?"

"But it's not finished," she said. "That *is* the point."

He shook his head. "That doesn't make sense."

"Yes, it does," she said. "We're all unfinished work. The mistake we make is thinking we can finish it. Troy, you can run away and be alone or you can stay here and be in the world, but either way, you're writing a story. You're making your life. You can't decide not to have a story. All you can decide is which story to have.

"You pushed away your girlfriend in Philadelphia and now you're pushing me away," she said. "Doesn't that tell you something?"

"Like what?"

"That the way you're trying to be… it's not possible."

He looked down, and she thought he was thinking about what she said. She hadn't spoken as artfully as her mother had in the letters. But she had made her point.

"No, it is possible," he said. "I just have to be smarter about it."

He pushed out a breath and walked past her to the driver's door. He grabbed the door handle. "Steven's coming up next week to put the house on the market. It's what my brothers have wanted to do for months now. I told him you're here, with your mother and your daughter. I'm sure he'll be happy to see you."

"You're not even going to wait until morning to say goodbye to them?" She gave a little smile. "Or even to Mo?"

"Tell them I said goodbye. Give Mo the beef. He'll know who it's from." He dropped his hand from the door and turned to face her. "I'm sorry, Jenna. But you fell in the love with the wrong guy. Back when we were kids, and this summer, too. I'm not capable of… of writing the story you want me to write. Okay? I don't agree with you. Not everything is unfinished. Sometimes things are… done."

He reached out and touched her cheek. "I never meant to hurt you. I thought we were on the brink of something the other night. I thought I could do it. But I can't."

"What will you do up there?" she asked softly.

"I don't know," he said. "I'll figure it out. I have a little saved up, and there'll be money from the sale of the house. I'm sure I'll find something to pay the bills. Pass the time."

She nodded and moved a step closer to him. She thought about telling him more from her mother's letters. But maybe it was time to admit to herself that those five days with him, back when they were young, were just that. Five days. And nothing more.

"I'll miss you," she said. "I wish…" She wanted to continue. But she was speechless. She didn't even know what the end of that sentence would be. He had given it his best shot, but he was who he was. Her mother had known when it was time to say goodbye to her first love out in Hollywood. She wasn't as smart as her mother. But she still should be able to figure out when it was time to say goodbye.

She put her hands on his waist and pressed the top of her head into his chest. She felt him kiss her hair. Then he took her arms and slowly pushed her back. With her chin lowered, she nodded. She brushed her hair away from her eyes and wrapped it behind her ears.

"Okay," she said. "Okay."

"Jenna…" he said. "I'm sorry."

"I'll be okay," she said. "I'm okay."

They stood there that way for a few moments, his hands on her arms, her head facing down. He squeezed her arms gently, then released his hold. He opened the car door and got behind the wheel. She backed up onto the lawn as he started the car. She raised her hand. He waved back and pulled out.

The fog was rolling in as she watched him drive away. It enveloped his car, and soon she couldn't see it anymore. She walked back to her house, stopping for a moment to look up toward her old bedroom window, the window behind which Sophie was sleeping, the window above the bluebell garden.

CHAPTER TWENTY-TWO

The next morning, Jenna went downstairs before either Sophie or Sweet was awake. She had barely slept that night, waking up every half hour or so and staring at the ceiling, remembering that Troy had left her for good. It was worse than when he had turned away from her, refusing to look at her, on the morning of his father's funeral. She could accept now that he had done that. He was devastated by his grief and his certainty that he was responsible for his father's death. But this was different. They were older, and the storm had happened so long ago. They were both alone and lonely, and they knew each other so well, and they cared about each other. And they'd had that kiss, a kiss she thought was the first step on their path forward. They had the opportunity to put the past behind them, to forgive themselves for whatever role they'd played in the horrible events of that night, to envision a new life. Coming together was their unfinished work, as her mother would say. But Troy wanted no part in it. He didn't want to feel anything anymore.

She made a cup of coffee, left a note on the kitchen table to say she'd be back before noon, gave Mo some breakfast, and then quietly slipped out of the house. She'd been meaning to go over to the hospital for a while, to thank Dr. Roberts in person and to let him know how well Sweet was doing. Sherry had mentioned that her grandfather worked on Saturdays during the summer, and Jenna was free to head there, since she didn't have to go to the newspaper office today and Sophie didn't have camp. She figured she would share the two letters she'd found in the safe with Sophie and her mother when she got back. She wanted to make the trip to the hospital sooner rather than later. Because she wasn't sure how many more weekends she'd be here in Lake Summers.

Not that she had decided for sure to leave. She didn't know what she was going to do. But Troy's decision to run off to Steven's cabin spurred her to re-examine all the decisions she'd made that summer. She'd been so happy to be back in Lake Summers, and so drawn to reconnect with Troy that she'd almost been living a fantasy. But there were other considerations as well. She'd been ignoring Matt for weeks now, and acting as though her life back in Rye didn't even exist. She hadn't told Matt she wanted to move here with Sophie for good, and she had no idea how he'd react once he found out. She also didn't know when Matt planned to tell Sophie about his engagement, or how she would help Sophie deal with what would surely come as a big shock. She had just shut her mind off to all of that. But maybe it was time to give it all some thought.

She closed the front door and headed to the driveway. Opening the door of her car, she looked up at the side of the house and noticed there were still a few bluebells in bloom. It was unusual that they'd lasted so long into the summer, but then again spring had come late this year. She went back into the house for a pair of scissors and a ribbon. She thought it would be nice to gather the remaining flowers together and give them to Dr. Roberts as a thank you gesture.

With the bouquet next to her on the passenger seat, she started up the car, and headed out for the hospital. She wondered again if it made sense to move here now. Could she possibly be happy living right next to Troy's house, knowing he was gone for good? It had been hard enough to do that the first time, back when her family arrived in town to find that the Jasons had left and couldn't be found. She didn't want to have to deal with that again. Still, she would be sorry to leave. She loved the lake, as she always did. She loved the market and the smoothie shop, she loved taking early-morning walks with Mo to get coffee and muffins from Mrs. Pearl's. She loved working at the paper, and had been looking forward to starting full-time in September. Her preview of the historical exhibit was coming along so well. She'd started off describing the photos of the firefighter she'd nicknamed Anthony, and the little girl on the station platform who reminded her of her mother, and she planned to reflect on how the past would never stop shaping the town and its residents. She now saw how she could draw inspiration from her mother's letters. She would conclude that history was neither a safety net nor a prison, but a springboard that propelled you to your next experience.

She turned onto Route 12, making good time as traffic tended to be light on weekend mornings. If she did decide to leave, she'd have to think about what would be next for her mother. The doctor had been clear that her mom could no longer live alone, so going ahead with Chloe's idea to move her to Long Island might be the best option—the only option. Chloe would be back in a couple of weeks for their mom's birthday. They could have a party for her, and then she and Chloe could start to make plans. Maybe it would work out. Maybe Sophie would be better off in Rye, so she could see her dad more often.

She arrived at the hospital, checked in at the desk, and asked how to get to the doctor's office. The guard gave her the floor number, and she proceeded to the elevator. But it turned out she hadn't even had to ask. She found him standing outside the elevator bank.

"Dr. Roberts!" she called.

"Jenna!" he said, his white mustache widening above his smile. "It's good to see you. And please call me Gavin. I've been hoping we'd see each other again. Sherry tells me your mother's doing well."

"She is," Jenna said. "We've had a good summer. She and my daughter have gotten so close. It's been great for all of us."

"That's terrific," he said. "You should be proud of yourself. It sounds like you uprooted your whole life to stay here with your mom while she recovered from that fall. I have no doubt that helped her a lot."

Just then the elevator opened and two women in blue scrubs came out. One of them came over and tapped him on the shoulder. "Gavin! I'm glad I ran into you," she said. "That was one amazing recipe."

"Did you like it?" he said. "It's one of my favorites."

"It was the best tortellini we'd ever tasted," she said. "And we're just as Italian as you!" She looked over at Jenna. "Tell him to give you his tortellini recipe. You'll never eat tortellini anywhere else again!"

She walked off with her colleague, and Jenna laughed. "So you're a cook, too?" she said.

He shrugged. "What can I tell you? I'm a man of many talents."

"But Roberts?" she asked. "That hardly sounds Italian."

"My real last name is Robertiadella. A long Italian name with too many vowels. Nobody could pronounce it. I started going by Roberts years ago."

Jenna nodded but felt her smile diminish. There was something odd about what he'd just said. *A long Italian name with too many vowels.* Where had she heard that before?

He pointed to the flowers in her hands. "Those are pretty," he said. "Virginia bluebells?"

"Yes… oh, I almost forgot. They're for you," she said, holding them out. "I'm sorry, I just got a little distracted. You know they're called Virginia bluebells?"

"I do," he said. "I grow them myself. I learned about them long ago when I lived in California. They were one of Abraham Lincoln's personal favorites."

He reached out and shook her hand. "Well, I'd better get going, I've got a meeting upstairs and a ton of paperwork to get done before the end of the day. Good luck, Jenna, and all my best to your family. Give me a call when you're settled and let me know how you're all doing."

He got into the elevator, and she watched the doors close, and then she stayed there, still, for a couple of moments, feeling people passing all around her. She could feel herself getting sideswiped, and she was sure people were wondering who this lady was who was frozen by the elevators. Did they think she just got bad news? Did they think she was going to faint? Was somebody going to hand her a paper cup of water? Another set of elevators opened just then, and she walked inside and pressed the button, glad she had asked the guard for his office location after all.

And as the elevator took off, she couldn't help thinking about unfinished work. And the one lesson that her mother hadn't mentioned in her letters. That sometimes you don't even realize you have unfinished work—even when it's right there in front of you, helping you bring your mother home. Encouraging you to believe you're up to the job. Sending you a granddaughter to help out. Sometimes unfinished business shows up when you least expect it. And presents itself right in front of your face.

She got off on the eighth floor and found Suite B, as the guard had instructed. She opened the door and walked right past the front desk, ignoring a voice that said, "Can I help you?" from behind. He was in a small office, sitting at his desk. She knocked on the open door, and he looked up.

"I'm sorry to bother you," Jenna said. "But I wanted to ask you… you see, my mother had Sophie on a journey this summer to find some letters about her long-lost love."

"Oh?" he said. "She told her that?"

"We found the letters, and they were all about this boy she met in California who was going to star in a movie. About how they met and how they spent all their time together and how incredibly in love with him she was. And I know this is ridiculous, how crazy this is going to sound—but something you said just now about the bluebells and Abraham Lincoln… I just have to ask it. Dr. Roberts… Gavin… are you the man my mother fell in love with?"

He looked at her a few moments more, then leaned back in his chair and pressed his palms on his desk. "I knew I said too much. I saw it on your face. I never meant to intrude on your life. I just wanted to see if I could help."

"So you are her long-lost love?" she said. He nodded. "Why didn't you tell me?"

"Because I didn't know if you knew about me. I didn't know if she'd want you to know. She put me behind her long ago. I wasn't even sure if she'd remember me."

"Not remember you?" Jenna said. "You were one of the most important people in her life. She wrote your whole story together in these letters she saved. She wanted Sophie to find them, to learn about love." Jenna shook her head. "But how did you end up here? You're not from around here, are you?"

"No, not originally," he said, gesturing for her to sit down in the chair opposite his desk. "After my movie was scrapped, I went home to Wisconsin. But I never forgot your mother. I remembered how she'd talk about Lake Summers, so I came out here to find her. And I saw her—at the lake one day. She was with a fellow, putting lotion on his shoulders, and she looked very happy. I heard someone call her Mrs. Clayton. That's when I knew for sure she was married and it was time to move on."

"But you stayed here anyway?"

"I decided I liked it here in the Northeast," he said. He leaned forward and clasped his hands on the desk. "I got a place a few towns north and eventually became a doctor and began working here at the hospital. Fell in love, got married, had a few kids, they had a few kids. My wife passed away three years ago."

"I'm sorry," Jenna said.

"It's okay," he said. "We had a good marriage. Lots of good memories. Anyway, I hadn't even thought about your mother for years, but I happened to be working the night she came in. The name Clayton rang a bell, and then I heard one of the nurses saying that people in town called her Sweet. So I knew for sure it was her. I was kind of tickled that she'd kept the nickname."

He paused. "I take it your dad passed away? How long ago?" he said.

"When Sophie was a baby," she said. "They had a good marriage, too."

He rubbed his chin with his fingers. "I'm really sorry I didn't tell you," he said. "I never meant to deceive you. I just thought she put me behind her years ago. I didn't realize our story still meant something to her."

"It means a lot," Jenna said. "It's nearly all we've talked about this summer. You were her first love."

"Do you…" He hesitated. "Do you think she might like to see me?"

"I think she would like that very much," Jenna said.

*

He came over the next day, wearing jeans and a button-down shirt, looking casual but just as handsome as he did in a white coat. Jenna had decided to keep his identity a surprise, so she just told her mom and Sophie that a special guest was coming for lunch. Sweet wore her peach dress with the fabric belt and the button earrings. Jenna thought she looked radiant.

She led her mother to the front step just as Gavin pulled into the driveway. Sophie followed behind, holding Mo in her arms. Gavin came up the walk and took Sweet's hands in his. "Sweet," he said. "You look beautiful."

"Gavin," she said. "You haven't changed a bit."

A few minutes later, the two old friends were out on the patio. Jenna brought Sophie into the kitchen to get lunch ready.

"So who is that guy?" Sophie asked. "Just some old friend?"

"Much more than that," Jenna said. "Soph, I know you're not going to believe this. But you know who that is? That's the movie star."

"What?" Sophie went to the window and looked out. "What do you mean? Mom, are you making this up?"

"Not at all," Jenna said. "I hardly believe it myself. But he's a doctor now. He works at the hospital where Sweet was taken when she fell. It was one big coincidence, and I figured it out when I went to the hospital yesterday. And you know what else?" she said. "I also found two more letters your grandmother wrote."

"No way!" Sophie said. "How is that possible? I thought we looked in all the boxes in the closet."

"It was in a safe in the closet," Jenna said. "Come, sit. Let me show you."

Sophie sat down, and Jenna pulled the two letters out of the drawer where she'd stored them. She gave them to Sophie and sat down next to her. "This is the rest of the story she wanted to tell you," she said.

Sophie read the letters to herself while Jenna watched her, twirling Sophie's ponytail around her fingers. She was glad Sophie now had the complete story. She was glad Sophie would now know her grandmother had been okay with putting her California adventure behind her. And suddenly it struck her as quite a coincidence that both she and her mother had fallen so deeply—and so secretly—in love when they were each seventeen. But then again, maybe not a coincidence at all. There was something magical about that age, she thought—an age when love could be boundless, because the responsibilities and limitations of adulthood were still in the future. She wondered for a moment what Sophie would be like at seventeen. She hoped her daughter wouldn't feel the need to travel across the country for love, or to climb out her window and steal into the night when a huge storm was approaching. Still, she did hope Sophie would know the kind of love both she and her mother had known when they were approaching the very end of childhood. She would never want her daughter to miss that experience.

Sophie sighed when she was done. "Wow," she said. "She was brave. She went all the way to Los Angeles by herself."

"That's true," Jenna said. "But you know what I think, honey? I think she was also brave because she came back."

"But she came back because her dad went and got her."

"But she also came back because she realized she didn't have to stay away anymore. That her life was her unfinished work, like the letter said. I think she was brave because she realized it was okay to come home. There'd be plenty more adventures in her life."

She watched Sophie crinkle her forehead as she considered this.

"So she was brave to run away and then she was brave for wanting to come back?" she said.

"I think so," Jenna said.

"Mom?"

"Yeah?"

"Did we run away this summer?"

Jenna thought back to the day she left Rye, and all that had been going wrong. The broken air conditioning. The sick dog. The angry daughter. The messed-up relationship with her ex-husband. The angry sister. The magical, unfounded belief that everything would be fixed if she came back to the town and the house where she had been so happy. The desire to turn her back on the things that were making her uncomfortable back home.

"I think, in a way, I did," she said.

"Do you think we should go home?"

"What do you think?"

"I like it here," Sophie said. "I like being with Sweet. But I miss being back home, too. I miss Daddy."

"I have mixed feelings, too," Jenna said. "We don't have to decide now. The nice thing is we have choices. We can talk some more later."

Jenna pulled from the refrigerator the tray of sandwiches she'd prepared that morning, and the four of them had lunch together. Seeing her mother so comfortable with Gavin, Jenna started to wonder if she'd been making a mistake, thinking she had to choose Rye or Lake Summers. Life wasn't a this-or-that proposition. She and Sophie could go back to Rye and deal with the unfinished work she'd left there—but they could always come back to Lake Summers, too. It was just as her mother had said in her last letter, the one she had written on the plane back to New York. In a way, life was always about starting over. Beginning new adventures. Flying into the dawn.

When lunch was over, Jenna and Sophie cleared the table, while Sweet walked Gavin to his car. "Mom?" Sophie said as she gathered up the napkins. "When did Sweet stop loving Gavin? Was it when she fell in love with Grandpa?"

Jenna thought for a moment. "I don't believe she ever stopped loving him," she said. "She just loved your grandfather, too. But in a different way, because she wanted to be his wife. Love doesn't have to end. You can still love someone even if you're not with them."

"Does that mean you still love Daddy?" she said.

Jenna put down the plate she was holding. "I never thought about it that way," she said. "But you know what? I guess in a way I do love him. Because if I hadn't married him, I wouldn't have had you."

She picked up the plate again and put it in the dishwasher. Then she folded her arms across her chest. She had surprised herself by saying she still loved Matt.

But it was a good way to feel as she approached the next chapter of her life.

She waited until Sophie took the napkins to the washer downstairs, then reached for her phone and punched in the familiar number. It was going to be strange to speak, but she knew it was time to do so. For far too long, they'd been communicating only by text.

She waited for a few rings, and then he answered.

"It's Jenna," she said. "I'm calling to say that we can't go on like this. We have to start talking to each other. We may not be a regular family anymore, but we'll always be a family because we share a daughter. And raising her is our unfinished work, and there's no way to do it unless we work together."

"Jenna," Matt said. "I'm glad you called."

CHAPTER TWENTY-THREE

Jenna watched Sophie and Mo through the patio door. They ran across the patio and down to the grass at the far end of the property as Sophie zipped and darted and made little circles and figure eights, looking over her shoulder to make sure Mo was keeping up.

She walked out onto the deck, pulling her sweater tighter around her shoulders. It was three weeks since she'd reunited Sweet and Gavin, and so much had changed since then. Even the weather. This morning was beautiful, the sky almost completely cloudless and the sun strong, but there was a slight chill in the air. Fall came early in the mountains. If she looked out on the horizon, she could see the very tips of the leafy trees in the distance starting to change from green to gold. Transition was in the air, still remote but unmistakable.

So it seemed a perfect day to celebrate a birthday.

"Anything else to do?" a voice said from the kitchen.

She walked inside, where Chloe was standing, surveying the platters on the table and the countertops. "Why don't I set up the glasses and plates?" she said. "And as soon as Ed gets out of the shower, I'll put him to work filling the ice buckets and bringing in the champagne. I cannot believe how good everything looks!"

Jenna nodded. It was quite an assortment of food. Mrs. Pearl had dropped by early that morning with dozens of muffins, croissants, and pastries she'd started baking before dawn. She'd also baked the birthday cake, with a devil's food base, layers of caramel cream and chocolate ganache, and shredded, sugared raspberries around the words "Happy Birthday, Sweet," which were written in vanilla bean icing.

"I think we're all set," Jenna said. "Sherry and Gavin are bringing over some pasta dishes, and Stan and Trey are bringing a huge vat of this new smoothie they invented for Mom." She remembered hearing them start to brainstorm the recipe when she stopped by the shop last week to invite them to the party. They thought it was too easy just to play off the name Sweet, so they decided to honor her invention, the Lake Summers Theatrical, instead.

"It's called Sweet's Theatri-cola Smoothie," Trey had said when she returned a few days later to taste the finished product. He held out a small sample cup. "It has a berry base and some almond milk for texture, and a touch of molasses for body, and some cola syrup for sweetness and flavor."

Jenna took a sip, and while the ingredients sounded a little off-putting all together, the result was delicious—refreshing and flavorful, with a mellow sweetness and a hint of caramel. "I love it," she said. "My mom will, too."

"You just have to get past the color," Stan added. And he had a point—the drink had a purple tint, kind of like pink chalk blended with coffee. "But don't worry, this is just the prototype. We'll have the color improved in time for next summer's relaunch. I hope you'll be coming back for the premiere."

"I wouldn't miss it," Jenna said. That had been one of the biggest surprises of the last few weeks—the Lake Summers Theatrical was staging a comeback. When Sherry had heard about the theater program that Sweet had once created, she confided in Jenna that she had once had the acting bug, just like her grandfather. She had never done anything about it, but now she wondered if the town would consider a reboot of the program, and if she could be in charge.

"I have the best qualifications in the world," she'd said. "Twenty-four-seven access to your brilliant mother."

And that wasn't even the biggest idea that Sherry had proposed. Learning that Jenna was thinking of returning to Rye at least for a little while, and Chloe was investigating Ocean Vistas as Sweet's new home, she'd asked Jenna if there was still time to consider an alternative. "I love my grandfather, but it's time I moved out," she said. "So I'm wondering what you think about my moving in with Sweet while I'm still in school? I would do the cooking and grocery shopping and make sure she's safe, and that way she wouldn't have to leave her home. I love her, and I love it here. Is this something your family might consider?"

Jenna didn't know how quickly to say yes. Sweet was thrilled when she heard the plan, and even Chloe had to admit it was a good arrangement. In the last few weeks, Sweet hadn't had any bouts of forgetfulness. Jenna liked to think that Gavin's appearance after all these years was the cause of her mom's improvement.

Standing now in the kitchen surrounded by all the birthday foods, Jenna looked at her sister. "I can't believe we're actually here," she said. "When I got Sophie's call about Mom in the ambulance, I was scared we'd never get to this day."

Chloe put her arm around Jenna's shoulders. "I know," she said. "But I wish other things had worked out well, too."

Jenna nodded, knowing exactly what Chloe was talking about. Last night, after everyone else was asleep, she'd told Chloe all about Troy, from the night they met at the footpath when they were kids to the moment he got in his car and left a few weeks ago.

"I'm okay," Jenna said. She was glad to be on good terms with her sister again. Chloe had read their mom's letters last night and realized that learning about Gavin did not in any way affect her memory of the happy marriage her parents had had.

"Are you sure you won't consider moving to Long Island anyway?" she asked. "I mean, even though Mom's not coming?"

Jenna nodded. "I'm sure," she said. "I think if I did that now, I'd be running away again. Sometimes the bravest thing is just to turn around and go back home."

Chloe reached out to hug her, and that's when their mother came into the kitchen. She was wearing an outfit she'd picked up when Jenna brought her to Lake Summers Fashions last week—a floral-print shirt dress with buttons down the front and eyelet trim above the hem—along with pearl drop earrings and a pearl pendant necklace. Jenna thought she looked glamorous, as though she'd stepped out of the pages of a fashion magazine. Maybe one published when she was seventeen. The year she went to Hollywood and first fell in love.

"Good morning, my bluebell girls," she said, as she gave each of them a kiss. "How wonderful everything looks! But where's my article? I want it on display where everyone can see it!"

Jenna smiled and pointed to the countertop.

"It's right there, Mom," she said. Jenna had taken some time last week to write a final story for the *Lake Summers Press* about the unlikely meeting of her mother and Gavin. She'd called it, "My Mother, My Daughter, and Some Unfinished Work."

"So is everything ready?" Chloe said. "Then let the celebration begin!"

She led their mother out to the back, while Jenna went to the front door to tape up a note directing guests to the backyard. As she was about to step back inside, she noticed Matt pull into the driveway. He waved to her, and she nodded and pointed toward the back where Sophie was. She had encouraged Matt to be honest with Sophie when she'd spoken to him on the phone, and he had called Sophie that evening to tell her about Felicity and his upcoming wedding. Sophie had taken the news well. She told Jenna she was glad her dad wasn't keeping secrets from her anymore.

She waved as more guests started arriving. Sherry and Gavin, both carrying stacks of foil-covered trays. Mrs. Pearl and Jake, the ponytailed helper from her store—Sophie had told her the other day she was glad he was coming because she thought he was nice and kind of cute. Samantha from the newspaper and Art from the resort. A few of the nurses from the hospital. Zoe and her boyfriend, the bookstore manager, and Claire and her husband, with a huge double stroller that held their twin boys. Stan and Trey, wheeling a cart that held their smoothie vat. Steven, her old playmate, along with his wife, who'd come to town to meet with a broker about the house.

And there, behind them all, was Troy.

He was wearing a green pullover shirt and a pair of jeans. It was a more relaxed outfit than she'd usually seen him in. And he looked relaxed. He stopped on the walk and looked at her, his lopsided smile still irresistible. He extended his arm to show her the bouquet of deep-blue flowers in his hand.

She folded her arms over her chest but couldn't stop herself from smiling. "Stranger," she said. "I don't remember you on the guest list. Your brother and his wife, yes. But not you."

"I guess I'm a crasher," he said. "But a crasher bearing a present. They're not Virginia bluebells, because you can't find those so late in the season. But they're called blue phlox and they're very nice, too."

"How did you even know about the party? Or the bluebells? Did your brother tell you?"

He shook his head. "My mail was forwarded," he said. "I got my copy of the paper these last few weeks. I read your piece about your mother. That was quite a story."

She nodded. She didn't know what to say. It was the same story she had tried to share with him the night she discovered her mother's final two letters. But he hadn't been interested then.

"So I guess your mom's doing well?" he said.

"She's great," Jenna said.

"Sophie, too?"

"Sophie's fine."

"And my man, Mo?"

"Mo's fine, too."

They were silent for a few moments, and Jenna looked at him hard. "So what are you doing here, Troy?" she said. She knew there was an edge to her voice, but she couldn't help it. He had hurt her when he left. She didn't want to be hurt again.

"I couldn't stop thinking about what you said that night," he told her. "You were right. I thought I was running away from my story, but I wasn't. I was just writing another one. A lonely, miserable one. I didn't want to write that story anymore."

Jenna looked at him, feeling her anger start to dissolve. He may have run away, he may have literally left her in the dark. But he proved just now that he had heard her. He had understood what she told him. Yes, she would have liked him to be there for her the night she discovered her mother's last two letters. But maybe what mattered more was that he had come back to tell her what he'd learned.

"I liked what you said in the article about unfinished work and second chances," he said. "It made a big impact on me. I'll never forget what happened to my parents. But that doesn't mean I can't find a way to move on."

She looked up at the sky, then brought her gaze down to the side of the house. The bluebells were gone now, just like the twisted oak. Years from today, what else would be gone? What would remain? She thought for a moment about what her legacy might be one day. What lesson did she have for her own grand-daughter, should Sophie have a daughter? What message about herself would she want to convey?

She smiled and accepted the flowers Troy held out, then took his hand in hers. She didn't know where she was going next, but she knew she would listen to herself now. And there was no place she'd rather be at this moment than right here in Lake Summers.

At her mother's home. Holding hands with someone she could see a future with. Toasting her mother's birthday. And sharing champagne with the people she loved.

A LETTER FROM BARBARA

I want to say a huge thank you for choosing to read *The Bluebell Girls.* If you did enjoy it, and want to keep up to date with all my latest releases, just sign up at the following link. Your email address will never be shared, and you can unsubscribe at any time.

www.bookouture.com/barbara-josselsohn

The Bluebell Girls will always hold a special place in my heart, as it was written here in my home state of New York largely during the depths of the pandemic. I grew up near New York City, and it was heartbreaking to see the places that have always been such a part of my life—Broadway theaters, the New York Historical Society, the American Museum of Natural History, Lincoln Center—shut their doors, and the amazing outdoor streets and spaces like Central Park, Times Square, and Fifth Avenue look so empty. I found that imagining and writing the two all-enveloping love stories in *The Bluebell Girls* provided a welcome escape, and I hope that sense of escape reaches out to readers as well. I'm so sorry for those who have suffered so much, and I look forward to the time when we can all return to the lives we love, maybe appreciating them even more.

I hope you loved *The Bluebell Girls*, and if you did, I would be very grateful if you could write a review. I'd love to hear what you think, and it makes such a difference helping new readers to discover one of my books for the first time.

I love hearing from my readers—you can get in touch on my Facebook page, through Twitter, Goodreads or my website.

Thanks,
Barbara

 BarbaraSolomonJosselsohnAuthor

 @BarbaraJoss

www.BarbaraSolomonJosselsohn.com

ACKNOWLEDGMENTS

I am so grateful to the many people in my life who have played a role in the creation of *The Bluebell Girls*. It's a pleasure to publicly thank you here.

First, thanks to my amazing agent, Cynthia Manson, who puts herself out for me every single day. You are an amazing source of support and brilliance to all of your authors, and I'm so lucky to be one of them. And huge thanks to my editor, Jennifer Hunt. Your wisdom, insight, and talent are off the charts, and I can't imagine ever again sending anything out into the world without its first stop being right in your hands!

Thanks, too, to the amazing team at Bookouture—I'm amazed at how much you all accomplish, and I enjoy every moment I work with you. I'm also grateful for my fellow Bookouture authors—you are all fabulous writers as well as terrific virtual friends!

My writing community continues to grow, but it remains filled with super-talented friends, colleagues, and mentors who become more valuable to me every day. Thanks to Caitlin Alexander, Jimin Han, Pat Dunn, Veera Hiranandani, Diane Cohen Schneider, Jennifer Manocherian, Marcia Bradley, Jamie Beck, Linda Avellar, Ginger McKnight-Chavers, Patricia Friedrich, Maggie Smith, Susan Schild, Emily Rubin, Tiffany Yates Martin, Phyllis Shalant, and Nancee Adams. Thanks, too, to the talented writers and professionals who make up the Women's Fiction Writers Association, the Writing Institute at Sarah Lawrence College, the Scarsdale Public Library, and the Scarsdale Library Writers

Center. And a special shout-out to Dr. Kim Greene-Liebowitz, a writer and physician, who wore both caps as she answered my medical questions.

I am so grateful to one of my favorite people in the world, Kathleen Pitrola, a fantastic friend and exceptional vet tech who provided much guidance for my scenes with Jenna's dog, Mo. Thanks, too, to Dr. Andrew Thayer and Hartsdale Veterinary Hospital, the inspiration for the caring veterinary clinic in my book. And, of course, thanks to the real Mo, my unwavering writing partner and the model for his namesake in *The Bluebell Girls.* Thanks for hanging in there during your own awful bout with pancreatitis!

While *The Bluebell Girls* evolved in surprising ways during the course of writing, the initial seed took root during a family visit long ago to Washington, D.C.—and to a small indoor-and-outdoor museum a bit off the beaten path. It's called President Lincoln's Cottage (*www.LincolnCottage.org*), and it provided an intimate, unique look at the sixteenth president of the United States. I encourage everyone to plan a stop there the next time they're in the D.C. area.

Finally, my deepest thanks to my family—my husband, Bennett, and our children, David, Rachel, and Alyssa. You are everything to me, and I love you guys more every day.

9 781838 889678